THE

CONSUL'S

WIFE

THE
CONSUL'S
WIFE

A Novel

W. T. TYLER

HENRY HOLT AND COMPANY
New York

Henry Holt and Company, Inc.
Publishers since 1866
115 West 18th Street
New York, New York 10011

Henry Holt® is a registered trademark of
Henry Holt and Company, Inc.

Published in Canada by Fitzhenry & Whiteside Ltd.,
195 Allstate Parkway, Markham, Ontario L3R 4T8

Excerpt from *Collected Poems* by Wallace Stevens
copyright © 1947 by Wallace Stevens.
Reprinted by permission of Alfred A. Knopf, Inc.

Library of Congress Cataloging-in-Publication Data
Tyler, W. T.
The consul's wife : a novel / W. T. Tyler.—1st ed.
p.   cm.
ISBN 0-8050-4425-6 (HB : acid-free paper)
I. Title.
PS3570.Y53C6   1998
813'.54—DC21   97-28210

Henry Holt books are available for special
promotions and premiums.
For details contact: Director, Special Markets.

First Edition 1998

Designed by Jessica Shatan

Printed in the United States of America
All first editions are printed on acid-free paper. ∞

10   9   8   7   6   5   4   3   2   1

The greatest poverty is not to live
In a physical world, to feel that one's desire
Is too difficult to tell from despair.

—WALLACE STEVENS

2351

I first heard about African sorcery at a Catholic mission sta-tion on the Congo River below Bumba, a few hundred miles north of the equator. I was drinking beer with Frère Albert on the second-floor gallery just north of the river, and he was describing the local Budja tribe and taking a long time with it. I sat in the wicker chair opposite, listening, drinking, and not paying much attention to the rumble of thunder rolling in from the west. I'm a good listener. I've been a good listener all my life, the only talent I can claim.

Only ten minutes earlier the day had been luminous under a cloudless sky, but now the verandah was shrouded in gray. Rain hammered overhead on the tin roof and curtains of water surged across the compound, lashing the raffia palms, wetting our faces, and bringing a wintry chill to the premature dusk of late afternoon. A flash of lightning exploded nearby, then another, both so brutally unexpected I flinched, jarring the wicker table and spilling some beer. As the shock of thunder reverberated away, rattling the windows behind us and shaking the gallery floor, Frère Albert told me a local sorcerer had threatened the storm.

His voice was so gently matter-of-fact I thought I'd missed something. Day swallowed by darkness, night shattered by light? Only five weeks in the Congo, I wondered what the hell he was talking about and whether we were both half crocked or just me. We'd been out on the Congo River that afternoon on an old diesel-engined scow, taking on mail and truck parts in the powerful brown wash of an Otraco riverboat pounding upstream toward Kisangani. As we came alongside, the drunken mate high in the wheelhouse backed off the engines, and the surge lifting our bow almost capsized us. I was bone-tired from heaving an iron-shanked grappling pole and both of us were a little dehydrated.

"Esprit malfaisant? Esprit malin?" Bothered about something, his gray eyes roamed the rain-swept compound and lifted to the ugly sky as he tried to be true to whatever memory he'd conjured up. He frowned and I knew neither satisfied him. "It's enough to shrivel the soul," he said in despair. He was a very gentle, very devout, very scrupulous man.

He was in his late seventies, but I wouldn't have guessed. His eyes were as bright as the perching fish hawk's I'd seen that morning, unclouded by age. Born in Antwerp, he had a medical degree from Paris but had abandoned his practice for Africa, where he had lived for more than forty years. He was as thin as a reed, his face weathered to the texture of dried tobacco leaf except for the sunburn he'd gotten that day, which had colored his long, thin, aristocratic nose like a boiled lobster claw. His fingers were broken and scarred and the thumb of his right hand holding his briar pipe was a cherry-bright stump. He'd lost it years ago in an accident in the mission sawmill we'd toured that morning. Sockless, he wore leather sandals and gray khaki shorts.

He was describing the power of African sorcery, but I had the feeling he was defining a condition rather than a man, some shapeless presence that lay outside the sorcerer and those he corrupted, like the sinister gray fog that had hidden the river that morning as I'd walked along the bank before the sun was up, a pair of binoculars hanging like a cowbell from my neck. The only thing I could think of was spiritual evil or the contagion of spiritual evil, but I was kidding myself if I thought I knew anything about either, not then anyway.

So I was curious and a little confused, but it was only my third trip to the bush and I was confused about a lot of things, including what I was doing in Africa and whether my diplomatic career would finally dead-end there, like so many others. I was with Ken McAuliffe, another embassy officer who had been roaming the bush for eighteen months and had visited the mission station before. He was in the machine shed in the back with Brother Felix, an ex–bank clerk fled to penance after some unexplained fall from grace, trying to replace a clutch plate on a 1955 Fiat truck.

The storm passed and the rain eased off. McAuliffe appeared out of the creeping mist and climbed the wooden steps to join us. Thin and blond-bearded, he was carrying an old carburetor wrapped in rags and a green wine bottle filled with gasoline. The bell rang from the cook house. Frère Albert and I emptied our glasses, McAuliffe brought a bottle of wine from his room, and we crossed the standing pools in the courtyard to join Brother Felix for dinner in the refectory. The Jesuit fathers were away that week for a conference with the archbishop, and we had the refectory to ourselves. It was a long narrow room with a vaulted ceiling and stone floors and smelled of woodsmoke and baking bread. The glimmering light from the mission generator dimly illuminated the long tables and sent our shadows flickering eerily against the whitewashed walls. We might have been in another century, and in some ways maybe we were. Against the far wall was a seven-foot cross carved from African mahogany and lit by tall white candles in metal sconces cut from powdered milk tins.

Brother Felix, as plump and bald as a eunuch, stood to say a prayer and serve our plates from steaming bowls of chicken, rice, and peas. McAuliffe poured the wine. We were tired and hungry and nothing more was said about the sorcerer or his storm. After dinner Brother Felix drank the last of the wine, rolled up his sleeves, gathered up the plates, and disappeared into the kitchen. McAuliffe returned to clean the carburetor he had left on the gallery and I sat with Frère Albert, drinking freshly ground coffee as he indulged my curiosity about local witchcraft.

The Africans of the savannahs and rain forests feared the sorcery of the lightning-maker more than any other, convinced he could invoke the storm and bring down the lightning the way some herbs from the riverbanks drew poison from an infected wound. His instrument was some sort of box hidden near the hut or village that had drawn his fury. Frère Albert had never seen one (it was rarely seen by a white man) but had heard them described.

The belief seemed simple enough at the time, but like everything else I learned about Africa, it wasn't simple at all. The deracinated bush traders I met on the track in the months that followed tried to sell me everything else from the slough of African tribal life, whether wooden carvings, ceremonial raffia, wooden fetishes, bone and iron weapons. But even after a few cigarettes, a bottle of beer, or a ride in my Land Rover, when I asked about local sorcery they wouldn't admit they knew what I was talking about, much less scout out a sorcerer's box for me for Blakey Ogden, the consul's wife. I picked up anything I could for her during my bush travels. The uglier a fetish or a ritual mask, the more authentic it was for her.

4

Except for Ken McAuliffe and me, few embassy officers ever traveled the bush and no one cared much about native art. If they bought something it was usually off the street in Kinshasa, a tourist shop or an ivory market fake. Not Blakey. The more fetishes and masks I brought back, the more her knowledge grew. She kept them in a rear closet, all tagged and identified. Her Little Boos and Big Boos I called them, as if they were just another of her odd indulgences, like me. But collecting can become an illness, whether it's Byzantine icons, New England scrimshaws, Flemish, impressionist, or pop art you're chasing, first a pastime, then a passion, and finally a sickness. Blakey wasn't that way. She planned to donate the most valuable to a Connecticut museum.

As it turned out, during my later wanderings on the savannahs of the Kasai, an old wizard tried to work his magic against Ken McAuliffe and me. One of the *Bena N'Kuba,* or bearers of storms, so a Presbyterian missionary I met near Tshikapa told me. He had once seen the sorcerer's mysterious box outside his rural chapel after Sunday evening worship services and remembered it as a crude twig box held together by dead vines and half covered with shards of broken mirrors attached by tar or pitch. Hidden inside was a hodgepodge of repellent animal, reptile, and human viscera whose mysteries only the sorcerer could explain. He was never identified. The missionary remembered the lightning and the storm that swept in as the worst he'd ever seen. No one was killed but two huts were struck and his congregation didn't return for six weeks or so. The Jesuits had once made bonfires of the idolatrous relics, but the Presbyterians tried in gentler ways to drive the belief from the savannahs in East Kasai, first of all by trying to persuade the villagers to move their huts from the hilltops where they'd be less exposed to the foraging fire and thunder of tropical storms. The incident had happened long ago but he said the tradition still survived, as I later discovered for myself. After twenty-eight years in Central Africa the missionary was a weird old bird, half blind with glaucoma and just as dim in his recollections. Like many Westerners too long in Africa, I wasn't sure he still knew what he believed. If he did, understanding somehow defied his capacity for words, as it had Frère Albert that stormy afternoon.

I finally tracked down a sorcerer's box. It was shown to me in a dusty bush town along the Kwilu River by a middle-aged Portuguese trader and mechanic named Ferrera who'd patched my Land Rover's leaking radiator hose. He was a short, bull-necked man with the arms of a blacksmith and a few faded purple-and-red tattoos on his forearms from his boyhood sailing days with the Portuguese White Fleet, fishing for cod off the Grand Banks. His bitter comments on the territorial administration and the government in Kinshasa told me his contempt for the postcolonial Africa had led him to despise everything else about the continent where he'd lived for so many years. He kept the box under the workbench in a half-collapsed battery shed at the rear of his weed-grown compound.

He led me into its shadows where it lay on the dirt floor. No more than eighteen inches long and half as wide, the box was made of Primus beer crate slats. Once painted black, it was termite-eaten and gnawed by dry rot, the broken mirrors that had decorated the sides were missing, and it looked like a small garden tractor battery. One of the dreaded *Bena N'Kuba* had made it, he said, moving aside the rotting lid with a screwdriver to show me the desiccated relics inside. He invited my exploration but curiosity led me no further. The smell was as powerfully corrosive as the smell of sulfuric acid in the battery shed. I didn't touch it. As he returned it to the shadows, I didn't think to ask why he kept it there among the carcasses of six- and twelve-volt batteries. I soon found the answer, supplied by a British Baptist missionary from Manchester who ran a Bible bookstore on a sand street in Kikwit and had invited me for dinner one night.

Ferrera's African wife was a Mupende woman with unusual healing powers, or so the Englishman explained as we sat in his gloomy dining room, his voice barely rising above the click-clack of soup spoons against discolored crockery. Her father and uncles had been fetisheurs. The missionary—his name was Stanhope—was a dried-up weed of a man with skin as pale as parchment. He and his wife spent their lonely evenings translating the Bible and psalm books into local tribal languages. "He suffers from migraine, suffers terribly," she told me in the kitchen as the two of us were washing dishes and he was getting his violin out of the closet and setting up his Victrola (they rarely had guests). I wondered if his migraine was brought on by all those African tribal dialects rattling around in his wispy Anglo-Saxon head. During my later visits I never saw a soul in their hot, dusty little bookstore, never once saw an African looking in the windows from the sand street, and I wondered if their lonely vocation didn't describe a kind of demon possession right there.

After the dishes were put away we sat in the parlor and he played his violin accompanied by the crank-up Victrola. I think it was Bach, but I wasn't sure. I wanted a cigarette but tobacco and alcohol weren't tolerated in their parlor. After his opening piece, his wife spread her knees, opened up her accordion, and joined in, but maybe it was a concertina. I don't remember. It was a very long, very dry, very tedious night. But I had my answer: Ferrera's African wife was born to the tradition. Despite the contempt that had poisoned her husband's memories of old Africa, his European rationalism had its limits. Mine too. I didn't mention the box to Blakey, knowing it was too menacing for her gentle curiosity.

But the foul little box and the sorcerer's reputation are only two of the elements that make it so terrifying. The other two are natural enough anyplace in the world but in Africa take on a malevolence all their own. One is the boundless energy of an African thunderstorm, the other the impenetrable darkness of the African night, and both are the sorcerer's apprentices.

There are few sights more ominous than that of the most powerful of tropical thunderstorms rolling toward you across the African savannahs. American homesteaders crossing the Great Plains in their Conestoga wagons to confront for the first time an endless horizon of rampaging buffalo under a black Nebraska sky must have known the feeling. The first growls of distant thunder from anvils of billowing cloud rising fifty to sixty thousand feet above the savannah come like a premonition, suspending the day. As the storm sweeps in, a different light, odor, and texture displaces the familiar. The air comes alive with an energy that soon invests grass, trees, metal, canvas, and hair and skin. As the dark curtain descends, thunder and lightning pour down from all directions, filaments of bloodred fire on the forward edge, great jagged white flares behind as the sky explodes and the earth seems to disintegrate in a devouring conflagration of wind, thunder, fire, and rain.

And then there's the darkness itself. On a moonless night the darkness was like no other I'd ever known, not in the Syrian Desert or the mountains of eastern Turkey. After the sun goes down domestic life retires to its huts and what stirs outside is as unimaginable as the phosphorescent shapes oceanographers search for from their bathospheres in the deepest trenches of the Pacific. In that world anything is possible. Traveling on such nights along the savannahs and the interravine forests, I could smell the smoke of the village fire on the evening wind long before I could find its embers.

I remember my second trip to the Kwilu with Ken McAuliffe. It was after nine o'clock at night and he stopped the Land Rover on the track, knowing from the woodsmoke the village was near but unable to find it. He'd been there many times but never so late. My arm and head were out the window searching the track ahead. I heard the quick scrum of bare feet nearby and dark hands gripped my shoulder before I knew they were there. They scared the hell out of me but McAuliffe only laughed. He had seen too much and I was still the embassy greenhorn. The villagers had recognized our cockeyed headlights, but I'd seen nothing and couldn't identify them, even then, when a half-dozen men from the village had surrounded us, shadows in a darkness without shadow, come to guide us into the firelight.

Others can imagine what they will—ethnologists, historians, foreign policy intellectuals, museum curators, or the Afro-American brotherhood in Washington—but most African traditions make no sense until you understand their complicity with the absolute darkness of the African night. So these are the sorcerer's apprentices and Africa is his theater: on such a vast continent on such a night, a sorcerer's box found in the trees behind the village, rumors of his sinister threats whispered by the women in the manioc patch, and then the light suddenly gone as the darkness descends, a familiar world torn apart by grotesque rituals of wind, thunder, rain, and fire. If you can imagine this maybe you can understand why its animus, like the chilling onset of some Hitchcock or Stephen King thriller in our own Tom Thumb popcorn theaters out in the suburbs, might seem a little personal to say the least.

I didn't know anyone at the embassy when I arrived at the Congo. I knew little about the country beyond what I read in the press during those earlier years of anarchy and bloodshed. I was in Beirut when the telegram came from Washington, living a lazy, comfortable life in promiscuous, laissez-faire Beirut, not the murder-torn, rubble-filled war zone that followed. From my fifth-floor office I could see the Mediterranean shimmering in the distance. Beyond the Bay of Jounieh were the white-peaked caps near Mt. Lebanon.

I had the first floor of an old mud-colored building dating from the Ottoman days that faced the green sea shallows between the corniche and the St. George Hotel. Moorish archways separated the four shadowy, high-ceilinged rooms. The deep balcony looked down on the turquoise-blue Mediterranean spilling over the rocks. The century-old building was owned by a Sunni who worked in the Ministry of Public Works. Tall, courtly, and French-educated, with a large balding head, thin gray hair, and heavy jowls, he looked more like an English Tory than a Lebanese Arab and was more a *rentier* than a civil servant. He owned a number of buildings in the quarter. He dropped by once a month to ask about my comfort and collect the rent. He always apologized for his poor English but insisted on speaking it with me, the only American in his many properties. He wanted to speak English like an Englishman, he confided one afternoon, bringing out a copy of the *Spectator.* He bought it regularly at the St. George Hotel. "One must take advantages of opportunities," he apologized, and I gave him his. He was my first lesson in Beirut's cultural mimicry, that thick, osmotic acculturation that had shaped so much of the Levant's history—Phoenician, Greek, Roman, Arab, French, and now American.

A few buildings away an old stone mosque sat on an escarpment overlooking the Mediterranean from behind its triple-arched *brise-soleil.* Atop the minaret three loudspeakers called the faithful to their daily prayers, the muezzin's voice transcribed on a scratchy phonograph record played on a turntable in the attendant's room far below. I was seldom conscious of it during the day. Lying in bed at night, the balcony doors open, above the sound of the sea I would hear a faint hoarse whisper from the darkness outside, like the sound of an old man drawing breath, and know the phonograph record had begun. A moment later the shrill, sad ululation of the muezzin would begin, astonishingly close, and remind me of where I was and the mystery of my being there.

On the far side of the mosque lay a small cove reached by a footpath where the fishermen moored their dories. Every morning walking to the embassy I passed them as they were hanging their blue nylon nets out to dry. Opposite was a coffee shop with tables out on the sidewalk where they sat in the late afternoon, smoking their water pipes. In a Moslem-owned shop in the neighborhood I often bought chicken and lamb roasted over an electric fire. Next door was a nut and sweet shop no larger than a broom closet where an energetic young Moslem ladled out toasted watermelon and sunflower seeds, cashews, and Syrian pistachios. The transistor radio on the shelf was always turned to Radio Cairo. On his walls, like those of most of the Moslem shops in the neighborhood, you could always find faded sepia and mezzotint photos of Gamal Nasser. Druze and Kurdish families lived in the old houses along the passageways opposite.

The cable arrived on a Friday afternoon in late June. The embassy was about to close. As I was clearing my desk I got a telephone call from personnel and went down in the elevator and looked at the cable. I had to laugh. "The Congo? They must be out of their minds," I told Rudy Fischer, the sour-tempered administrative counselor who was nearing retirement and impatient with the younger generation. "I don't know anything about Africa."

"That's your tough luck, Mathews. Two years in Beirut and they're going to send you to Paris? Not a chance. But you screw up with the jungle Mau-Mau down there and I'll tell you, this time no one's going to bring your goddamned bones back either."

He knew nothing about Africa but was annoyed with me for an incident that had happened a few months earlier. I had been hunting francolin and partridge on the eastern slopes overlooking the Bekaa Valley and had been picked up by a Syrian army patrol along the Syrian-Lebanese frontier. I didn't have a dog or a compass and had walked far ahead of the two footsore Lebanese I was with, tracking a covey I had flushed. The border was unmarked except for an occasional triangular yellow sign warning of minefields and tank traps. Both seemed unlikely so I didn't pay much attention to them until a squad of Syrian soldiers in olive green and Afrika Corps–style forage caps came loping through the cedar and pine trees. I thought they were on maneuvers and stepped aside to let them pass. They didn't pass. Barking fiercely in Arabic, they surrounded me, two seized me from behind, another grabbed my shotgun, and a sergeant smelling of garlic searched me and took my wallet and keys. Wrists shackled behind my back, I was led away, put in a Soviet jeep, and taken to a Syrian army cantonment where I was held for over twenty-four hours, kept in a lock-up with a wolf-faced Syrian farmer and a Lebanese taxi driver. Arrested for currency smuggling, both spent most of the night shouting obscenities at their captors through the bars. The following day, still in shackles, I was interrogated by a young lieutenant from G-2 who believed enough of my story to telephone his headquarters and the Foreign Ministry in Damascus. Fischer had to drive up from Beirut to meet me the next night at a desolate frontier post east of Tripoli. I was handcuffed and kept in the back room until he arrived. They brought me out, took off my handcuffs, and delivered me to Fischer, unshaven, tired, hungry, and stinking like a pissoir.

"You're a goddamn disgrace," Fischer grumbled when he saw me, ashamed and embarrassed as a half-dozen Syrian soldiers stood watching us.

"It's just a sideshow, Rudy. Don't make it any worse." My 12-gauge Beretta shotgun wasn't returned. It was five in the morning when we reached the corniche in Beirut.

There were few people I would miss at the embassy. It was more difficult leaving Simone Coulet, a young Belgian woman I was seeing at the time. Slim and dark-haired, her laughing brown eyes had attracted me one torrid August afternoon when we met in the sea off Khalde, both of us snorkeling alone. We bobbed in the waves together far from the beach, introduced ourselves, talked, and swam back together. She was an administrative officer with the UN and shared a beach cottage nearby with two secretaries from the Belgian embassy.

"I still believe I'd be good for your career," she said sadly that evening as we were having drinks on her balcony near Pigeon Rocks. She had said so before and now she was even more convinced. "It's true, I know it's true. You'll find out. You can't escape it." On Sunday mornings in her flat or mine, she gave me useful lessons for my bachelor kitchen. "Never keep tomatoes in the refrigerator." "When you're boiling something on the stove, keep the handles pointed to the rear." "When you're making an omelette, don't overdo it. Five or six quick turns with a fork, you see? is enough." But as she became more serious about our affair, her spirit dimmed. The long silences came, punctuated by sighs, and an occasional tear. On a sunny morning two weeks later she drove me out to the airport, wet-eyed and silent. It was painful saying good-bye. Tears splashed down her cheeks as I kissed her and promised to write.

So I had come to Africa on direct transfer from the Middle East, from vast open spaces and the thick amber light of the Mediterranean and the smell of the sea to arrive in the capital late at night after an all-day flight from Brussels. Dan Ritchie, a redheaded embassy political officer, welcomed me in the sultry reception room, a damp seersucker jacket hanging like wet wash from his slight shoulders. It was a torrid, breathless night. The airport was far from the city and the streets we sped through were sinister, dark or badly lit, smelling of decay, overripeness, and rot. What I sensed in the days that followed was a lurking anarchy, a pervading sullenness waiting to explode. What I saw were ragged skies torn by storm clouds, dirty streets, skin-and-bones street vendors, morose, sullen policemen in gray khaki who couldn't read a driver's license or an identity card, and civil servants who spoke a demotic Belgian French. Entering the cool silence of the embassy, a bright modern two-story building a few blocks from the port, you might believe you were in Brussels, Bonn, or Madrid. During the first weeks I saw little to encourage me. I missed my afternoons on the Mediterranean at Khalde with Simone, missed the mellow golden light of late afternoon, the suqs, the sea, and the mountains.

I had been assigned as a political officer but Owsley, the middle-aged officer I replaced, was still there, awaiting orders for Milan. Kim Johnson, the political counselor, described my temporary duties the morning after my arrival. A tall, willowy easterner with a mannered drawl, Johnson was out of the European Bureau and knew as little about Africa as I did. With Owsley still in residence and his onward assignment up in the air—passed over for promotion once too often, Johnson informed me behind his closed door—he was sending me off to the Afro-American Institute every morning to learn Lingala. In the afternoons I would be loaned out to Carl Turpin, the economic counselor, helping with a backlog of annual reports in the economic section. It would be temporary, he promised as he led me through the suite of offices to introduce the other political officers. It was a four-man political section and Owsley was the oldest, a sad little man with gray hair who mutely raised his head to nod. Time, drink, and disappointment had dulled his eyes. He monitored the parliamentary circus and did a bang-up job, so Johnson told me in a loud, cheerful voice. Owsley took no comfort from this bonhomie and returned to his newspaper. Ken McAuliffe was missing that morning. Off in the bush, Johnson explained.

The consulates at Kisangani and Bukavu hadn't reopened after the rebellions, and McAuliffe spent most of his time traveling the provinces to report on political conditions. A few minor insurgencies still smoldered deep in the bush but were burning out, kept alive by a handful of ragtag rebels with old muskets and bows and arrows. As a bachelor, the travel worked less of a hardship on him than the married officers, none of whom showed much interest in the interior anyway. For them, like the embassy, the capital and the daily round of diplomatic exchanges, dinners, and receptions were the heart and soul of diplomatic life.

I had a cramped little bachelor flat on the sixth floor of a modern blue-tiled building three blocks from the embassy. The living room, dining room, and small bedroom were all painted a pale green; the furniture was government issue and could have come from a hospital waiting room. The small balcony overlooked the ivory market, an open square filled from dawn to dusk with chattering native traders and honking horns. I couldn't find a decent car and had to depend on the embassy motor pool for transportation. I was considering buying a motorcycle I'd seen advertised on the embassy bulletin board. Dan Ritchie told me over lunch that it wouldn't be wise. No motorcycles, no beards.

At Durban, his previous post, he'd grown a beard, but the embassy at Kinshasa was larger and more cosmopolitan, or so it saw itself, a kind of mini-Brussels. Kim Johnson told him to shave it. At the time Vietnam had created a division between the older and younger officers and Johnson was one of the believers, not so much in Vietnam or the Third World, although he'd served a short tour at the embassy in Saigon, but in the traditional establishment institutions. That was often the way with most senior diplomats: Duty is everything, but passion counts only in tennis and love affairs. Trimming the beards and the long hair was Johnson's way of muting the differences and keeping the grunts in the barracks.

I didn't buy the motorcycle. My relations with Johnson were already prickly enough after I told him I was wasting my time working for Turpin. After the first several weeks I was a fish out of water and thinking about bagging it. At the time State was trying to round up volunteers for the rural provinces and I was considering signing up for the CORDS program in Vietnam.

"I'm Blakey Ogden," she said the night we met. **"You've just** arrived, haven't you?" It was at a dinner given by Pickersgill, the deputy chief of mission. She sat to my left at a candlelit table on the terrace under the stars, a slender blond woman wearing a dark dress, her face partially hidden in shadow. Forgetting that name cards marked our places, I was surprised she knew who I was.

"Just arrived. How about you?"

"Oh, no. Almost a year now. My apartment is on the floor below yours."

"The flat with the piano?" I had heard someone playing and not very well.

"Jeffrey plays. I hope it doesn't bother you."

"Not at all. Jeffrey?"

"My husband, the consul." I remembered him then, a man in his early forties in a pale linen suit rising from a cluttered desk in his first-floor office during my introductory rounds. His blond hair was thinning on top and a mustache as fine as corn-silk decorated the colorless lip. His voice was dry, his hand limp and damp, barely offered.

"I've met him."

"I imagine this is quite a change from Beirut, isn't it?"

"I haven't gotten around enough to compare it to Beirut, not yet."

"It's hard in the beginning, I know. I was terribly shy at first too."

I laughed and said no one had ever accused me of being shy. She smiled and asked me a few questions about Beirut. There was something in her face that encouraged me, and I told her about my apartment near the corniche overlooking the Mediterranean and my landlord who looked more like an English Tory than a Lebanese Arab. She talked a little about her two years in Oslo. So we reminisced, laughed, and fiddled with our wine-glasses while the candlelight danced in her eyes and we waited for the lamb curry and rice. I wasn't sure of their color. Her fingers were long, delicate, and finely tapered. Lovely in all her parts, I decided.

There were six at our table. The others were all older, talking of events and people I knew nothing about. All were from the embassy. To Blakey's left sat Ralph Philips, the sandy-haired Agency station chief, who asked her about Louvanium University. I didn't know Blakey was auditing a few classes there. The orange-haired woman to my right leaned across me from time to time to interrupt, inquiring about the new ambassador's wife.

I don't recall what else was said during dinner. I didn't have much to say. As Blakey's attention turned elsewhere, it was her gentle voice and unfailing graciousness that struck me. I imagined the innocent trust of a privileged childhood, an education in a fashionable university, probably a women's college in the East, followed by a socially predictable marriage; if not a lawyer, banker, or broker, a diplomat would do. There would be small children at home just as lovely; they would be learning French and taking tennis lessons; they would have an African nanny. It wasn't my world and never would be. Nevertheless, watching her face and listening to her voice that night, I knew the occasional despair of the bachelor life.

The weekly country team meeting was held each Friday
morning in the embassy conference room, a large sunny room on
the second floor behind the ambassador's suite. Kim Johnson
sometimes asked one of his political officers to accompany him,
the invitation intended to give the younger officers a better sense
of those momentous events their seniors were grappling with
there in the high ozone of the second-floor conference room. I
went with him my second week to be formally introduced to the
senior embassy staff, most of whom I had already met.

Ambassador Graham, who had arrived a month before me
from Brussels, led off from the head of the table with a discussion
of the morning cable traffic and how Washington's queries were
to be answered. Pickersgill, his deputy, kept his eye on house-
keeping matters and noted a few instructions for the administrative counselor. Before he gave his political brief, Kim Johnson
turned to me in my chair against the wall, introduced me, and
mentioned my Lingala studies. Philips, the Agency station chief,
was next. He gave up no secrets but after a growling commentary
on recent staff changes at the Soviet embassy said he was worried
by a report he had heard from one of his people that McAuliffe
was missing. Did that mean trouble in the region?

No trouble at all, Johnson said quickly. McAuliffe had been
three days missing but had safely reported in the previous afternoon through the British Baptist radio net. He was traveling
four hundred kilometers to the southeast near the Angolan border. I still hadn't met McAuliffe but was intrigued by his
absences, envying someone able to knock around the bush like
that. I was also curious about the stories I had heard.

The ambassador also was perplexed. A New Englander and an economist by background, he was a precise little man, slim and silver-haired, with cool manners and a lively curiosity about his new country and his staff. I knew this from the thirty minutes I spent with him my second day when he said he was very pleased by my studying Lingala. He knew McAuliffe reported on the interior but was surprised he was traveling alone in such a remote backwater. What was the relevance of the region and why was he traveling there? "Observing for the most part," Johnson said, coloring. "Monitoring local stability."

The answer didn't satisfy Ambassador Graham, who asked the name of the village from which McAuliffe had radioed in. Kim Johnson didn't know and neither did anyone else. None of them traveled and each had his reasons. Pickersgill suggested they give the ambassador some sense of the general area McAuliffe was visiting. Johnson got up to search the 1:10,000 map on the far wall. Colonel Harris, the red-haired defense attaché, went to help. They stood awkwardly at the map, pointing to a general area along the Kasai-Shaba frontier about the size of Texas.

"Terra incognito, it seems," Ogden drawled from the foot of the table. As consul, he was the low man on the country team totem pole, his presence titular, not substantive, as Kim Johnson was fond of saying, and one to be endured rather than welcomed. With nothing to contribute to the weekly strategy sessions, he would have been better off keeping his mouth shut, but modest restraint wasn't his style. Graham ignored him and so did everyone else. Were any AID officers with him? he asked, looking at the AID director and Turpin. In addition to his other problems, Turpin was a diabetic and as worried about tropical diseases as he was of flying in unpredictable weather. Both shrugged and looked at Johnson. None, it seemed. Not satisfied, and irritated by their common ignorance, the ambassador said he'd like to see McAuliffe's trip report as well as his earlier reports when he returned, and let the subject drop. Pickersgill vigorously nodded his head in approval.

Kim Johnson was annoyed as we went down the stairs. Philips had ambushed him and neither Turpin nor the AID director had come to his defense. He had been made to look a fool. I said he hadn't looked the fool and suggested he seize the initiative and tell Turpin he was sending me along with McAuliffe on his next trip. He said he would think about it but his mind was elsewhere, still pondering his humiliation in the conference room. I went off to my Lingala lesson.

It was drudgery. I was the only student in the class, a three-hour morning session taught by a nervous Maluba professor in a dusty, windowless room in a building a mile from the embassy. He wasn't a language professor but a librarian who worked part time for the USIS library. There was no textbook, just a sheaf of pages he typed out himself, then mimeographed and handed to me with a shaky hand at the end of each day's session. Lingala was as useless as Sanskrit or Navajo outside the Congo River basin where I intended to serve my time and move on. I was out to see the world, not join the cause, whether in the Congo, Vietnam, the Middle East, or anyplace else. So I didn't much like the screw-up in my assignment or those long listless afternoons in Turpin's economic section two blocks from the embassy. By the third week I had finished the late economic reports, but Turpin couldn't find much for me to do. A middle-aged mediocrity out of the AID ranks, he was a hapless administrator in a listless embassy backwater.

I saw Blakey Ogden several times that first month at the odd cocktail party or diplomatic reception. Her smile always drew me through the crowd to her side. Her name continued to puzzle me. It was the sort of name clever schoolgirls give each other as they grope with the confused, sexless identities of female adolescence, and I wondered how it had survived marriage. I asked her about it one evening at a reception given by Kim Johnson for a visitor from Washington. We were standing poolside near a frangipani tree. The moon shimmered through the trees and lay broken on the water on a warm, musky night.

"Blakey?" She looked up in surprise. "Blake's my maiden name."

"From your school days?"

"From school, yes. From summer camp, I suppose. I've never thought much about it. Why?"

"Just curious." I remembered the girls from Sacred Heart, Kentucky Home, and Collegiate on a long-ago autumn afternoon in Louisville's Seneca Park, pulling on their long socks and shin guards before a hockey game. I had a feeling she would have been there among them, tall, lithe, and loose-jointed. "Field hockey, tennis?"

"Both. But not very well." She smiled, amused by something. "Are you always like this?"

"Like what?"

"Your questions."

"Not always. Just sometimes."

"You're very bold, aren't you?" I didn't know whether it was a compliment or not.

"Not bold, just not shy."

"But that's what you said before, wasn't it? So tell me, how are you managing? Is it any better? The last time you said you were bored."

"Not much change. A little monotonous." Her glass was empty and so was mine. We strolled on toward the bar at the rear of the pool.

"You miss Beirut, I suppose. But I'm sure it will get better. Just give it time."

"Maybe. I wouldn't mind doing what Ken McAuliffe is doing."

"Traveling the interior? Then you ought to suggest it."

"I have. Nothing seems to be happening."

Before we reached the bar her husband called to her from across the pool and came to intercept us, briskly moving through the crowd on the poolside terrace like a ballroom dancer—a quick two-step, a few whirls, a bow, a few words, and then on toward us.

"Ah, yes," he said to me, smoothing away a frown as he reached Blakey's side, his hand at her elbow. "Making your way, are you? Margaret tells me you've been dragooned into Turpin's shop. Studying Lingala too, are you?"

"Still studying." I had forgotten Blakey's name was Margaret.

"Rather a waste, I'd say." He wasn't easy to talk to. He fancied himself a lively conversationalist but had no private voice, only a public one. He had a way of blinking his eyes after one of his quips, waiting for others to share his cleverness. Older than Blakey, he had a master's degree from Tufts, where he'd taught. Like so many academics turned diplomat, his conceits didn't so much advance the conversation as embroider it. But his possessiveness was always obvious. So was her sense of duty as the obedient diplomatic wife. They left me there and he led her away to meet someone.

One particularly empty afternoon not long afterward another circular telegram from the Department crossed my desk soliciting volunteers for the rural provinces in Vietnam. It was three o'clock and Turpin hadn't returned from lunch. I told myself that if he wasn't back by three fifteen, I would sign up. At three fifteen, I put the cable in my pocket and walked over to the embassy to tell Kim Johnson I was bagging it and volunteering for the CORDS program in Vietnam.

"Volunteer! You must be joking. You can't volunteer!" He quickly got up and closed the door. I showed him the cable but he dropped it aside, indignantly plucked out his cuffs, and gave me a testy lecture on career responsibility—sticking it out, making the most of career opportunities, putting the best face on it. The first political counselor he had served under in Bonn had been a complete jackass, he remembered, yet he had disciplined himself, had quietly bided his time. If he hadn't, he would be in Edinburgh stamping visas.

I asked what had happened to his former political counselor in Bonn.

"Do we know, do we care! What's that got to do with it? I haven't the foggiest idea!" But then he calmed down. "So you see, it's largely a matter of perceptions. How we're perceived, a young chap who throws it all over after less than a month at post." I suppose he thought my decision would reflect badly on him. He asked me to think about it for a week. It was no coincidence that Marcia Johnson called me later that same afternoon, inviting me to brunch *en famille* the following Saturday.

In Beirut after the embassy closed in the early afternoon I would sometimes climb the hill away from the sea and catch the little red tram on Bab-Idriss to old Beirut and prowl the suqs. In the narrow passageways were Shiite farmers in kaffiyehs from the south or the Bekaa Valley, Druze shepherds in ragged Turkish trousers, square-headed Armenian goldsmiths, Kurdish women dressed like gypsies, Syrian porters in their woolen caps carrying merchandise from the ports, and Palestinian money-changers. Anything could be bought there: pottery, copperware, silver, furs, cheeses, gold, sheep, goats, hashish, shoes, and Persian rugs. The rough cobblestones, twisting passageways, and open ditches filled with blood and offal were those of a medieval market town, mixing the smell of herbs, green olive-wood, Turkish coffee, and freshly slaughtered sheep.

To the west along the Hamra and Pigeon Rocks was French Beirut with its shops and sidewalk cafés. The shops were vacant at midday, sterile and overpriced. Beyond were the beach clubs that lined the Mediterranean toward Khalde, where the scalding sands made the sea seem tepid. Few swam but in the summer Beirut's bourgeoisie flocked to the cabanas, bars, and beach houses, older men and women, boys, gamines, foreigners, the British and French showgirls from the casino across the Bay of Jounieh, the local bankers, brokers, fleshpots, and skin-traders, all crushed together in that dense, sprawling, sun-sweltered intimacy that has little to do with swimming or surfing but instead was a local variant of Côte d'Azur narcissism that made the Lebanese bourgeoisie so vulgar and similar beaches in France, Greece, or Italy so depressing.

In Lebanon I could escape on weekends to hunt quail among the Shia of the south or shoot partridge on the eastern slopes of the Bekaa Valley along the Syrian frontier. The impoverished Shia never showed me anything but generosity; their hillside villages lined by septic ditches smelled of fourteenth-century poverty and shamed the proud Sunni landlords in Beirut. If social improvement was to be their lot, it would be gained not through smashing the political charter, as the Shiites of Iran would later do, but through petty accumulation, harder work, or immigration, or so I thought, but time and Islamist fundamentalism proved me wrong. So that's what I had left for raw, primitive, undisciplined Africa and a different kind of social and political reality.

But in Kinshasa there was little to escape to after the embassy closed. I missed the mountains, the sea, missed my afternoons on the beach at Khalde, especially on weekends. A few weeks after my arrival I learned that on Sundays Ambassador Graham opened his pool on the residence grounds to the embassy crowd. I didn't care much for embassy socializing but decided to take a look.

I arrived a little after twelve on a brilliant sunny day with a few wispy clouds hovering over the river. Children were splashing in the far end of the pool while their parents sprawled in the lounge chairs nearby. As I crossed toward the dressing room a woman in an orange bikini lifted from the springboard in an effortless jack-knife and sliced into the water without a splash. The blond head bobbed to the surface and she kicked her way back to the ladder where two boys waited. She climbed out, her lean brown body leaking water, the orange suit sagging on her breasts and hips. It was Blakey Ogden. I watched as she led the taller of the two back to the board and stood behind him, positioning his hands and feet on the edge of the board. After a minute she stepped back. He stood there uncertainly, hesitated, and then cannonballed off the board with a drenching splash. I thought the two boys, probably seven and ten, might be her sons.

I changed into my trunks in the dressing room. When I returned to the pool the two boys were cannonballing off the board and Blakey was sitting alone on a lounge chair at the other end of the pool area. She waved and I went over to say hello. Draped in two red towels, one worn like a sarong, the other over her shoulders, she was writing on a tablet in a green leather portfolio on her lap. She put it aside and dropped her sunglasses over her nose as I joined her.

"Hi. Welcome to our country club. You haven't been here before?"

"The first time. It's nice."

"It is, isn't it? Sit down. I come almost every Sunday before the crowd when I have the pool to myself."

Jeffrey was off at the Belgian Club, playing doubles with Pickersgill. I asked about the two boys. They weren't her children but belonged to an embassy communicator and his wife—the couple on the lounge chairs at the far end of the pool. More couples with children were arriving and she told me I had better take advantage of the pool while I could. Dan Ritchie and his wife, Linda, were among the arrivals and stopped to talk to Blakey. I took her advice and swam for a while. She sat on the lounge chair, writing in the green portfolio open next to her. When I saw her again she was leaving the dressing room in a dark-blue skirt and a white blouse, the green portfolio under her arm. Wide shouldered and wide breasted, she carried herself easily and effortlessly. From her fluid, unconscious grace, I thought the name Blakey made a little more sense.

The Ritchies invited me to share their picnic basket with them. We spread out a mat on the lawn beyond the shrubbery enclosing the pool. Linda Ritchie kneeled at the picnic basket, unpacking the ham sandwiches, chips, and beer, but was suddenly motionless as she looked out across the lawn toward the residence.

Genevieve Graham, the ambassador's wife, was walking with Blakey among the flower beds on the far side of the drive, a basket over her arm. Blakey was carrying her green portfolio.

"Very much the lady, isn't she," Linda said, watching Blakey kneel among the flowers, knees to the side. "It must be nice. But I suppose we should be grateful." I didn't know what she meant until Dan explained it was Blakey who had persuaded Genevieve Graham to open the pool on Sundays. She was her social secretary.

"Even so, she's too much her own person," Linda said. I didn't know what that meant either but I didn't ask.

During lunch Dan Ritchie described Kim Johnson's humiliation at the country team meeting. It seemed to please him. He either didn't know or had forgotten that I had been there too, but I didn't say anything. "Isn't that perfect?" Linda said. "Kim's so sanctimonious, he had it coming." Ritchie had dug out seven of McAuliffe's earlier trip reports for Kim Johnson, who sent them to the ambassador. He got them back with the ambassador's scribbled comment: "These might have been improved by the addition of more detail on local economic life: price indices, availability of food staples, transport, bridge and road repair, etc."

"Can you imagine Johnson telling Ken McAuliffe that?" Linda said. "I mean, for God's sake." She asked what I thought of McAuliffe. I said I hadn't met him yet.

But I had heard stories. Marcia Johnson told me he had grown up on a ranch in Montana and eastern Oregon and seemed to believe his western boyhood explained everything anyone needed to know about him. Turpin's young secretary said I couldn't miss him, that he drove a battered Honda motorcycle like a madman through the streets of the capital where he was sometimes mistaken for a Peace Corps volunteer, a Mennonite missionary, an Oxfam volunteer, or a teacher from the American School where he got his grass, anything but a diplomat. He had been a Peace Corps volunteer before he joined the foreign service.

The next morning I called Kim Johnson and again suggested I tag along during McAuliffe's next trip and handle the economic reporting. Johnson said he would have to discuss it with Turpin. Before he could a cable arrived from Washington recalling Owsley and abolishing his position in the political section. I was to stay on to replace Ken McAuliffe, due for a transfer in three months. That solved the problem. It was McAuliffe who told me. He appeared unexpectedly late one afternoon at my office in the economic section, a stranger wearing wrinkled khakis and dusty engineer's boots. Of medium height and slight in build, he had a blond beard and startling blue eyes the color of cornflowers. Misled by the beard, I didn't know who he was until he introduced himself.

We had a long talk and the next afternoon he invited me out to dinner. He had a small whitewashed cottage shaded by mango trees in a compound out near the river in a section where a few of the international organizations and missionary groups were housed. A dark-haired, full-breasted young Danish woman in a halter and shorts greeted me at the door. Her name was Gretchen. I thought she was his wife at first but after she returned to the kitchen McAuliffe told me she worked for a Scandinavian relief agency. The cool shadowy living room was sparely furnished. There was a small studio couch, camel chairs, and Afghan cushions scattered about the floor. Books were everywhere, on the bookshelves, tables, and floor. He didn't have a cook or a houseboy and didn't do much entertaining. We drank Primus beer on the small patio outside the kitchen door where Gretchen rejoined us. She was as silent as a gazelle at first, but her dark brown eyes were lively enough so that it didn't matter. Her cottage was nearby on the other side of a small hedge. I concluded they were probably living together, an arrangement that probably displeased Kim Johnson as well as Fishbeck, the post security officer.

McAuliffe and I began the first of our trips together the next week. We flew out of Kinshasa in the five o'clock morning darkness on the U.S. military mission's old C-119, a kind of flying boxcar that rattled its way up to 12,000 feet and lumbered on through broken clouds to drop us off in the Kwilu several hundred miles to the east. We spent a day and night in Kikwit, the sleepy little provincial capital, before hitching a ride in a missionary Cessna the following afternoon to a grass airstrip to the north. We were to spend the night at an isolated palm oil plantation, and the Congolese manager had sent his Land Rover for us. We were exhausted after our long talks with provincial officials and an endlessly talkative official dinner the night before.

It was a cloudless afternoon as we drove away in the Land Rover down the shadowed sand roads between sheltering palms, the track so silent the Land Rover seemed to be as engineless as a pirogue gliding under the trees. We emerged at the landing on the Kwilu River where a lopsided old ferry was waiting. Painted red, it looked like a garbage scow with a queer little wheelhouse to the side. The Congolese farmers who had been waiting silently filed aboard carrying their parcels and merchandise. After we got out the Land Rover drove on.

The immense river was sheeted with silver, the western sky tinted rose and lavender in the dying afternoon sun. Swallows skimmed the surface and the smell of woodsmoke drifted over us from a hidden village nearby. Crossing the Kwilu that afternoon brought it together, the great silence, the immense sky, the green corrugations of forest in the distance, the silent figures sitting and standing along the sides of the ferry, resting after their long, long journey on foot. I suppose it was the beauty as much as the immensity, the immensity as much as the solitude, the tranquility, and the people. But there was something else, something timeless and uncommunicable, too vast and too enduring even for the government's criminal talents. I didn't really feel it until that afternoon. I don't know what it was but for the first time since I'd arrived in the Congo I knew where I was.

I grew up in Kentucky along the Ohio River and maybe that had something to do with it, a vast river flowing by and a boundless frontier beyond waiting to be crossed. As a boy I could no more imagine living in a riverless town than a Sioux or Comanche on the Great Plains could imagine living without a sea of grass stretching away toward an endless horizon or an infinite sky overhead. Part of my inheritance, my memory and imagination, the river was always there, broad, swift, and unchanging, marking the frontier of a world long vanished but still alive for me. Where the cornfields, brick buildings, or cobblestone boat landings ended another world began. The green corrugations that lifted across the plain of brown water could be Ohio and Indiana but in my earliest years conjured up the world of my grade-school history books, a world of eighteenth- and nineteenth-century

31

Kentucky, primeval forests, salt licks, pioneer forts, buckskinned frontiersmen, and war-painted Indians.

I remember arriving once in my grandfather's Buick at the old steamboat landing at the foot of 4th Street above the falls of the Ohio to hear the calliope from an excursion boat. We'd come too late and found the paddle wheeler gone, just a faint black speck upstream by now. Looking out across the immense plain of river, it seemed to me the paddle wheeler had already passed into the world of Simon Kenton and his Kentucky frontiersmen, a world still alive for me in memory and imagination. My heart ached to be with them but history had denied me, leaving me stranded on the cobbled boat landing in my summer shorts and Buster Brown shoes, the prisoner of my grandfather's house, the sedentary habits of his declining years, the backseat imprisonment of his Buick sedan, and those long evenings alone with him at his long dinner table. On summer evenings after we returned I would race up the back stairs to my room, take a book from the shelf, and lie sprawled across the bed, looking at the black-and-white engravings of eighteenth-century Kentucky.

The following morning I left the guest cottage a little after sunup and wandered down the sand road to the river. There was a small native market under the trees near the ferry landing, no more than three or four thatched huts with wooden counters. A wrinkled old woman was stooping behind the plank counter in front of a lean-to made of rushes, humming to herself. Standing again, she saw me there, smiled as if ashamed, and lifted her small wrinkled hand over her eyes. When she took it down, I was still there, looking at her plantains and mangoes. I bought two of each. As I paid I put my hand to my eyes and asked in my crude Lingala why she'd made the gesture. I was a *Flamand,* she said with a wrinkled smile. Her small hut had nothing to offer a White man. Surprised to find me there, her eyes had nowhere to hide.

I laughed and asked if she had any cigarettes. She pointed to the neighboring hut. I lifted a pack of Belga cigarettes from the counter but I had spent all my *makuta* with the old woman, and the old man with a flocculence of tight gray hair didn't have change for my five-zaire note. He bent down and rattled around in his wooden chest under the plank counter, brought out a burlap bag, removed an old wooden mask, and held it out. I took it and lifted it into the broken sunlight. It was old, no doubt about it, fissured by dry rot and weevils. The face had been half repainted with dull maroon and white marine paint, the kind you use to paint a boat bottom. I knew it was old but didn't know whether it was authentic or not. By then a few of the ferry passengers had gathered around, watching curiously. It appealed to me, maybe because of the mystery of its facial expression, which looked out at me with a primitive curiosity as puzzled as my own, maybe because of the fragrance of woodsmoke that permeated every grain of the light African wood. I bought it for the zaire notes he owed me in change to remind me of my first visit to the bush.

After the embassy closed, my late afternoons were silent and empty. I didn't play golf and hadn't played tennis in two years, not since I threw my racquet over the fence at one of the American University courts in Beirut. At loose ends, I would drive over to the Belgian Club in the secondhand Volkswagen I had bought from a departing embassy secretary. I hadn't joined the club but dropped by occasionally for a drink, to watch the tennis players and the golfers, to wander, listen, and observe. It was a large stucco building dating from the Belgian raj with an open verandah surrounded by English hedges and banks of flowers dividing the neatly trimmed emerald-green lawns. To the rear was an open terrace surrounded by frangipani, bougainvillea, and poinsettia trees. Beyond were the tennis courts and the golf course.

The grass was even greener that day after the early-afternoon rains, and the air was sweet, crisp, and clear. Seeing Colonel Harris trundling along the path to the first tee in his red plaid knickers, I followed at a distance to watch him tee off. He addressed the ball well enough, but his vicious swing topped it. The ball veered away for thirty yards and hopped across the asphalt path. He took a mulligan, sliced the next ball into the trees, and teed up another.

Returning by another walk under the trees, I saw Edna Pickersgill and Blakey Ogden sitting on one of the green benches near the courts. Edna Pickersgill saw me and said something to Blakey, who turned and waved. I wandered over.

"I hear you've been traveling," Blakey said. "How very lucky. I told you it would work out." She was wearing a white sundress and sunglasses, her blond hair sleekly gathered behind her head, tied with a brown velvet ribbon.

"So you did. How've you been?" I sat down next to her.

"The same. Always the same. Was it lovely?"

"Different. Not like this green mirage."

"Mirage?" Edna Pickersgill asked, peering at me from the end of the bench. She was a small sparrow-headed woman with short gray hair and a fringe of gray bangs that made her face seem even smaller.

"The diplomat's burden," Blakey said as she turned to the tennis court. "Their wives too."

Jeffrey and Pickersgill were warming up for an evening doubles match two courts away. Jeffrey was eager but erratic and constantly out of position. Pickersgill, taller and stouter, had a strong backhand and outmatched Jeffrey, even in volleying. After two missed balls Edna Pickersgill called to her husband to ease up a bit. Disgusted, Jeffrey came to get a drink from the Thermos at Blakey's feet and Pickersgill followed. Jeffrey insisted on shaking my hand, his eyes suddenly cool. He stood mopping his face with a towel, troubled and irritated.

"I've lost my rhythm for some reason. I don't seem to be following through on my backhand."

"It's your feet," Blakey said, rising. "You're out of position for both your backhand and forehand." Pickersgill agreed and they led him back out on the court. From the way Blakey set her feet and shoulders, the way she moved the racquet and the way Jeffrey tried to follow, I knew she was the stronger player. She would have beaten his socks off.

Edna Pickersgill excused herself and went off to meet her dressmaker. Blakey and I sat and watched the tennis players. Her advice had improved Jeffrey's stroke and seemed to stir his competitive fire as well. I stood up, ready to leave, when a Congolese trader called to me from the path. He brought a few hand-carved wooden figures from a sack and held them out. Blakey saw him too and we crossed behind the bench to look at them. She took off her sunglasses, examined a wooden figure, turned it in her hands, then smiled at me, thanked him, and gave them back. It was the first time I had clearly seen her eyes in the bright sunlight. For some reason they surprised me. A clear ash green, warm and quick, they had an astonishing clarity to them, like the clear, bright transparency of a tropical sea, registering depths you don't expect. Putting her glasses back on, she said they were nice but not authentic.

"Fakes?" I asked, wondering how she knew.

"No, not exactly fakes, just not authentic."

"If the figures aren't authentic, they're fakes, aren't they?"

"No, you're confusing the two." A gifted woodcarver had made them, she said, a man who took pride in his work but who'd mixed his own unique style with that borrowed from an authentic tribal tradition. The result was intended to be sold, like much airport or curio shop art, not to deceive.

"How can you tell when a piece is genuine and not deliberately faked?"

"Just a feeling. I'm not always sure, but the more I see, the more I know."

"Intuition maybe?"

"Not entirely."

"Then you've been studying."

She told me she had majored in art history at Bennington and had studied at the Rhode Island School of Design. During Jeffrey's assignment to Washington she had worked part time for a Georgetown interior decorator who collected African art. Her interest had begun there. A college roommate was now assistant curator at a Connecticut museum and from time to time sent her books on Central African art. Since her arrival she had bought a few pieces of her own and added to her small library of ethnological texts, African art books, and museum catalogs. She had begun auditing a few anthropology classes at Louvanium University.

I was surprised. "So you know what to look for. You're an expert now."

"Hardly. But I know what I like. Because so much on the local market isn't authentic, collecting is difficult. Never getting out of the capital makes it all the harder. You're lucky if you're able to travel here, very lucky."

Pickersgill and Jeffrey joined us, sweating and out of breath, and then retreated to the dressing rooms for a shower and a rub-down before their seven o'clock match.

Blakey and I followed slowly along the path where the shadows had lengthened across the lawn under a still-luminous evening sky. Head down, choosing her words carefully, she told me she didn't think of the Congo as a nation at all but as a quilt-work of tribes, each best identified by its art. The more primitive the tribe, the less interesting the art, but each was unique. For her the country only made sense if you knew something of the tribes: Bakongo, Bayaka, Bapende, Basalampasu, or Baluba. The Basuku too, the Bakusu, Bakuba, Bolia, and Basonge, to name a few.

Embarrassed, she hesitated and raised her eyes, as if her knowledge went far beyond my interest. "It's a little confusing sometimes, I admit."

I said the names meant nothing to me except one and told her about the Bapende mask I'd bought in the Kwilu, probably because it reminded me of the woodsmoke of the interior and my first trip to the bush.

"You're a romantic."

"Probably."

We reached the foot of the terrace steps and a Congolese waiter joined us with his tray and asked if we wanted a table. I looked at Blakey, who glanced at her watch and hesitated.

"Why not?" I suggested.

So we climbed to the terrace and sat there for another thirty minutes or so. Listening to her describe the country in terms of its art made more sense than many of the discussions I had heard at the embassy. Her knowledge struck me as much as her modesty that first night on the Pickersgills' terrace. The dinner crowd began to arrive, American and Belgian couples moving loudly among the nearby tables. "But I've been talking too much," she said. "You haven't told me anything about the rest of your trip."

I described crossing the Kwilu River that afternoon, the immensity as much as the silence, and mentioned the Ohio River and my Kentucky boyhood. I told her about my visit to the native market and the old woman rising from behind the counter, seeing me and hiding her eyes. The smile in Blakey's eyes touched her lips and transformed her face.

"That's lovely," she said, still smiling as if she was a little surprised by my familiarity and embarrassed in some way. "Just lovely."

A few minutes later Jeffrey called from the bottom of the steps, dressed for his seven o'clock match. He frowned, tapped his wristwatch with his racquet handle, and turned away. We got up and went down the steps. "Thanks for the drink. And the story. It was wonderful. And without your Lingala, it would have been completely different, wouldn't it? I told you it would work out." She followed after him, then turned and waved, still backing away. I went back to my table and finished my drink alone, feeling the emptiness of the afternoon. Her glass was still on the table, still wrapped in a napkin. I missed her, missed her even more as I realized how much I had shared with her that afternoon that I wouldn't have shared with anyone else.

The next morning she was still on my mind. I put the Bapende mask in the burlap bag, bound it tightly with hemp cord, and attached a note to her, saying I wanted her to have it. On my way down the stairs, I stopped on the floor below, looped the rope over her doorknob, rang the bell, and went on without waiting. Later that day I thought I had been too presumptuous. When I returned that afternoon an envelope in blue vellum was waiting in my downstairs box. Inside was a note from Blakey. "The Bapende mask was marvelous," she wrote in her bold, fluid handwriting, "one of the loveliest gifts I've ever received. You're too generous and I'm very grateful."

It was the first and last time she ever mentioned it.

Ken McAuliffe and I traveled regularly after that, sometimes by regular airline flights or packet boat along the Congo and Kwilu Rivers, sometimes hitching rides on the U.S. Military Assistance group's C-119 ferrying military advisors to Lubumbashi. Occasionally we cadged seats on single-engine missionary aircraft, other times we were dropped off by the defense attaché's Cessna—"The Bug Smasher," we called it, its front window crusted with tropical insect life lifted on the savannah fires as the farmers burned their fields. We flew in fair weather and foul, in twelve-seat DeHavillands crowded with chicken coops, crates of vegetables, and squalling children, and sometimes leased two-engine aircraft, *petit porteurs* flown by young

Belgian pilots accumulating enough flying time to qualify for their European licenses.

The towns and villages of the sparsely inhabited wilderness were separated from one another by vast distances, most inaccessible from the capital except by air. The scars of the rebellions and government neglect were everywhere apparent. International aid money poured in but none reached the interior. Roads were impassable even in the dry season, bridges and ferries were out, riverboats idle for lack of parts. Palm oil, maize, coffee, and cotton plantations were abandoned for lack of roads to evacuate their products or agricultural credits to restore the ruins. Government teachers and doctors were recruited from the capital but went unpaid, like the remote local administrators, and worked without textbooks, medicine, or buildings. The provinces we traveled were much the same, all bankrupt, victims of abandonment, venality, and neglect. Villagers survived by foraging, gathering, and subsistence farming, government officials by their wits, by petty peculation and thievery.

We camped out in the rotting guest houses of abandoned palm oil and coffee plantations still unoccupied after the rebellions, in decaying colonial hotels in dusty provincial capitals, in bare-as-bones Catholic hostels, in spare bedrooms or on cots in the front rooms of isolated missionary outposts with their oil lamps and oilcloth-covered kitchen tables, as bare, primitive, and sparse as those on the Kansas and Nebraska prairies, circa 1850. We slept on reed mats in village huts and sometimes in the back of the Land Rover.

There were still pockets of rebellion in a few regions we visited. In the mountains high above Uvira south of Bukavu a group of rebels were still holding out. They'd never been pacified, not by the Belgians, not by the missionaries, not by the

40

army. We spent the night on the shores of the lake below in a strange caravansary whose high adobe walls with the mountains looming high to the west made it seem like something out of the Hindu Kush. It was run by Italian priests in dirty white soutanes who had a collection of Italian gangster films.

In the forests of Kilembe below Idiofa we spent two nights on a palm oil plantation just reactivated after the rebellions. The palm oil processing plant had been attacked two nights before by a handful of guerrillas with muskets and bows and arrows, the survivors of Pierre Mulele's ragtag rebel army. I spent the hottest, most miserable night of my life in an abandoned coffee plantation above Lac Leo II a few degrees south of the equator. Mosquitoes made sleep impossible. I ended up sacking out in an old Victorian bathtub filled with pea-green lake water brought up in a teakettle. God knows what bacilli bedded down with me that night.

The next morning a Black wash boy in tattered shorts appeared at the front door with an invitation for breakfast. The old house was occupied after all. We walked up the lane between the raffia palms and were greeted on the front steps of the porticoed house by a ruddy-faced coffee planter in khaki shorts and white knee-length hose, a .45 automatic stuck in his belt. He told us he was a Polish-born Belgian and so was his wife, maybe twenty years younger and as pale as a ghost as she came down the long staircase from upstairs.

There was a long table in the dining room smelling of mold and bat dung where whitewash had peeled from the walls and ceiling. We sat under a cobwebbed chandelier with the morning sunshine leaking through the dusty windows and across the dusty floor, served coffee, rolls, and English jam by the Congolese houseboy in white gloves while the planter told us of his plans to organize a commercial fishing operation on the lake with European venture capital. A copy of the *London Financial Times* lay on the table next to him. The fish would be frozen or smoked. The frozen fish would be shipped to Europe, the smoked fish to markets in West Africa. Despite the paper folded at his elbow, he didn't convince me, I don't think he persuaded McAuliffe, and I don't think he reassured his young wife, who listened silently, her eyes as pale as a weimaraner's as she turned to me and McAuliffe in turn as her husband droned on, trying to learn by our faces whether we believed her husband. I didn't. She wasn't wearing a wedding ring and I didn't think he was Polish-born at all or that she was his wife. He offered us a brandy as we left but we declined. He was holding a brandy snifter and smiling ambiguously as he said good-bye on the front steps. I think he knew I didn't believe him.

It was after that trip that I began borrowing books from Blakey's library. She occasionally used the second-floor embassy conference room to work on Genevieve Graham's social schedule. Late one morning she was coming down the stairs as I was going up and we stopped and talked for a minute.

"How do you keep all the names straight?" I wondered.

"What names?" She stopped, puzzled.

"The tribes, the names, the art, the masks. All of it."

Her face lit up. "Oh, that. It takes a lot of study, a lot of reading, like anything worthwhile. Why? Are you really interested?"

"Yeah, very much. But I can't find much on the Kwilu in the library."

"Why don't you drop by this afternoon? I'll show you my library. It's not much but you can help yourself. It's a beginning anyway."

I showed up at six, admitted by a small moon-faced Bakongo houseboy in a white jacket. It was a nice apartment, far larger and better furnished than my own. There were Persian rugs in the hall and a thick beige carpet in the living room. The walls were hung with prints and a few modern abstracts, one an original that looked like a Miró. Behind one of the two long couches was a bar, next to it an upright piano. Blakey came down the hall from the kitchen and led me into the study across from the living room. On the bookcase above the studio couch were three shelves of art books, museum catalogs, and ethnological texts. She put on her glasses and brought down a history of the Bakuba kingdoms of the savannahs written by a Belgian scholar, a small monograph, and a museum catalog from Brussels.

"Start with these. Some of the text will probably bore you but the illustrations will help. Try to associate each tribal name with a piece of art. That's what I do." She gave me a mimeographed list of other books sent to her by her curator friend in Connecticut. She had abstracted a half-dozen titles from the same list and sent it to the USIS library, suggesting they buy them.

I returned her books a week later, a little awkwardly I suppose, unfamiliar with the etiquette of calling on a married woman. She was in the kitchen with her part-time Bakongo cook, wearing a dark dress and an apron, getting ready for two guests Jeffrey had invited for dinner. She told me to help myself from the books on the library shelf and left me there while she went back to the kitchen. I browsed for a while and found two museum catalogs that looked interesting.

As I was leaving Jeffrey came in. I don't think he liked my being there but Blakey quickly joined us and explained. "Ah, yes, Margaret's student scholar, is it. Seeking barbarous enlightenment, are we?" She asked me to join them for a drink before the guests arrived. I thanked her but said no. I didn't want to push my luck.

After nine years of marriage, their formality still had too much a public aspect. He still called her Margaret, she still called him Jeffrey. People who live such unrelenting public lives don't have much of a private one; marriages intended for public performance are usually dishonest as well. I suspected Jeffrey was responsible. His self-awareness seemed as theatrical as it had during our first meeting and explained a lot, including her interest in African art and her lonely Sundays at the pool. I thought him a domineering bore, someone who interests you less each time you see him, like a bright candle burning down. Maybe that's what I wanted to think. But what do bachelors know? It probably happens with a lot of marriages.

Blakey's books began my tutorials and I soon moved on to other texts from the library. Not having much else to do with my free hours except study Lingala, read, drink, and listen to my record collection, in time I got interested.

As it turned out she was right. The Congo I'd read about was a political and diplomatic abstraction; the Congo I came to know with her help wasn't a nation at all but a patchwork of tribes, each most easily recognizable by their art. Mobutu's army and his national political party were the stitches holding the tribal patches together, both as brutal as they were corrupt. At first the hundreds of tribes were no more than a congestion of unpronounceable names, but in time Blakey and the library books taught me to sort them out. Like Blakey, I suppose I have a visual imagination anyway, and the masks and fetishes helped, a kind of mnemonic device.

Because of her art books, museum catalogs, and ethnological texts as well as my trips to the bush, I recognized the truth of what she'd told me: The most politically mature tribes were also the most interesting artistically. If the discovery increased my interest, I had no one to share it with. No one at the embassy cared about native art; "nation-building" was the new diplomatic dynamic and "economic takeoff" the miracle engine that lifted it from poverty, hopelessness, and deprivation. I picked up anything I could for her during my bush travels. Her interest wasn't limited to the aesthetics of a piece. The uglier and more sinister a fetish or a ritual mask, the more authentic it was for her. Since she never got out of the capital, her knowledge was incomplete. She never knew the absolute darkness of the African night, never saw her weird little figures dancing their ghoulish jig in the coals of a dying village fire.

But I didn't like dropping by her apartment. Late one afternoon Jeffrey appeared unexpectedly in the study door, still in tennis shorts and a damp tennis shirt, a towel around his neck. We hadn't heard him come in. I don't know whether he'd crept in trying to surprise us but we both looked up from the couch. "Ah, yes," he said, seeing the museum book on Blakey's lap. "Art must have its way, mustn't it." He left and returned with a glass of soda and sat down in the leather chair, a towel around his neck, blond legs crossed, his cold eyes on Blakey. His presence broke her concentration as well as mine. After a few minutes I left.

We began meeting casually on Sundays at the pool or at the Belgian Club. I would show her the itinerary for my upcoming trip and ask what I should be looking for. Jeffrey was usually off somewhere on Sunday mornings or in the late afternoon, at his little theater group, playing tennis at the ambassador's court, or learning to water-ski on the Congo River with the Dutch chargé d'affaires. We would go through one of the books she had brought looking for details about the territories McAuliffe and I would visit, not only the tribes and the art, but the first European discoverers, the tribal rivalries, the mission stations, the old Belgian outposts, the flora and fauna. I think she got a lot of pleasure from that and I learned a lot more about the Congo than I'd intended. Later I was surprised at how much I'd soaked up.

McAuliffe made traveling easy. He'd seen it all before and nothing ever bothered him, not strange couples telling lies in abandoned houses, not the long hours waiting at some remote grass landing strip for a flight that wouldn't come, not the hours spent on a mosquito-infested riverbank waiting for a broken-down ferry, a Land Rover, or a truck to be repaired in the light of a battery lantern. He had patience, I didn't, and never understood where his came from. He always had a few books in his kit bag and it didn't matter whether we were broken down on the track or waiting in some dusty little provincial office for the local administrator to show up. Out would come one of his paperbacks. In the Peace Corps he'd taught shop mechanics in a Karachi vocational school. One book he always carried with him was a worn manual on small engine repair bound in red leather. Mechanical problems interested him more than the abstractions of political reporting (in this he was typically American). I don't suppose we ever made a trip together that he didn't end up on his back under a truck or humped over a balky generator or pump with a flashlight, fingers silver-black with graphite.

He had lost faith in our ability to make a difference any other way. For almost two years he'd reported on the conditions he found in the interior but nothing had changed; the diplomatic and social minuet continued.

You could never tell what other books he might have. I remember crossing the Lualaba River in the Kasai that July and he opened his kit bag and took out Livingstone's journal. He showed me Livingstone's entry as he'd crossed the Lualaba just two miles upstream a century earlier. There were other books too, obscure yellow-paged volumes in crumbling octavos he had picked up at the bookstalls along the Seine and in London, tales of the eighteenth- and nineteenth-century travelers in Africa and the Middle East.

In the dusty streets everyone seemed to know him, to recognize the dark-blond hair, the beard, the khaki hiking shorts, and the cleated engineer's boots he wore in the bush. Black street orphans would wait for him on the steps of our hotel and then troop after us through the streets, rural administrators would ask for office furniture, vehicles, scholarships for themselves or their cousins, or reassignment back to the capital. America was invincible in those days, America could do anything, or so they thought, and McAuliffe was their hope for the future. Village women waved at him from their manioc patches, missionaries regaled him with their tales of government corruption; their plain, prim, unpainted wives put on rouge and a bright dress, set out their best dinner plates for supper, and afterward brought out their broken appliances.

He always knew someone interesting to talk to, whether native or European, whether an old Belgian mercenary turned planter, a Greek trader mining secretly for gemstones or cobalt, or a defrocked French priest who was living with his sixteen-year-old native bride in a crumbling old cottage near Luluabourg. The priest was an emaciated man in his late fifties with long thin hair the color of ashes, palsied hands, and a racking cough. He was writing his memoirs, he said, rising from his armchair and shuffling across the hot little room to haul out a notebook-filled cardboard box from under the table where he kept his gin, whiskey, and cordial bottles. "A pure Cartesian screw-up," McAuliffe said that afternoon as we left. "Screwed up, screwed in, and screwed out. Dead in six months."

McAuliffe knew everything worth seeing, even if he didn't always tell me where we were going. I'd sit there in the borrowed or rented Land Rover, bouncing crazily over the track, and after thirty minutes or so think he'd gotten us lost again, as he did once or twice. Then he would stop and point down a trail and there would be a Pygmy village or a dozen fishermen wading a whitewater river to set their fish traps below a thundering falls, or an incredible view of the mountains of Rwanda in the distance. He wouldn't say a word, just shake his head and smile. If our journey came at the end of the day, maybe we'd open a bottle of beer from the twelve-packs of American commissary beer he always brought with him, whether warm or cold, and we would get out and sit there on the fender in silence enjoying the view. He never took a camera with him. After a few trips neither did I. Just being there was enough.

He had studied at Harvard, or so he said. I didn't know that until that night outside the palm oil plant near Kilembe when we sat on our sleeping bags over the wood fire drinking beer and talking until one o'clock while our two night guards sat in the fringes of the firelight, old carbines across their knees, their eyes hyena-bright as they stirred at every sound in the surrounding forest. He had drunk four or five beers that night and was more talkative than usual.

After Harvard he'd done postgraduate work in Paris and Geneva, where he'd worked on a research grant at L'Institute des Hauts Etudes before moving on to Paris as a research assistant at CBS News. His French was far better than mine and the best at the embassy, with an idiomatic Parisian quickness that often eluded me and approached that of a native-born French speaker.

I asked him why he left Geneva. He was lying on his back in front of the fire, one leg lifted over the other, looking up through the fringe of trees at the star-strewn sky. His grant was for a study of French policy toward Germany, 1945–1955. After six months of research, he read through his first three chapters. "I'd never read a more treacly collection of clichés, lies, and half-pissed plagiarisms in my life," he said, laughing. Whether in writing history, biography, or anything else, putting words to paper was a moral act. His weren't. So he had burned it, all of it.

He hadn't grown up on a ranch. His father had been a history professor at a small New England college. When he was ten his father had taken orders, become an Episcopal minister, and moved his family west, first to Montana and then Idaho and Oregon. He was something of an enigma to others but wasn't sly the way I was. Like most incorrigibly honest people, he had no sense of the mystery in himself.

My restlessness was plain enough. I'd been a drifter since college and still was, searching for something I couldn't find. As an undergraduate I'd been in and out of four universities in the West, the Midwest, the South, and the East before I finally took a degree. After two years in the army I went on to graduate school but lasted less than eight months. My friends and classmates were planning to be doctors, lawyers, architects, or engineers. Some would follow their fathers into the family firm, into banking, real estate, insurance or the law, into the brokerage or distillery, into industrial lacquers, frozen foods, aluminum foil, or bathtub fixtures while I prowled the anteroom, waiting to be summoned as I had as a boy, reading dog-eared *National Geographic*s in the dim Heyburn Building office of Dr. Bradford Ryder, my grandfather's physician, who hadn't changed his wallpaper, his chairs, rugs, suits, ties, or mouthwash in the dozen years I'd been going to him.

In time they would move on into marriage and family, into suburban homes on Cherokee Circle, Vauxhall Road, or Old Lyme Lane, and on into the Louisville Country, Boat, or Pendennis Clubs, into respectability, security, and middle age while I still prowled the margins, awaiting my summons. I didn't know what secrets they possessed that had been denied me. I imagined they were in full command of their lives while mine eluded me. All I knew was that there was far more to my life than I understood or could reveal to others. What moved me on wasn't the certainty of truths possessed but the mystery of everything uncommunicable, a world too complex, too chaotic, and too vast to imagine any all-embracing unity in medicine, commerce, or the law. After six years abroad I was little more than a vagabond turned diplomat. Living abroad indulged my wanderlust and gave me an excuse for postponement. Always restlessly moving on, never satisfied, always pushing toward a frontier I would never cross, maybe I imagined too much, waiting for something miraculous to happen. But it never had.

I didn't know what McAuliffe was looking for. What was obvious was that after eighteen months of writing up trip reports that were soon forgotten in the political section safes and the African Bureau archives back on the fifth floor at State, he no longer took his reporting seriously. He said it was the same dead end as Geneva and Paris. The interior was still prostrate in its misery; now that the rebellions were dying out, no one cared. I suggested a new ambassador meant a new beginning, a new opportunity, but he didn't agree. He had grown indifferent in his reporting; he often abandoned his drafts and I had to finish them myself, adding detail he'd neglected. It wasn't that he was lazy. He lived in the moment, in the practical world of making things work today, not tomorrow, lived for the physical pleasure of the here and now, whether it was meandering through the villages we visited, the beer, the cigarettes, the occasional grass, the chickens he so carefully roasted over an open fire, the *mwamba* he cooked, the vegetable stews he concocted, or the easy sensuality of his bedtime companion back in the capital. He had left the world of abstractions; reflection didn't matter much either, except as melancholy, sadly remembering a past that no longer mattered to him. After his junior year at Harvard, he had left for a year or so, roamed around, spent some months as a merchant seaman. He learned French as an auto mechanic's apprentice in Paris.

He annoyed the senior embassy staff, maybe because of his indifference to rank or protocol, because of the way he dressed and the way he talked, sometimes a kind of cryptic argot mockingly borrowed from the Beat hangouts and coffee houses of San Francisco where he had spent some time. Maybe it was because he baffled them, because they resented his independence. Bureaucrats are sometimes like that, levelers in their own way, avenging their mediocrity on the more daring, the more imaginative, and the more able. Turpin was one of them. One time a few days after we got back from one of our trips, he called me from his office and asked me to drop by. I had moved to the political section in the chancellery by then. I didn't know what he had in mind when I arrived. He went into his office and he carefully shut the door, listened for a moment, and then squeaked his way behind his desk.

He was chairman of the board at the American School and his fifteen-year-old daughter had told him McAuliffe brought back grass from the bush and sold it to the young American teachers at the school. As school board chairman, it was Turpin's responsibility to know these things, just as it was mine to tell him.

Turpin had it backward. McAuliffe sometimes bought grass from a botany teacher at the school who had his own plot of marijuana hidden back in the scrub near his cottage, protected against discovery with a couple of fake green mambas dangling in a bamboo glade. We had a few joints from time to time at the small cottage he was sharing with Gretchen near the river. Twice in the bush, I'd heard him turn down offers of grass, once by a young Belgian bush pilot who had flown us to Mbandaka and a second time by the screwed-up son of an American missionary visiting his parents at their mission station outside Kindu. I told Turpin it wasn't true, that it wouldn't have mattered if it were, and that the rumor was as idiotic as the other stories I'd heard about McAuliffe.

"So you deny it," Turpin said, working his thick porcupine brows and giving me the benefit of a prickly frown. Frowning ferociously was his way of showing displeasure and terrorizing his supine office staff.

"Sure I deny it."

"What do you mean 'other stories'?"

"Just what I said. He sometimes rides a motorcycle, stays away from cocktail parties, and doesn't heel like the other diplomatic spaniels around here, so what?"

His short, stubby fingers drummed impatiently on his desk and his little gray-flecked sunflower-seed eyes were screwed up as he leaned across his desk. "Look here, Mathews. He's not someone I would recommend you imitating."

"Don't then. It's none of our bloody business, is it?" Our talk was over but I knew it wasn't forgotten.

Not long afterward Ambassador Graham decided to make his first trip to the interior. After a few indecisive talks with Pickersgill, Kim Johnson, and Colonel Harris as to which province he should visit, he thought of abandoning the trip. Then one Friday afternoon he summoned McAuliffe and me to his office and led us to the map in the conference room. What would McAuliffe recommend? McAuliffe asked what sort of trip he had in mind. A ceremonial visit to a provincial capital, long on protocol and short on local color, interest, or usefulness, or a more informal tour of the countryside?

"I simply want a much better sense of what's happening out there," Graham said, his small hand wandering vaguely over the map. "Three days, I should think. However you can manage it. But Genevieve says no tents and no sleeping bags."

McAuliffe didn't hesitate. He pointed to East Kasai and the capital of Mbuji-Mayi at the center of that vast plateau that lifts from the Congo River basin and ends in the Rift Valley lakes along the Tanzanian frontier. "Then why don't we begin here?" he said. After a few questions, Ambassador Graham agreed and asked McAuliffe to fly to East Kasai and make the arrangements.

Blakey and I left the Belgian Club terrace where she had been waiting and walked out the path under the trees along the eighth and ninth fairways. It was a brilliant cloudless afternoon. The blue sky was washed clean after the late-morning rains.

"When do you leave?"

"In the morning. Wheels up at five thirty."

"So soon. Maybe this will help." She had brought a book and handed it to me. "My friend in Connecticut sent it." We stopped in the shade of a tulip tree. It was published by the Musée de l'Homme in Paris. Folded inside was a tattered colored photograph clipped from a two-year-old issue of *Town and Country,* taken in the study of a posh country house in East Hampton. On the wall was a Kifwebe mask, one of the rarest and most valuable of all African masks.

"From the Basonge people in the bush to the east of Mbuji-Mayi. It would be nice to find something like this. But it doesn't belong in a private collection but a museum. Keep the picture, the book too."

We walked on and returned past the tennis courts where Jeffrey and a German counselor were playing doubles two courts away.

"He never gives it a rest, does he?" I said.

She stopped. "He only plays out of a sense of duty." Her voice was far away. "He has talent but it's wasted on the tennis court. He never wanted to be a consular officer. He's always had problems working with others. For some odd reason I think he likes the title."

Her comment surprised me but for the first time said something about their marriage, a subject I stayed away from. I wondered how much loyalty she had. Maybe no more than I did. We walked back to the terrace. She seemed especially tired that afternoon.

"What's the trouble?" I asked, knowing there was something else on her mind. I had seen that same quiet sadness before.

"What you said. 'Wheels up at five thirty.' It would be nice going someplace, getting away." I told her she would be going to Mbuji-Mayi with the ambassador's group. "I suppose so," she said. Then she told me Jeffrey had been a little touchy recently. A few people had commented about seeing us so often together at the Belgian Club and the residence pool. They had had an argument and after a long talk she had persuaded him to calm down and be sensible.

"Sensible how?"

Her head was down, her eyes on the path. "About you and me. Our relationship. An 'intellectual relationship,' so Jeffrey put it."

I laughed. "Is that what he said? That's so goddamned stupid I can't even think of an answer. What intellectual relationship?"

She flushed in a way I had never seen before. "What else would you call it? Our being together like this."

"I don't know. Is that what it is, an intellectual relationship?"

"Of course. What else could it be?"

"I don't know. Give me time. Maybe I'll figure it out. Do you want me to talk to him?"

"No, please. Don't make it difficult." We climbed the steps to the terrace. "It's hard enough as it is. Don't make it impossible."

We found our table and ordered drinks. The look on her face still bothered me. As well as I thought I knew her, she sometimes puzzled me, so quick, lively, and animated at times, laughing easily and naturally, and then just as suddenly silent and withdrawn as the silence lengthened and her smile faded, as if there were something she was denying in herself, her spontaneity, her loveliness, or maybe something else. That afternoon I watched her face as she followed Jeffrey and the German counselor coming back through the twilight under the trees and saw the same look again. I suppose a negative sense of oneself is inevitable with those who suppress their own individuality for the sake of another. I'd known a few women like that, women late in finding themselves, some realizing who they were only after the knowledge came too late and they'd married the wrong man. But I suppose that's a bachelor's view.

"I'd better go," I said as they disappeared toward the locker rooms. I didn't want to talk to him, knowing I'd say something I'd regret. "I've got to start packing."

She looked up, not answering for a minute, as if I weren't really there. "Don't do anything foolish." Then the smile came, lighting up her face the way it always did. "And don't be angry about what I said. Please. It will be all right."

It was noon when our Air Congo DC-3 dropped to the sunny tarmac at Mbuji-Mayi, the sleepy provincial capital six hundred miles to the east. It was McAuliffe's fifth trip to the Kasai, a region he favored, and my second. Through the missionary radio net we had sent word asking that a local Maluba planter by the name of Kalonji be notified of our arrival. Greeting us instead at the gate was the Reverend Virgil Moody. He told us Kalonji was in Lubumbashi so he'd come to invite us to be his guests. In his mid-sixties, he was a bowlegged missionary from Kansas with stiff gray hair, jittery gray eyes, and a prairie twang as dry as cracked corn. I'd met Moody during my first visit and wasn't impressed. For reasons I could never quite identify, I didn't trust him. I don't think McAuliffe did either.

We would have preferred to stay elsewhere but the alternatives weren't appealing. One was Madame Onema's decrepit three-story hotel on the edge of the native market where I'd spent two sleepless nights during my first visit, trying to keep unwelcome intruders out of my bed. The small rooms had little ventilation, hard thin mattresses, and no baths. The bed linen on my narrow iron cot hadn't been changed since the last occupant, the washbasin taps hadn't worked, and the door chain was missing. The girls from the bar below were appealing enough with their dusky faces and seductive smiles, beckoning with henna-stained fingers as they watched us from across the bar before dinner. They had a habit of roaming the upstairs halls after midnight in their long cotton waxes and rubber thongs.

My first night I spent a few hours answering discreet raps at the door. I finally backed a chair under the doorknob to keep the hallway courtesans out of my room and drifted off to sleep.

Around two o'clock I was wakened by soft hands and the fragrance of jasmine. A young girl had crept into my room, dropped the cotton robe from her shoulders, and slipped into my bed. She was mother naked, as sinuous as a seal and just as slippery as we wrestled about. If I'd pinned her to the bed Greco-Roman style the interlude might have ended differently, but I didn't. I picked her up, cradled her in my arms, dumped her out the door, and tossed her the wax and rubber thongs. She thought there was something personal in my throwing her out and maybe there was, but it was her youth, not her cunning little body. She couldn't have been more than thirteen years old.

The other option was an air-conditioned guest house belonging to the Belgian-managed diamond company, but the Belgians posed problems of another kind. The *Société*'s senior officials were tireless in their efforts to enlist American help in eliminating the illegal diamond mining. Reducing the illegal trade in diamonds would increase the Congo's foreign exchange earnings, or so they claimed, but the claim was disingenuous. The diamond syndicate wanted to reduce their own cash outlays in buying up the illegally mined diamonds that found their way abroad. One proposal was to equip the syndicate's security force with American Huey helicopters, another to transfer U.S. military sensor systems from Vietnam to the Kasai diamond reserve. Since the alluvial diamond mining area was the size of Connecticut, that crackpot idea made no better sense in the Kasai than in Vietnam. But for old Belgian *colons,* anything was possible in the Congo and everything had its price. They were as far out on the lunatic fringe as everyone else. When he visited Mbuji-Mayi, McAuliffe felt obliged to decline the *Société*'s offer of a guest cottage, as I would later, since neither of us wanted any misunderstanding about their hopes or our obligations.

We didn't welcome Moody's invitation but had no choice. We piled our luggage into the back of his rattling Land Rover and his driver drove us over the sand roads to the small sun-scaled stucco cottage a mile or so away. In a large guest room in the back he kept two sets of army-style bunks atop one another available to traveling missionaries and church functionaries. Donations for room and board were contributed to a quart mason jar on the table inside the door.

McAuliffe had brought a bottle of Irish whiskey for Kalonji, his Maluba planter friend. As we unpacked our bags in the back-room dormitory he offered the bottle to Moody. It was a gesture, nothing more, and I thought it odd when Moody accepted it and even odder when he insisted on paying for it. He hurried away to find his cash box, still wearing his dark serge suit, rayon tie, and black shoes. He looked a little like one of those nineteenth-century Indian agents on the Wyoming frontier and I said as much to McAuliffe, who only smiled.

A widower without a pulpit since the Africanization of the Protestant churches, Moody had lived in the Kasai for over twenty years and had remained on as a kind of unofficial vicar to the local Congolese clergy, who still gathered in his dining room for guidance, gossip, and prayer. The churches had fallen on hard times since independence. Foreign missionaries had once carved out denominational kingdoms in the old Belgian Congo, but nation-building was the new state religion, its apostles the thugs and bullies of Mobutu's single political party, *Le Mouvement Populaire de la Revolution.* Intended to create a new mass consciousness to displace those divisive tribal loyalties upon which the Protestants and Catholics had once built their congregations, it was as much an oppressor among the peoples of the interior as the old Belgian colonialism, intimidation and brutality as much its tool as forced servitude and the ten-lash law had been in King Leopold's Congo.

The passing of church authority had also been accompanied by that decline into backbiting, hypocrisy, and bitchery that corrupts disinherited clerisy everywhere. Not strong enough to break with the past and begin anew, as Moody should have done, they were too weak to do anything except whine about their fall from grace. For men of the cloth, the Congolese pastors I listened to at Moody's dining room table that night were a pretty disgraceful lot.

The next morning after breakfast McAuliffe and I eluded Moody, who was at his ham radio in the radio room, shouting into his microphone and trying to raise some retired missionary in Nebraska. "Yes, ma'am, that's right! Reverend Virgil Moody, WDXZQ, Mbuji-Mayi, the Congo! You hearing me now, sister? . . ."

We left the picket gate in front of his cottage and walked down the sand road through the stippled morning sunshine to the provincial offices. A Congolese flag hung from a rusting flagpole in the clay yard of the cream-colored stucco building that had once housed the old Belgian territorial administrator, now gone to decay and badly in need of paint. A newer flag hung alongside bearing the bright green banner of the national political party.

The nine o'clock appointment with Governor N'Debo had been scheduled by telegram through the Ministry of Interior, and we were ten minutes early. The policeman on duty at the front desk summoned the governor's *chef du protocol,* a plump frog-eyed Congolese in a too-tight European suit who was confused by our arrival and bewildered by our appearance. He'd instructed the policeman on duty to watch for the car bearing two American diplomats but we'd come on foot, wearing khakis, polo shirts, and hiking boots. We looked less like diplomats than two footloose American knockabouts roaming the bush.

Only after we showed him our pink diplomatic identity cards was he persuaded we were the visitors he'd been expecting. He was impressed but still confused and visibly nervous. The ministry telegram had informed him of our arrival but didn't explain our purpose. He led us into his small dusty cubicle of an office and offered us refreshment while we waited for Governor N'Debo. The *chef du protocol* was newly arrived, like the governor. He hadn't welcomed his assignment so far from the capital among an alien people and complained of his homesickness now. The local *mwamba* was inedible, the local women sullen and treacherous, like the men. His wash boy was a thief.

N'Debo joined us ten minutes later and invited us into his larger but just as empty office. Tall and portly, he was impeccably tailored in a blue shantung Mao suit. His handshake left my hand smelling of eau de cologne. He was of the Bakongo tribe from the Atlantic coast six hundred miles to the west, newly assigned to the Kasai after several years of parliamentary obscurity. His aquiline face was jet black and his bearing impressive, like many from the Bakongo mercantile aristocracy. He smiled constantly across his desk but his smile was facile rather than warm, like his light, dry French chatter. He had none of that melancholy that troubled the more serious politicians I'd met.

He was surprised the American ambassador was coming but pleased and honored. He'd been in Mbuji-Mayi for less than three weeks, was still settling in, as much a stranger to East Kasai as I was, and knew far less of the region than McAuliffe. After the rebellions the provincial legislatures had been abolished as centers of tribalism and sedition, governors were assigned who weren't natives of the provinces they ruled, and men like N'Debo were the result. Like Roman proconsuls, they seldom spoke the local tribal dialects, hadn't the trust of the local populations, and were often indifferent to or contemptuous of their welfare.

Our courtesy call lasted twenty minutes. I'd met a number of governors by then and thought N'Debo was less a serious administrator than a parliamentary dandy with substantial business interests on the side. He had no advice to offer on the ambassador's itinerary. Knowing Mbuji-Mayi and the Kasai as he did, McAuliffe had already prepared a draft itinerary. N'Debo suggested we discuss the plans with his deputy, Pierre Matanda, a Mupende from the Kwilu McAuliffe had dealt with during his earlier visits.

McAuliffe's draft schedule for the ambassador's three-day visit included an overland trip to Chief Job's remote village out on the savannah some fifty kilometers away. He'd met Chief Job a year earlier while traveling alone and they'd become friends. Three times his guest during his travels, now he wanted the ambassador to visit the village.

Matanda frowned when he saw McAuliffe's schedule. The village was too far from Mbuji-Mayi, Chief Job too minor a chief to deserve the honor and too poor to afford the hospitality offered by the more important Baluba *chefs cotumiers,* or traditional chiefs, whose villages were larger, wealthier, and more accessible.

"Oui. C'est exact," McAuliffe told him, and that was the point. Visiting a poor, obscure village was one purpose of the ambassador's trip, to discover for himself the conditions of remote rural life.

Matanda lazily disagreed. *"Non, non, non, non! Ecoutez-moi encore un peu, cher ami."* Chief Job's village was far too isolated to have shared in provincial development and wasn't typical of anything except its own backwardness. The people there were treacherous, inhospitable, and unapproachable. Compared with the larger villages of *les chefs cotumiers,* they were hay-seeds, louts, nosepickers *"à la merde,"* sauced in their own filth. *"Ils font rien, ils dorment!"* They did nothing but sleep all day. Ragpickers, cretins, mental retards!

McAuliffe tried to persuade him to accompany us, but Matanda didn't know Chief Job, had never visited his miserable village, and had no intention of doing so now. Besides, he had a bad back, a slipped disk so the Belgian doctor at the *Société*'s clinic had told him, a condition that could only be made worse by bouncing over rough roads through choking dust that aggravated his bleeding sinuses. He pulled a handkerchief from his jacket pocket. How he suffered sometimes—nagging headaches, nights without sleep!

Tired of the impasse, I got up and told McAuliffe we should forget bringing the ambassador to the Kasai and think of the Kwilu instead. McAuliffe nodded and stood up. Matanda daintily returned his handkerchief to his pocket and followed us to the door. Okay. Enough! *"Puisque c'est ça, allez!"* If that's the way it is, go ahead. If Chief Job was willing to entertain the ambassador and not ask the provincial government to finance the traditional feast, he might think about it. But he wouldn't give the chief a single *makuta* and we were to tell him that. We'd then see for ourselves he had no interest in entertaining the American ambassador. But McAuliffe had visited Chief Job's village three times and the chief had never asked him for a thing, no bags of rice for a Food-for-Work Program, no scholarships for his village youths, no pumps, not even hand tools for his farmers.

Matanda had a police Land Rover sent around and we were driven back through the sand streets to the Reverend Moody's cottage. Moody was in the back room, talking by radio to the Presbyterian mission at Bibanga. He'd been surprised the previous evening when McAuliffe had told him he knew Chief Job and had eagerly volunteered his Land Rover as well as his services as interpreter. Now he was surprised the visit was still on. We climbed into his Land Rover and set out across the savannah, trailed by two provincial policemen in a gray Land Rover.

The Kasai had been a rebellious province years earlier and the scars were everywhere apparent—bridges out, roads unrepaired, and farms abandoned. The Balubas believed they were being punished for their earlier rebellions but their lot was no different from the other provinces we traveled. All were victims, not so much of retribution but of venality, corruption, and neglect. In East Kasai, once a fertile cotton and agricultural region, the illegal mining of the province's alluvial diamond reserve had become the principal industry of the impoverished local population as well as local officials. The government's response was to strengthen the police constabularies and army caserns. Since both the police and the army were involved in the illegal trade and both had vehicles and aircraft at their disposal, the policy only increased the efficiency of the trade and the profits of senior officials back in Kinshasa.

Chief Job's village lay fifty kilometers to the east atop a solitary mountain lifting a thousand feet above the scrub. I saw it first as a hazy blue shadow in the distance, not as impressive as the African peaks in Tanzania, in the Tibesti, or even the Kivu, but unique enough for the savannahs of the Kasai. The switchback laterite road leveled off at the top of the final grade and we drove through a small village of no more than a dozen thatched huts.

I saw no signs of life in the dirt clearings. No cooking fires burned, although the pots were there, and no village men lounged under the raffia-roofed shelters that protected their idleness from the torrid midday sun while their wives toiled with hoes and machetes in the patches of manioc, maize, and sweet potatoes. The village seemed deserted. I wondered if the villagers were off on bivouac on the vast diamond reserve or maybe inside the huts, resting after a night of illegal digging. I asked McAuliffe if he knew anything about the village. He was as puzzled as I was.

Moody said nothing, head turned with ours toward the deserted huts, abandoned to the midday sun. He didn't tell us the village was the sorcerer's village, guarding entrance to the loaf of mountain and frightening away meddlesome government officials, itinerant Protestant pastors, and vagabond American diplomats. He didn't tell us the sorcerer and his village were Chief Job's bitter tribal enemies.

The sorcerer's power was legion among the Balubas of the region, the most feared of the local *Bena N'Kuba,* as we would learn later. Because Moody was a tireless source of local color, anecdote, and gossip, as he had been for the past hour with his babbling travelogue on the passing landscape, explaining what needed no explanation, like the fresh elephant spoor we saw on the track or the bundle of orange plantains carried by a young woman we passed on the road, his silence was curious if not inexplicable. But if he told us nothing about the old wizard and the bad blood between the two villages, the sorcerer would know of our visit. Vehicles were rare on that remote mountain-top, and three white men followed by a police Land Rover soon attract attention.

Three kilometers beyond the rutted sand road petered out at the edge of a draw and was replaced by a worn footpath leading up the hill through the trees. The village in the clearing at the end of the path was as small and poor as McAuliffe had said, no more than eight thatched huts lying under the raffia palms and African hardwoods on the final knoll before the mountain dropped away.

Chief Job had heard our vehicle and was standing on a patch of bare earth in front of his own thatched hut, puzzled, a hand mattock in one hand, a clump of onions in the other. He recognized McAuliffe and came to embrace him as he would a native son returned from the capital. He was a small man, five foot four or so, small and shrunken but with lively cinnamon-brown eyes and an imposing Buddha-like head too large for his dwarfish body, covered with a flocculence of gray-white hair. He was in his late sixties, I suppose, and was wearing foam thongs, a tattered white shirt, and ragged khaki shorts, like a wash boy back in the capital, the torn patches stitched and restitched with a quilt of sewing machine thread, like much of the European clothing sold in the interior, transported in bales from the sec-ondhand clothing marts of Europe and America and unloaded from the ships at Matadi by the wholesalers in Kinshasa, many of them Greek Jews from Rhodes.

He welcomed me in his broken French and turned to Moody with a nod. Yes, he had heard of the Reverend Moody. His glance didn't linger. McAuliffe suggested we take a tour of the village, and Chief Job led us about on his thin leprechaun legs, showing me first his own large hut and then two others, all dark, their earth floors recently swept, all smelling richly of woodsmoke, which by then had become the smell of Africa for me. In the last hut a pregnant woman and two girls sat in the shadows weaving raffia mats. His wife and two of his daughters, he told me. Outside again, he explained the cultivation of the two small patches of field nearby where manioc, yams, and stunted maize grew. By then we had been joined by a few men of the village, all following curiously but respectfully at a distance.

I asked about their hand tools. The chief summoned one villager, took a mattock from his hand, and showed it to me. Crudely hand-forged and very old, the handle was polished to the smoothness of coin silver. As old as he was, he said. He spoke easily and familiarly, with none of those wooden mannerisms that characterized the other tribal chiefs I'd met, usually in their ceremonial capes and cowrie-beaded caps, always addressed through an official interlocutor and always under government auspices, coaxed and prodded about by party officials like children in a grade-school pageant.

As we were standing at the top of the rise above the village looking out over the vast plain below, the savannah bleached white by the midday sun, the silver river bickering and flashing along the rapids, he turned to McAuliffe and asked if the Americans were still on the moon. McAuliffe laughed and said no, the American astronauts had come home.

McAuliffe's second visit to the chief's village had come just after an Apollo moon landing. The USIS cultural center and the embassy in Kinshasa had made the most of it, a public relations bonanza after the bloody stalemate in Vietnam. There were press releases for the national radio, photographs for the local press, and NASA films for private viewing for cabinet officials. Through the secretary of the MPR political party, the embassy had arranged a film showing of the Apollo landing for the senior party leadership at the national theater. The crowd left the theater in a late-evening gullywasher, thunder booming over the rooftops, whitewater raging through the gutters and flooding the streets. Running blindly for their Mercedes, many of the party dignitaries got soaked. The same week an article on the front page of *Le Matin* reported that the old women soothsayers in the market believed the Americans had infuriated the sun god, first landing on his lunar consort in their grasshopperlike vehicle and then stomping about in their heavy boots to defile her virgin beauty. The sun god was punishing the earth with the violently unseasonable weather.

I don't know whether Chief Job believed all this or was even aware of it but he remembered the Apollo moon landing. He told us some in the Kasai thought the Americans were still on the moon, men better informed than he, men who knew of such things. His own poor head couldn't confirm it any more than his senses could. The moon seemed to him the same, hanging in the night sky as it had since he was a boy, just as the stars and the sun were the same. He and his villagers knew about the moon landing only because others in the Kasai who owned transistor radios had heard the transmissions in Lingala and told them it was true. He was speaking in Tshiluba now, not French, and Moody was translating; yet from the sly way Chief

Job looked at McAuliffe and me as he spoke, I knew he wasn't talking about the American moon landing. In his native language he was saying he had no faith in Mobutu's national radio.

As we moved back toward the village, he told us he owned no radio; he and his villagers were as isolated as ever. The territorial administrator and the local party officials left his village alone, like the Congolese pastors. I asked him why and he pointed down the path toward the track and said something in Tshiluba as Moody translated. Moody explained Chief Job believed his village too small, poor, and inaccessible to interest the provincial administrators in Mbuji-Mayi. Although at the time I had no reason to question Moody's translation, I later came to doubt this was what Chief Job told us. I suspect he was explaining that it was fear of the old sorcerer at the far end of the mountain that kept Mobutu's political apostles and Moody's ministers away.

Returning to the chief's hut for a glass of palm wine, I saw a large bleached skull lying half hidden in the grass behind the hut. It was an elephant's skull, the chief said, the skull of a marauding elephant that had terrorized the village for an entire planting season six years earlier. One evening the elephant had appeared there where the skull lay, the enormous legs rooted like tree trunks in the high grass. That same afternoon the chief had walked all the way from Mbuji-Mayi and was very tired. He'd gone to his hut to rest and at dusk was wakened by his three village elders whispering that the elephant was behind his hut. No one else knew how to fire the village's single musket and so the chief had gotten up, muzzle-loaded the old firing piece with a wad of powder, crept outside, dropped to one knee, and shot the elephant where he stood.

He stooped over like an old woman, eyes shut, hands over his ears as he described how the elders had waited nearby. Afterward he had left the skull in the high grass as a kind of memorial, not to the dead elephant, although it was a very old elephant, not to other marauding elephants, and not to his marksmanship in shooting elephants. He meditated for a moment, head turned away, resisting Moody's prompting and speaking again in French. He had left the skull there as a memorial to the harshness of life here in this poor remote village where the government still hadn't come to dig a well and where the women still drew water from the river far below, despite marauding elephants. But the luck hadn't been in the shot, the luck had been in the weapon.

He led us inside and from its burlap wrapping brought out an ancient octagon-barreled Belgian musket. It fired no cartridge, no ball, but a spear, the heavy shank thrust in the bore and discharged by a thunderous explosion of black powder ignited by flint and iron. Now, of course, weapons weren't fired that way. When the elders had wakened him that evening and asked him to fetch the old blunderbuss, they had no idea of its risks. It wasn't simply a matter of killing an elephant or being entertained by a fiery explosion on a feast day—*Non! Non!* It was risky business.

From a battered tin trunk at the head of his pallet he brought out the hand-forged iron spearpoint, as large as his hand, still wired to the thick wooden shaft. In the bottom of the trunk were the two elephant tusks, still wrapped in raffia. Holding the ancient musket in one hand and the wooden shaft in the other, I knew what he meant. Unfired for years, the old rogue musket he had raised that evening had a hairline crack at the breech and was probably as dangerous as the elephant he'd brought down with a very lucky shot, probably by severing its jugular vein. Yes, I said, he'd been very lucky. He nodded and brought out a corked bottle of palm wine and four green plastic glasses. As he poured out the palm wine, he said he hoped he would never again have to fire the old musket. Once a lifetime was enough for any man, even a chief. Perhaps the skull outside was to remind him of that too.

As we were saying good-bye at the head of the footpath, McAuliffe finally told the chief of the ambassador's coming visit to East Kasai and our hope he could come visit his village. Surprised, Chief Job solemnly searched McAuliffe's face, then mine. He turned silently to study the clutter of thatched huts and the handful of villagers watching us, and then looked away to the east. Moody started to say something but McAuliffe shook his head, waiting for the chief's answer.

Nodding, the chief finally turned back to us. Yes, he would be honored if the ambassador would visit his village, but what could he offer this important man, this ambassador from a country that had sent a man to the moon? Only the same friendship and hospitality he had offered McAuliffe, and of course he would offer that.

No one said much as we drove back the mountain. Moody was behind the wheel. I didn't give much notice to the sorcerer's village as we passed through. Neither did McAuliffe.

We met with Matanda the next morning in his office, bright with midmorning sunshine and drowsy with flies from an open window. He'd been with the Belgians the night before and was sleepily hung over. He'd discussed the ambassadorial visit with a few of the *Société*'s senior officials and had drawn up an itinerary that he was anxious to share with us. The Belgians had volunteered their guest cottages for the ambassador and his party, but we'd expected that. Given the size of the group there was no alternative. The first day would begin with a motorcade tour of Mbuji-Mayi followed by a luncheon hosted by Governor N'Debo at the *Société*'s main dining room. The first day would end with a traditional feast hosted by one of the traditional chiefs of the region whose village was three kilometers from Mbuji-Mayi.

McAuliffe said no. The motorcade and luncheon were fine but the day would end with a trip to Chief Job's village, not the traditional chief whose village was so often visited by official visitors from the capital that the entire village had become little more than a claque of professional entertainers, like the folk dancers in the capital.

"Parlons serieusement! Voilà une plaisanterie, n'est pas!" Matanda broke in. Let's talk seriously now! Are you joking! Chief Job's village was out of the question. His village! Those clods? Those hayseeds? *"C'est pour rire, eh?"* A joke, wasn't it? Be serious! It would be an embarrassment to everyone! No more jokes, please!

McAuliffe said it wasn't a joke and reminded him of what had happened two years ago when the previous ambassador had toured Mbuji-Mayi. He had visited the same traditional chief, who'd entertained him, given him a feast, and presented him with a pair of ivory boxes. As it turned out, the gift had been bought with U.S. AID money given the chief's village for a self-help project. The money had ended up in the pockets of the chief and his business partner, a Greek trader in Luluabourg who'd supplied the ivory boxes. The self-help project was never begun, everyone in Mbuji-Mayi knew about the deception, including the syndicate, the Greek had bragged about it, and U.S. AID as well as the American embassy had been made a laughingstock.

Matanda snickered from behind his desk. Yes, it was true, but no harm had been done. Out of one American pocket into another. McAuliffe was on his feet by then, shouldering his kit bag. He said he was sorry we couldn't agree on details and told him we were canceling the visit. We left the office, leaving Matanda in fly-bothered bewilderment behind his desk.

"The traditional chiefs bought him off," McAuliffe said as we went down the front steps and out into the broken sunshine of the clay yard. "Matanda's in everyone's pocket and always has been."

We didn't return to Moody's cottage but walked down the sand road to the native market and prowled the stalls. I stopped at a small lean-to where an old woman sold Chiclets and packets of five or more cigarettes and bought a package of Belgas. Next to the lean-to a Maluba trader had spread out his goods on a raffia mat and was sitting on his tin trunk, smoking and scratching his bony legs. On the mat were a few wooden bowls, leather belts, a brass candlestick, a few colobus monkey and lynx pelts, and several small Tchokwe masks, all newly carved. I didn't see anything worthwhile, but McAuliffe picked up one of the belts, looked at it closely, and handed it to me. The belt was old but I doubted it would interest Blakey. It was made of cowskin, very old and very brittle, ornamented with discolored beads, but the pattern had been broken and some beads were missing. McAuliffe said it was Lunda, once worn by a Lunda chief, probably made from the skin of one of his own cows. Only the Lunda chiefs had once had cattle herds on the savannahs.

"How do you know?"

He shrugged. "I read a little too."

"So you're sure it's genuine."

"Pretty sure." He held it toward the trader and asked what it was but the trader didn't know. I offered him a few *makuta* for it anyway, and we bargained for a few minutes and I bought it. Twenty minutes later we found an old Lunda woman selling pottery and raffia baskets at the edge of the market and I showed her the belt. *"Malopwe wa Bantu,"* she said as she identified it. For her at least, it was a Lunda chief's belt.

"Does Blakey know about this talent of yours?" I asked him as we walked back to the missionary cottage.

"A little, maybe, but I've never pushed it. Does Jeffrey?"

"Know what?"

"Never mind," he said, and smiled.

As we went down the sand road we saw Matanda's black Mercedes waiting at the picket fence, the driver leaning against the front fender, waiting to drive us back to the provincial offices.

Matanda had relented, undoubtedly at Governor N'Debo's urging, and agreed the visit to Chief Job's village could take place. We spent an hour or so working out the remaining details and then met with N'Debo, who quickly approved the itinerary. McAuliffe and I flew back to Kinshasa in midafternoon.

The sorcerer must have learned of our plans the following week. His power and influence had been ignored, first by McAuliffe and me, then by the provincial administration, led by the newly arrived governor, the intruder from the Atlantic Coast, and now by an American delegation arriving from the capital. Probably it was then he decided to take matters into his own hands.

McAuliffe and I still know nothing about him, not even his name. A tiny man, Chief Job would have told us, as black as a shadow, his Western clothes contemptuously cast aside, his wizened face daubed with kaolin, his arms and legs gray with wood ash as he prepared his magic in the thatched hut at the edge of his village. He wasn't demented, I told Blakey later, just stubborn and proud, an unlucky old wizard whose time was running out, like all of old Africa's, one of the dreaded *Bena N'Kuba*, a bush apothecary who'd survived the Belgians, the missionaries, the anarchy of independence, and Mobutu's brutal political cadres on his remote mountaintop only to be provoked to action by the most naive of all intruders, a pair of footloose American diplomats poking around in the bush for some idyllic remnant of the African past.

In a whisper that traveled down the mountain and out across the savannah to the provincial capital, he vowed our visit to Chief Job's village would never take place. He chose the most terrifying instrument in his arsenal to use against us and committed his reputation, which was also his existence, to its success. How much he would dare, how little the rest of us. Chief Job and his villagers soon learned of his warning and so did Governor N'Debo and Matanda. Unlike N'Debo, Moody, the old hypocrite, had always known of the sorcerer's awesome power. Now nodding over his Irish whiskey on his front verandah or gossiping around his dining room table with his Congolese parsons, I suppose he thought that with our help he could finally put an end to the sorcerer's terror. McAuliffe and I, the embassy's two bush experts, were back in Kinshasa by then. We didn't know a bloody thing.

It was late October. The dry season was almost over and the rains would soon begin. The ambassador and his entourage flew into Mbuji-Mayi in late morning in the sluggish old C-119 belonging to the U.S. military mission. It was adequate for military cargo but with only a dozen or so temporary seats less comfortable for passengers. There were fifteen of us, led by Ambassador Graham and his wife.

Most of the country team members had brought their wives, festive in their bright sundresses and broad-brimmed hats as they left the cargo door, some carrying umbrellas against the sweltering sun. They might have been descending to a weekend polo match at Middleburg or a yachting outing at Newport. Colonel Harris had brought his two DIA cameras and his blue-and-red golf umbrella. Turpin had his nylon pill bag, Mrs. Turpin had her leather poker chip canister and card carrier. Kim Johnson appeared at the airport dressed in the tailored Abercrombie and Fitch safari outfit he'd worn in Saigon. On his hip was a holster but instead of the small .25-caliber pearl-handled revolver he'd worn in Vietnam, it now held a miniature Minox camera. The ambassador was sensibly dressed in a blue seersucker suit. Jeffrey wore seersucker too, although he wore an ascot rather than a tie. Blakey, summoned early in the flight to sit next to the ambassador's wife, was wearing a sleeveless blue sundress. Arriving together at the airport that morning, Jeffrey and Blakey looked quite handsome, very much the American consul and his lovely wife.

Under a cloudless sky Governor N'Debo had assembled his provincial cabinet and senior army and police officers to greet us. After a few formalities and some confusion as to who would ride where, McAuliffe got the seating straightened out and we were whisked off by motorcade for a dusty tour of the provincial capital. The ten-vehicle caravan was led by a police Land Rover followed by N'Debo's black Mercedes carrying the ambassador and his wife. McAuliffe and I were in the rear in Moody's clattering Land Rover, driven by Moody's Maluba driver. Blakey and Jeff were somewhere in between, like Moody, invited by the AID director who'd never been to Mbuji-Mayi to share his vehicle, a government-provided Toyota.

The tour was to take forty-five minutes, but it was soon obvious N'Debo was taking liberties with our carefully planned schedule. We were first delayed by impromptu stops at the concrete-block shells of half-completed buildings, suspended for lack of funds. As the ruins of more government clinics and schools were added, I knew what was happening. The unspoken assumption of most Congolese officials was that the American ambassador was the second most powerful man in the Congo. It wasn't true and no one had the power to move Mobutu except maybe his fetisheur, but whatever their fantasies about American power, provincial governors were pitifully weak and under no illusion about it. However much they might bully their subordinates and terrorize their local constituency, they were utterly without influence in the capital, where the American ambassador was believed second in importance only to the president. Previous American ambassadors had done nothing to discourage the myth, and Ambassador Graham was no exception.

At each stop, standing in the deteriorating rubble of a new clinic or new school surrounded by a rabble of the Congolese poor, he listened to N'Debo's capital and equipment needs with a gravity that suggested omnipotence. Turpin and the AID director were soon summoned to take notes. As more trumpets and flourishes were added to the farce, N'Debo's smile grew broader, his imagination bolder. By the time we reached the Belgian compound where we were to have lunch, morning had lengthened into afternoon and we were an hour behind schedule.

N'Debo was the host for the long and lavish luncheon. The air-conditioning wasn't working, the dining room was oppressively hot and the meal heavy, delightful in Brussels on an autumn afternoon but not the torrid African savannah. Service was slow because of the many guests the Belgians had crowded in, most of them Europeans from the *Société*'s administrative staff. The wine was enervating, like the speeches. The Americans, all of whom had been up since four o'clock that morning, were all sleepy, but not N'Debo, who was at the top of his form, lively, witty, and irrepressibly optimistic. Listening to him and watching his face as he talked to the ambassador and his wife during the long meal, I knew how much I had underestimated the man. As usual, Matanda had drunk too much and was incoherent and beginning to stagger as he sought out McAuliffe and me after lunch.

McAuliffe and I followed the ambassador and his entourage back to the cool comfort of the Belgian *Société*'s guest houses under the palm trees where they had two hours to rest and relax. I saw Blakey outside her cottage and got out to say something to her but Jeffrey took her elbow, turned, and led her away. Moody's driver drove us back to the cottage. The pleasures of the African bush are those of improvisation, not protocol, and we'd accepted Moody's offer of his guest rooms to be at some distance from the ambassador's group and its nagging uncertainties about detail that accompany ceremonial travel in the bush. Three times that morning the ambassador's aide and Kim Johnson had sought us out to clarify some point or another. At four o'clock we were to begin the overland trek to Chief Job's village.

A little drowsy ourselves, we sat on the shadowed porch of the missionary cottage. It was a brilliant windless African afternoon, the sky cloudless, the breath of air from the savannahs suspended in that transparent hush that settles upon sleepy provincial towns soon after midday. Most of the shops and small markets were closed, the government offices empty. Nothing stirred in the metallic heat of the clay and sand roads except a few squabbling magpies, and even their cries were muted. McAuliffe sat slumped in a rattan chair, frowning over his itinerary as he tried to work in a visit to an agricultural project suggested by the AID director for the following day. Since the project was funded in part by an American Protestant mission, both of us knew who'd suggested the idea. Moody sat nearby in his wicker rocker, fanning himself with a sun-faded rattan fan from a Topeka, Kansas, funeral home. I was bone-tired, looking again at Blakey's photograph of the Kifwebe mask, wondering what she was doing and whether I had time and the energy to stroll down to the market and search out a Baluba or Basonge trader.

"I wouldn't worry about it too much," Moody offered. "I reckon it'll all work out in the end one way or another, the good Lord willing." He usually took a nap at midday. The rocking chair creaked and he disappeared inside. Sleepy himself, McAuliffe got to his feet. "Me too, I think. You going to stand watch?"

We heard the car a minute later, McAuliffe at the screen door, me in my chair. I got to my feet, thinking it was either Kim Johnson or the ambassador's aide. Instead N'Debo's black Mercedes came speeding up the road and stopped at the gate. N'Debo's *chef du protocol* scrambled from the front seat, unlatched the picket gate, and came running up the front walk. *"Bonjour! Bonjour!"* He was out of breath, his face dripping sweat, still wearing his damp coat and tie from the luncheon.

Governor N'Debo wanted to see us immediately. He didn't explain why. His message delivered, he turned and trotted back to the car. We followed, climbed into the backseat, and were driven back in silence over the sand road.

N'Debo was waiting alone on the rear terrace of the white-stuccoed governor's villa, reclining on a red-cushioned lounge chair in the shadows of the bougainvillea. The protocol chief led us around the side of the house past the detached kitchen to the rear steps of the terrace. He didn't accompany us but turned and hoofed it back around the side of the house toward the kitchen. N'Debo greeted us like old friends, warmly shook our hands, and brought two deck chairs near. Then he summoned his houseboy for drinks and sank back down again.

"Il est très intelligent" were his first words as he complimented the ambassador with an intimacy I hadn't heard before, not even during our after-luncheon talk. *"Très, très intelligent,"* he added in that same soft voice I'd sometimes heard from other Congolese in praising a man's intelligence. For them it was the ultimate compliment but always a whispered one, a legacy from the colonial past when the Congolese, so often humiliated in public by his Belgian master, heard the compliment only behind closed scullery doors, its beneficiary a secret exception in the White Man's Law. His whispered voice told me we were fellow conspirators.

He talked about the morning tour. He was gratified by the ambassador's interest in his province, pleased by the questions he'd asked, and optimistic at the many notes his counselors had taken. Help was badly needed and from whom could he expect help if not the Americans? A houseboy brought Simba beer in brown quart bottles and we sat in silence as our glasses were filled, gazing out through the flame and frangipani trees and rows of raffia palms and beyond the tin roofs of the monetized economy toward the great grassy silence of the savannah.

N'Debo's face grew thoughtful after the houseboy retired. As the silence lengthened, broken only by the mild wind stirring in the trees, he put his glass aside on the wicker table. Avoiding our eyes, he said he was sorry to tell us we wouldn't be able to travel to Chief Job's village that afternoon. He asked us to tell the ambassador and extend his apologies.

Surprised, I asked why. He avoided my eyes, his face turned away, and it was a long time before he answered. The visit would create impossible problems. The ambassador was his guest and his responsibility, unpleasantness was to be avoided, and therefore the visit to Chief Job's remote mountaintop was to be canceled. He had no choice in the matter. He still hadn't turned toward us.

Watching his averted face, I remembered the old woman I'd met during my first trip to the bush along the Kwilu River and how she had smiled, ashamed to find me there, and told me her eyes had nowhere to hide.

N'Debo's eyes seemed the same. I asked him what kind of unpleasantness. "Serious unpleasantness" was all he would say. McAuliffe tried to draw him out but N'Debo only shook his head. An embarrassed smile lingered on his face and his flushed eyes pleaded for understanding: *I can't discuss this,* they seemed to say. *Ask no more. I can't talk about this at all.*

The afternoon was already passing, the light changing. Our caravan of Land Rovers was scheduled to leave at four o'clock, and it was approaching four now. We would have an hour on the track and an hour in the village before darkness fell. To arrive with the night would mean confusion and failure.

"What are we supposed to tell them?" McAuliffe asked. "The ambassador will want an explanation. What do you expect us to say?"

"That there will be very serious problems." Abruptly, N'Debo left his lounge chair to prowl the verandah.

I asked him if he'd considered an alternative. If the group remained in Mbuji-Mayi that night, who was to be their host? Who would feed them? The Belgians again?

N'Debo grimaced and shook his head. His chief of protocol reappeared at the foot of the terrace steps, his wet froggy face lifted as he awaited N'Debo's signal to be invited to join us. Lifting his arm, N'Debo pointed back toward the kitchen. *"Je vais faire pipi,"* the protocol chief whispered, hand at his crotch.

"Allez pisser. Allez-y vite!" Arm still raised, N'Debo told him to take a leak someplace else and sent him away. I thought his rudeness unusual. If he wouldn't share his problem with his protocol chief, why would he share it with us?

"So you haven't thought about where we'll go," McAuliffe said.

I said, "So maybe we'll go to Mama Onema's for *mwamba* and warm beer. Is that what you want?"

"Qu'est-ce-que je peut faire?" N'Debo cried with sudden passion. "What am I to do? What can I do?"

He couldn't entertain the ambassador and his group. How could he? His protocol resources were meager. Forced by rank to entertain more lavishly than their miserable budgets allowed, most provincial governors were shameless spongers, and he was no exception. Although he'd promised himself his administration would be different, it wasn't different at all. He was a sponger, a parasite, his ceremonial life lived off the cuff. "It's true! It's shameful but true! I shame myself but what can I do?"

The Belgians had paid for the luncheon, a humiliation and an embarrassment. They had tricked him by generously offering their dining room, kitchen, and serving staff and then had filled the front tables with their petty clerks and their wives while members of his provincial cabinet had been seated to the rear. The local Maluba businessmen from the Chamber of Commerce would pay for dinner the following night, but most were diamond smugglers, far richer than he. He wasn't a Belgian *Société*? How could he offer whiskey, dinner and wine, cordials afterward? Was he a resident European ambassador in Kinshasa? No! He was alone, his wife hadn't yet arrived from the capital, his larder was as empty as his pockets and the pockets of his provincial government.

"La caisse est vide." He collapsed miserably in his lounge chair, shaking his head. "Empty, all empty."

I sympathized with him but was puzzled as to why he would confess to these humiliations but not the reason he'd canceled the trip to Chief Job's village. Something deeper than pride?

So I told him we were both in difficulty. McAuliffe and I could help him with two or three hundred dollars from official funds, maybe more, but it was a little late in the afternoon for that and time was passing. We had on our hands a dozen or so restless Americans, all in bush attire by now, camera bags ready, eager to be driven out across the savannah to this remote mountaintop village they'd heard so much about. We could manage the cocktail hour. The ambassador's aide had brought liquor and most of the country team as well. Christ knows they drank enough in Kinshasa to float every Otraco boat on the Congo

River, so they weren't traveling dry in the bush. But who would feed them? The Belgians again? I could call the Belgian dining room manager and ask if he could cater dinner at the guest cottages, paid for by the Americans. Is that what he wanted?

N'Debo shook his head. What was the alternative? Lousy, just as Ken said: Mama Onema's cathouse hotel where the diamond traders gathered to be served warm bear, cassava, beans, and chicken *mwamba* while the prostitutes eyed them from across the room and the nearby bar.

N'Debo smiled briefly, grimaced, and closed his eyes.

Remembering Matanda's unhappiness at our choice of Chief Job's village, it had occurred to me N'Debo might have been warned against the visit by the same prominent tribal chief Matanda had suggested host the traditional feast. Angry that Chief Job's miserable village and not their own would receive the American ambassador, a few traditional chiefs may have warned N'Debo against the visit, prepared to make trouble for him in Kinshasa, where money ruled and their clansmen had foreign bank accounts earned by their illegal diamond trade.

"Who's going to make trouble?" I asked. I told him the ambassador's itinerary had been seen and approved in the capital. The Foreign Ministry saw it, the Ministry of Interior, and so had Mobutu and his *chef du cabinet* up on the hill. All of them knew the ambassador would visit Chief Job's village and all had endorsed it.

N'Debo was listening with interest. So was McAuliffe, who looked at me with a smile. Maybe it was a small lie, but that was what diplomacy was all about, wasn't it?—little lies protecting bigger ones.

"So who can object to the visit?" I concluded. "It's the ambassador's decision and he'll take full responsibility. If there's any trouble, the ambassador will deal with it, the U.S. embassy, all of us."

N'Debo's ears perked up. He was intrigued but continued to ponder in silence for a few minutes, brow furrowed, head turned away again. An interesting point, he admitted finally, smiling mysteriously as he got to his feet. He would think about it. He waved us away, still smiling, and asked for us to return at five for his decision.

N'Debo's chauffeur drove us back to the Belgian compound. Inside the gate the vehicles were waiting, assembled in the sand drive under the raffia palms in front of the guest cottage. I told McAuliffe I doubted we'd see N'Debo again that day.

"It was my fault," he said. "I should never have suggested the trip."

"It wasn't your fault. You did everything you could do."

Colonel Harris in his safari and bush kit was taking pictures of a few wives standing in front of the Land Rovers. Chief Job's mountain was a dim unseen shadow far in the distance. Moody was also there, standing on the verandah of the ambassador's cottage, talking to Jeffrey Ogden and Kim Johnson. He was rumpled and sleepy, dressed as he had been that morning on the tarmac in a dark serge suit, white shirt, gray at the collar, and his clip-on red nylon tie.

"What's going on?" Kim Johnson called testily from the top step. "Do you realize what time it is?" McAuliffe told him it was a little complicated.

Ambassador Graham had finished his nap and was having a drink in the front salon with the AID and USIS director, his aide, and Turpin. Jeffrey Ogden and Johnson followed us in. In moments of uncertainty, the ambassador's face betrayed a hint of dyspepsia, as it did then as McAuliffe explained N'Debo had canceled the visit. We'd tried to convince him otherwise but doubted we'd succeeded. The wives came drifting in to learn the sad news, Blakey among them. The ambassador asked for an explanation, as I knew he would. McAuliffe turned to me.

I told them what seemed most plausible under the circumstances. Our visit to Chief Job's impoverished little village had offended the major Baluba clan whose traditional chiefs had always received the American ambassador. Their Baluba clansmen in Kinshasa would also be offended. Aware of their influence in Kinshasa, N'Debo had decided to cancel the trip. McAuliffe and I tried to assure him the embassy would take full responsibility. Although N'Debo might have weakened, he hadn't changed his mind.

"Why in the world didn't we think about this?" Johnson demanded.

His editorial *we* had become tiresome and I was annoyed. "Think about what? I'm not a mind reader. Neither is Ken. N'Debo agreed to the trip two weeks ago. Even as late as this afternoon at the Belgian luncheon, we had no reason to think he'd change his mind."

Doubt and uncertainty are the bane of an ambassador's existence, whose exalted presence is intended to resolve problems, not get caught up in them. My explanation seemed to satisfy the ambassador, but he was annoyed. McAuliffe and I had embroiled him in a nasty little provincial squabble he wanted no part of. He was disappointed with Ken and me for not anticipating the problem, irritated at N'Debo for his irresolution and cowardice, and troubled at the prospect of a long evening spent in the Belgian guest cottage playing bridge with the embassy wives or listening to his counselors and their tiresome chatter. Looking again at their faces, I didn't much blame him.

Kim Johnson, who'd known N'Debo as a parliamentarian back in Kinshasa, suggested he and the ambassador go talk to the governor immediately and reassure him the embassy would take full responsibility, as we'd promised. The ambassador declined, as I knew he would. He preferred to hold himself above the fray and let N'Debo make the decision himself. Turpin, Colonel Harris, and Jeffrey quickly agreed with his wisdom and congratulated him for it, but I knew from his face it wasn't wisdom but bewilderment and irresolution.

But there was no doubt he was disappointed. "I was keen to travel," he said, looking about forlornly at faces that brought him no comfort. Standing behind the small divan, Blakey suggested a sensible solution: "Why don't we have a picnic of our own out on the savannah? Couldn't we?"

Ambassador Graham's face brightened. "That's a splendid idea," his wife said gratefully, looking at me. "Chicken, ham, deviled eggs?" Could an appropriate place be found? she asked McAuliffe. If not a picnic, we could at least take advantage of the caravan waiting outside to drive out on the savannah for drinks and watch the sunset. The husbands agreed. I was sent to telephone the manager of the Belgian dining room to ask if he might cater a small picnic paid for with embassy funds. McAuliffe found a map in his kit bag and spread it out on the coffee table as he described a few possibilities along the river.

Unable to reach the Belgian manager, I'd just returned to

the front salon when I heard a car entering the drive. Moody, who'd remained outside all this time, put his head in the door and beckoned me outside. Governor N'Debo was coming.

I watched from the front steps as the governor emerged from the backseat of his black Mercedes, cheerful and smiling, dressed in his dark-blue shantung Mao suit and dark glasses. A leopard-skin cap was cocked jauntily on his dark head and he carried an ornately carved ebony walking stick with an ivory handle, a veritable bush dandy, a provincial facsimile of the president himself.

"Nous y allons!" he called to me triumphantly, waving the stick aloft and then vigorously shaking my hand, as irrepressible as he'd been that morning as he'd herded us through the misery of abandoned clinics and schoolrooms. The astonished ambassador immediately joined us followed by McAuliffe, Kim Johnson, and the others. N'Debo didn't mention his tardiness and the ambassador asked no questions. As he and the others dispersed to gather their jackets, cameras, and bush bags, N'Debo drew McAuliffe and me aside.

"We'll all take responsibility," he whispered, "all of us together." He raised McAuliffe's hand in his, then mine, both of us clumsily clutching his carved ebony walking stick as he turned toward the savannah to declare the victory that would be ours. An hour earlier he had conceded defeat, now he was claiming his triumph. I had no idea what had changed his mind, but it was his ebullient confidence that most puzzled me.

There was some confusion as vehicles were filled according to diplomatic rank. Kim Johnson was the first to protest, then Turpin. In the melee I saw Blakey look toward me, as if hoping we might share a Land Rover, but then Jeffrey appeared at her side and led her away. The motorcade soon circled out of the compound, down the sand roads, and out of Mbuji-Mayi.

McAuliffe and I were with the Reverend Moody and his Maluba driver in the second Land Rover behind a police Toyota. As we left the Belgian compound Moody turned to tell us he'd heard rumors that the visit had been canceled.

McAuliffe stirred and looked at me, puzzled.

"When was that?" I asked. Moody wasn't sure. Yesterday or the day before. Now he was pleased it was taking place. Beyond that his shrewd gray eyes told us nothing. He nibbled his sunflower and sesame seeds and stared past us from time to time out the rear window at the awesome parade of vehicles lumbering through the dust behind us.

The sky had turned to brass as our long caravan crossed the savannah. Grassland and scrub that an hour earlier had seemed empty and bleached to dust took on density and color. It was the hour of transition, the hour of flux from the parching bone-white heat of the day to the softer, gentler ambers of the deepening afternoon. The thickening light darkened the shadows along the laterite road, along the streams and the glades of acacia and palm. It magnified the figures visible near the roadside huts where the villagers stirred, busy at the wood and charcoal fires and cooking pots, absorbed in those small tasks that in the capital were hidden behind the ugly clay-and-concrete-block walls of the native communes but on an open savannah under a limitless sky gave a renewed dignity and grace to these small daily acts of existence. I was grateful Blakey was there to see it. The spectacle might have made her own carved figures seem less important.

We climbed the serpentine track up the mountain and passed through the first village. The huts again seemed deserted, the cooking fires unlit, the doorways draped with raffia cloth, like those of a village shut away in mourning or in sickness. McAuliffe wondered what had happened as he looked out the window and told the driver to slow down.

In my ignorance I thought Chief Job might have invited his neighbors to share his feast at the far end of the mountain, but no, they were gathered inside in the darkness and so was he, the most feared of the local *Bena N'Kuba,* waiting somewhere in the early twilight of a closed hut, his drained body slack as he listened to our vehicles passing on the track outside. It must have seemed to him the passing of an era: first the Reverend Moody, McAuliffe, and me, followed by N'Debo's black Mercedes with the blue-and-yellow pennon of the Congo flying from one fender and the American flag from another; behind them the AID director and economic counselor and their wives, the political counselor and the American consul and their wives, the defense attaché and the USIS Public Information officer, followed by the senior territorial administrators, the MPR political director and his sound equipment, and finally the Land Rover from the national police. We had come despite his warnings.

The track narrowed as it traversed the plateau, lightly forested with scrub and stunted trees. Because he thought it would interest McAuliffe and me, the Maluba driver pointed to a fresh elephant spoor along the track. For some reason Moody told him it wasn't fresh but a spoor we'd seen during our previous visit, but he was wrong. That spoor had been along the track near the foot of the mountain. The driver only shrugged and said no more.

Conscious of the fading light, I was leaning forward, scanning the road ahead for the first sign of the path that led to Chief

Job's village. We were more than an hour late and the village soon would be swallowed in darkness. I was worried Chief Job had given up in despair, dispersed his villagers, and retired to his hut to meditate upon marauding elephants, his sickly crops and undug wells, and the fickleness of moon-traveling foreigners.

As we approached the village McAuliffe pointed to the raffia palms cut from the trees and stuck at intervals along the verges. From the final rise we could see the villagers assembled in the clearing in front of the thatched huts at the end of the footpath. We parked along the track in front of the turnabout above the draw and the other vehicles lined up behind us. McAuliffe and I went back to fetch Governor N'Debo and the ambassador and led them across the draw and up the path. The others followed.

Chief Job was standing in front of his villagers, dressed as he had been on our previous visit in tattered shorts and a tattered white shirt except for the mustard-colored cotton cape that descended from his shoulders to the ground. On his great Buddha-like head was a faded cloth cap of the same color, ornamented with beads and ancient brown-toothed cowrie shells. The women of the village began their ululations as soon as we crossed the draw below the path and continued as N'Debo, the ambassador, and his entourage joined the chief. The din made it difficult for Moody to translate Chief Job's words of welcome. The ambassador had to bend to hear, his head turned, the fingers of his right hand pressed delicately against that finely sculpted right ear.

The chief was astonished by the size of our caravan and said as much to Moody, holding up one finger first, then seven more. He had expected one elephant, Moody translated with a chuckle, not the entire Indian circus. The ambassador and N'Debo laughed and so did everyone else. I suppose it didn't matter but I doubted Chief Job had ever heard of an Indian circus and wondered how accurately Moody had translated his remark. I'd twice heard Moody mention traveling circuses during our conversations at his dining table and suspected it was a metaphor drawn from his Kansas boyhood and a long-remembered summer day when the traveling circus paraded the main street of his dusty Kansas tank town.

During our bush travels McAuliffe and I had been invited to several banquets and receptions organized by provincial officials in honor of visiting government dignitaries from Kinshasa at which tribal chieftains and their retinue were sometimes present. They always came as performers, never as guests, fetched on-stage like traveling mummers and jugglers at a medieval court. Afterward they were fed banquet scraps from the kitchen door, like the hunting dogs of the dukes of Burgundy. This explained why McAuliffe had been so determined to visit Chief Job's village; it wasn't that way that evening.

Chief Job's words of welcome, the tour of the village and the quick look at the nearby fields, the singing and the feast that followed were something like a community picnic on a village green. Protocol was forgotten as the hosts and their guests mingled together, talked when an interpreter was available, and communicated in other ways when one was not. It was chaotic for a few minutes as a few confused chickens and squalling pigs got mixed up underfoot but no one seemed to mind, not even Kim Johnson. In Chief Job's hut gifts were exchanged, but too many people had crowded in and I didn't see the gifts or the exchange.

Moody's driver and I went back to the Land Rover to bring back the case of beer and box of paper cups and plates we'd brought from Kinshasa. Dinner was served and the local *mwamba* dished out by the village women. There was no banquet table, just a crude plank resting on two portable palm tree stumps. Four wooden stools were the only chairs, reserved for the host and the guests of honor. Palm wine and beer were offered. Several Americans tried it for the first time but few liked it.

Jeffrey Ogden and Turpin stood at the edge of the crowd, their heads turned away, washing out the palm wine with warm beer. There were wooden bowls of red-skinned bananas, plantains, mangoes, and roasted caterpillars. The Americans were most intrigued by the tub of yellowish-gray meat that was set out. Beef? Pork? What? Colonel Harris sampled it. Monkey meat, McAuliffe told him, traditional at village feasts. Harris's jaws worked as he edged his way to the back of the crowd. Except for McAuliffe, who knew and liked it, no one else was tempted except for Blakey. I'd eaten it a few times in the past but found it stringy and tough. Chief Job was amused by all this.

"It's marvelous, all of it," Blakey said as she stood next to me. "Is it always like this?"

"Not always."

"I think I'm beginning to understand."

Jeffrey joined us. "Understand what? What didn't you understand?" Blakey moved away without answering.

Colonel Harris had brought out the DIA camera and so had the USIS chief and a few others. Would it be impolite to ask Chief Job to pose for a photograph? they asked Moody, who put the question to the chief. Putting his plate at his feet, he stood with great dignity, and the ambassador, his wife, and N'Debo stood with him. He remained standing proudly long after the last shutter had clicked and so did the others. N'Debo finally suggested they all sit down. The photograph Colonel Harris showed me later in Kinshasa was a poor one. That great Buddha-like head was a lump of faceless ectoplasm, the proud features dissolved by someone else's flash.

As dinner was ending, N'Debo yielded at last to the pleas of his territorial commissioner, Mr. Kifumbi, the pint-size territorial chairman of the national political party who'd been making a nuisance of himself since the feast began. A microphone and sound equipment were brought from his Land Rover by one of his party militants. Kifumbi's three aides, all thugs dressed in the green twill of the party *jeunesse,* or youth wing, herded the villagers on the far side of the clearing in front of the chief's hut facing the chief and his three guests of honor on their four stools. The village children stood in the front row, the elders in the rear. Kifumbi stood in front at his microphone, which wasn't working properly. After a few minutes of tinkering, it still didn't work, but Kifumbi commenced without it, instructing the villagers in the lessons of the party. He spoke in Lingala, the old commercial lingua franca of the riverboats, a language of command, not social discourse; its brutal imperatives made grace, courtesy, and even politeness impossible. It was now the language of the nation and the party, as remote from this village and its richly inflected Tshiluba as the thundering falls of the Congo River below Stanley Pool, far too subtle even for Moody's Kansas ear.

The lesson was interrupted by two pigs loudly grunting from the rear where they'd found some scraps left from the feast, maybe Colonel Harris's monkey meat. One of Kifumbi's militants was sent to chase them away. A few villagers were amused but not Kifumbi.

"Are we vigilant!" he shrieked, waving his small hands toward his chorus. Untrained in the MPR's bullying school, the villagers' response was hesitant; Kufumbi's three party thugs joined them and thundered the reply: *"Yes, we are vigilant!"*

Kifumbi wasn't satisfied. *"Are we vigilant!"*

The response was less faint this time: *"Yes, we are vigilant!"*

Americans leaving civilian life for army boot camp, as I did once, know the desolation of an existence disciplined by the raucous commands of a barracks-room bullhorn wired from a distant orderly room. In that way I thought some of the Americans present, the ambassador and Kim Johnson in particular, might have better understood the relationship of the president's political party to the natural rhythms of remote village life. Whether they did or not I don't know.

"Are we working for the revolution?" Kifumbi bellowed.

"Yes, we are working for the revolution!"

Kifumbi seemed demented, bellowing and gesturing so violently in front of that small group of children and elders. Come to crush that unique tribal identity that endured in villages as remote as this one with the mindless thunder of mass dementia, his frenzy fell on fearful hearts and frightened faces. Behind him the ambassador's wife, who during the day had shown herself to be a sensible woman, looked on in horror. But for children chanted words and rhythms are also games, just as imbecilic stump orators are also clowns; when a few shy smiles began to appear among the youngest in the front row, Kifumbi stopped and gave them a hysterical lecture over the now-working loudspeaker. The noise was deafening.

Embarrassed, N'Debo grimaced, stood up, and waved his hand to signal Kifumbi to end the performance.

The light had changed by then, the air thick and oppressive as an ugly yellow glare drifted in over us. The wind began to stir, softly at first and then with steadily increasing violence. A few angry gusts brought the first warning, followed by a savage glare of lightning. A crack of thunder drove the frightened Kifumbi from his now-whistling microphone. The sound gear was hastily packed away as the villagers began to scatter. The dust had whipped up, stinging our faces and blowing the white mounds of cooking ashes fiery red. Ash swirled across the banquet dishes; they were covered and quickly taken away. Looking up I saw a darker scud racing like smoke over the treetops. Above it the boiling, crocodile-yellow underbelly of a towering thunderhead queerly reflected the light to the west, lifting the curtain of twilight that had descended just a few minutes earlier.

The storm had swept in without warning. The wind slashed savagely through the raffia palms, flogging dust and chaff everywhere, tearing free the cut raffia boughs decorating the banquet plank and sending them soaring out against the sky. The rain began to fall as the thunder reverberated across the savannah, heavy random drops at first and then in torrential sheets. Wild with wind, the sheltering trees swayed and pitched, clumps of thatch lifted from the hut roofs and were blown away. Lightning and thunder slashed in from all directions in deafening bursts, now behind us, now in front, now darkness, now shocking white

light, every living detail drained away as it struck, faces and figures dissolved in ghoulish luminescence, the stuff nightmares are
made of, and I remember thinking stupidly "spiritual evil," whatever that was, the power that shriveled Frère Albert's soul,
remembering the stormy afternoon we sat beneath the shelter of
the mission verandah drinking beer and I wondered what the hell
he was talking about.

Not quite pandemonium, but nearly, but we had come, all of
us, come successfully, and now the feast was over. It wasn't the
end McAuliffe and I had in mind, but maybe there was a lesson
in the storm's havoc too, as much a part of the villagers' lives as
the undug wells, foul water, and marauding elephants. The
farewells were brief and breathless, everyone maintaining some
final shred of civility—wet faces, wet smiles, wet handshakes,
and slippery feet in the mud gumbo as the villagers scattered to
their huts and the damp visitors fled to their cars.

N'Debo, Ambassador Graham, and his wife left immediately, huddled under Colonel Harris's red-and-blue golf umbrella, not a wise shelter, I remember thinking in the glare of a
lightning bolt. Moody shot ahead of them, bounding like a terrified jackrabbit down the path, coattails flying, less dignified
than his arrival but more the measure of the man. I looked for
Blakey but couldn't find her.

McAuliffe and I had brought bags of rice and flour for the village and I sprinted through the rain to unload them. It was dark
now and the slick path was deserted. There was some congestion
at the turnabout on the far side of the draw as the vehicles waited
to turn around and begin their journey back down the mountain.
They had their lights on and the windshield wipers ticking furi-
ously. Moody wasn't in his Land Rover and neither was his driver.
I unlatched the back door and hauled out a bag of rice. A horn

honked and then another as two vehicles passed. Blakey was with Kim Johnson and his wife; she waved through the rain-streaked glass, her face illuminated by the lights of a waiting vehicle. Moody was with Colonel Harris in the Land Rover behind them. The wind and rain had diminished by the time I reached the knoll but the thunder was still rolling across the savannah to the east and I could see the shimmering pulses in the distance followed by the faraway rumble of the moving thunderhead. Wet and muddy, I delivered the rice to Chief Job's smoky hut and found McAuliffe and Moody's Maluba driver alone with the chief inside.

The chief was standing at his battered tin locker, a bright pressure lantern at his feet, explaining something in French to McAuliffe, who was obviously upset. As he spoke he was wrapping a small silver bowl in raffia before placing it in his locker. The bowl was the ambassador's gift. McAuliffe had recommended giving Chief Job a breeding sow, but the country team believed the gift of a pig undignified for an ambassador. McAuliffe had told them it wasn't for the ambassador but a village chief. He'd lost the argument but that error was forgotten now and I didn't think that was why he was angry. The chief's ceremonial cape and cap, beaded with cowrie shells, both dark with rain, hung forlornly on a stick propped against the side of the hut.

Moody's driver and I went back to the Land Rover and brought the other bags of flour and rice to the hut. Chief Job wasn't expecting them. He thanked us, we said our farewells, and he embraced McAuliffe a final time before we left.

"He's a fool," McAuliffe said softly as we crossed the clearing in the light rain.

I turned. "Who's a fool?"

"Moody."

"He's always been. What happened?"

"I'll tell you later." The caravan had long departed and the rain had eased to a whisper, almost invisible in the lights of our Land Rover as we drove away. I sat in the rear behind McAuliffe and the driver. We crossed the plateau and as we passed through the dark village, the Maluba driver slowed to a stop and looked out the window. "*Il est parti maintenant.* He's gone." No fires were burning and there were no lights. I didn't know what he was talking about.

"Who's left?" I asked. McAuliffe opened his door and stood for a minute in the doorway, looking across the Land Rover roof toward the village as we waited. I couldn't see anything. "Who are you talking about?" I called. "Who's gone?"

"The sorcerer," McAuliffe said. That made no sense either. He got back in and we drove on.

"I don't know what the hell we're talking about. What sorcerer?"

"The one in the village. The fetisheur who ruled the mountaintop, the one who kept everyone away."

Moody's driver had told McAuliffe the whole story, Chief Job had repeated it ten minutes earlier in his hut, and now McAuliffe told me. The old sorcerer had warned against the visit, vowing it would never take place. Chief Job's villagers had known, the driver knew, many in Mbuji-Mayi knew, just as N'Debo and Moody knew. His was the strongest power in the area, that perverse power that had kept away Moody's meddling pastors, the local provincial officials, and the territorial party cadres. Chief Job's villagers had known of the warning but at the chief's urging had awaited our arrival, standing terrified at the end of the track under a murderous open sky. After the long delay, they were convinced the sorcerer's magic was too strong, the Americans wouldn't come, but then our caravan had arrived, the feast had taken place, and the storm had come too late. The American ambassador's magic was too powerful, the sorcerer's power had been broken, and now the chief and Moody's driver could tell McAuliffe the whole story. The old sorcerer had fled in humiliation. A villager returning along the road had brought word to one of the village elders just before Kifumbi's political program commenced.

Too late, McAuliffe and I understood the dilemma Governor N'Debo had been struggling with so indecisively on his verandah that afternoon.

We descended the mountain, the official caravan far ahead of us. As we began our trek across the savannah, our headlights caught a small solitary figure trudging along the road. McAuliffe told the driver to slow, but the man bounded into the scrub and disappeared. I wondered if he was the sorcerer. The driver said no, the man we'd seen was an illegal diamond digger. The sorcerer would go north into the equatorial jungle, a prophet to the most primitive, to the disinherited who made of smashed traditions new prophets and new mythologies, like the half-mad fetisheurs who'd accompanied the Simbas during their war against the national government in 1965, some of whom faded off into the most primitive bush up near the Sudan border after their defeat.

It was a long drive. Not a drop of rain had touched the countryside we were crossing. The track was bone-dry and the stars were out.

At the Belgian guest cottage the ambassador and his group
were in dry clothes by now, in the midst of a cocktail happy hour
as they celebrated their return. McAuliffe and I joined them out
of the darkness. The voices were loud, the lights punishing, and
the drinks strong. N'Debo wasn't there, nor were any other
provincial officials. Pleading a mild headache and a damp suit,
N'Debo had returned to his residence, tired but happy, or so the
ambassador's aide told us.

The ambassador was also pleased. The visit had been a success. He congratulated McAuliffe, as did everyone else. "Per-
fectly delightful," the ambassador's wife said, putting her hand
on his arm. McAuliffe was embarrassed. His shoes were as
muddy as mine and his shirt was still damp. What had Chief Job
said afterward? the ambassador asked, sitting back down on the
divan. Was he pleased?

"Very pleased," McAuliffe said. Lying on a swatch of smoky
raffia on the coffee table in front of the divan was Chief Job's
gift, an ivory tusk from the elephant shot with his father's rogue
rifle.

McAuliffe asked if the chief had told him how he'd come to
shoot the elephant. No, the ambassador didn't know the story.
"Did he shoot it?" he asked, surprised and eager.

"Just outside his hut," McAuliffe said. "At dusk one evening.
Reverend Moody knows the story."

"Come to think of it, someone did mention something," the
ambassador said, "but it was so noisy I couldn't follow." He
looked around for Moody but he was in the far corner, describing for the AID director the urgency of his Protestant pastors'
needs for health clinics and agricultural subsidies. Others

joined us, including Jeffrey and Blakey, who'd been with Kim Johnson's wife across the room.

"Everything was a little confusing," said the ambassador's wife. "You say he shot it. How marvelous. Tell us about it."

"It's a little involved," McAuliffe said. "Hugh tells it better than I do." Erect and proud, he said nothing more, lapsing into that silence I knew so well.

She looked at me. "Tell us, please. You must. We're absolutely fascinated."

I told them and they listened with interest. "That's marvelous," she said. "We couldn't have gone home without knowing the story. But we were a little worried coming back, wondering whether the storm did any damage. Did it?" She looked at McAuliffe.

McAuliffe said Chief Job had told him a palm tree was struck but no one was hurt.

"I'm so relieved," she said. "All of us."

"What did N'Debo say?" McAuliffe asked.

"The governor? About what?"

"The storm."

"Naturally he was worried too, wasn't he, dear?"

"I think he was, yes." The ambassador nodded. "Very worried."

"Did he say anything else?"

"Not that I remember. Why?"

"He didn't mention the sorcerer in the next village?" I asked, knowing he hadn't.

"Sorcerer? What sorcerer?" The ambassador looked at McAuliffe and then at me. "I'm afraid I don't understand."

"The sorcerer in the next village," I said, "the one who brought on the storm."

"The storm?"

"The storm that swept in too late."

"A sorcerer's storm?" Kim Johnson broke in. "Are either of you serious? You certainly can't be serious."

"I think they're jolly well pulling our legs," Jeffrey Ogden said.

"Not in the slightest," I said, conscious of Blakey looking at me queerly.

"A storm? A sorcerer's storm?" Seeing my face, Johnson laughed suddenly. "My God, man—"

The whole episode was so preposterous I suppose I was a little angry. "You think I'm not serious?"

"You don't mean you take it seriously." He laughed again.

"That's not the point," McAuliffe said. "It's not what we believe but what they believe." He turned to me. "Tell them."

"If anyone's interested."

"We are, certainly," the ambassador said. "By all means."

"Please," Genevieve Graham said. "You must."

So I told them about the *Bena N'Kuba,* the lightning-maker and the bearer of storms, about the box shown to me by a Portuguese in the Kwilu who kept it in the battery shed at his weed-grown lot, the foul little box you never see, not even among the bush traders you meet on the track or in the tin shacks of the urban slums, some of them disgraced fetisheurs themselves, their power broken, selling off the relics of their order to the European curio hunters. I saw Blakey looking at me with a strange smile, as if remembering our secret, the collection hidden away in the back of her closet where she kept the ugliest of the relics I'd brought back and no one had seen except me. It seemed that except for Blakey and McAuliffe, they were all strangers, everyone in the room.

I described the threats against Chief Job's village by the sorcerer at the far end of the mountain and the delicacy of Governor N'Debo's problem earlier that afternoon. I told them why it wouldn't do for a westernized Congolese civil servant to admit to a pair of American diplomats he was powerless against the threats of a primitive bush sorcerer whose magic was so murderous: villages struck, huts burned, villagers maimed or killed. I explained why N'Debo wouldn't admit he believed in such rubbish. But he did believe and that's why he'd canceled the visit and refused to explain his reasons, changing his mind only after we'd assured him the ambassador and the embassy would take full responsibility. His logic was simple enough. Whose strength would be greater than the fury of an obscure African bush doctor if not that of the American ambassador? Hadn't we put a man on the moon?

I'd said too much. The ambassador sat looking at me in bewilderment, head lifted, his blue eyes glazed dumb.

"How absolutely fascinating," his wife said, recovering herself, but from her face I knew she was just as horrified. They had thought of it as a pastoral evening in a pastoral village but I had made it something sinister. Blakey's baffled look told me the same thing. I should have kept my mouth shut the way McAuliffe always did.

"Certainly, but I'm sure it's nonsense," Kim Johnson said quickly, conscious of the ambassador's confusion. "N'Debo's Belgian-educated."

"What's that prove?" I said. "Except that he'd never admit to what I just said."

With the ambassador looking on, Johnson was irritated. "I'm sure it proves he believed no such thing."

"Why don't we ring up and ask him?" Jeffrey said.

"Ask N'Debo?" Johnson said, coloring. "Of course I won't ask him." As usual, McAuliffe turned to wander away. "It's degrading nonsense. I know the man. I've known him for two years."

"Of course it's nonsense," said the ambassador's wife, rising to put a reassuring hand on Kim Johnson's sleeve. "But it's such dear nonsense."

I heard a voice at my ear. "I thought you said N'Debo didn't want to offend the traditional chiefs." It was Turpin whispering at my right elbow, wagging his eyebrows and screwing up his sunflower-seed eyes. "Isn't that what you said this afternoon?"

"That was before I knew."

His damp shoes creaked as he crept closer. "Knew what?"

"About the sorcerer in the next village."

"You believe that." I thought I saw his nostrils twitch suspiciously. Maybe he thought he'd finally sniffed out a few ounces of what had made me and my tale seem so insensible, a joint of *Cannabis sativa* I'd lit up coming back. First McAuliffe, now me. If I'd had any pot with me, I would have lit up right there.

"Christ, Turpin. Don't you understand? It doesn't make any goddamn difference what I believe."

But I knew I'd said too much. I saw Blakey smiling from across the room, but then Marcia Johnson drew her away. I'd hoped earlier we might take a walk out under the stars and I'd show her the immense African night as it was far out on the savannahs when it seemed you were on the far edge of the universe, looking back across the dust of drifting galaxies toward our own constellation. The room had grown warm, the drinks were strong, and everyone was tired. Turpin creaked off in his damp shoes, leaving me alone with the ambassador and his wife. She thanked me again and went off to look for the AID director's wife. From the ambassador's weary expression, I knew he preferred to believe what I'd told him earlier that afternoon about provincial political rivalries, the simpler law diplomatists live by.

Now that we were alone he seemed uneasy. "A very entertaining tale," he said, rising from the divan. "Very entertaining indeed." His misty blue eyes drifted away, searching out the drinks tray carried by the Black houseboy in white gloves supplied by our Belgian hosts. Seeing his empty glass, I went to fetch him.

McAuliffe and I left twenty minutes later. Moody was already gone. We walked down the sand road carpeted with ribbons of raffia palm under a sky brilliant with stars. I'd seen only disbelief behind me, but what could I expect? The room was bright, civilized and congenial, its energy civil and domesticated, pulsing into lamps, air conditioners, and fridges, cooling drinks and lighting up costumes and cocktail-hour faces, never dumb, raw and uncivilized like the terrorizing thermal violence out over the savannahs. I didn't know whether they believed me or not.

At the missionary cottage, Moody's front porch bug light was on. Thick-jacketed beetles, bat-size insects and moths clicked against the glass, flinging swallowlike shadows across the floor and walls. I'd expected Moody to be there waiting, as he usually was. He wasn't but he'd been there. The wicker rocking chair was still moving.

"He paid Chief Job for the tusk," McAuliffe said sleepily as he stopped at the foot of the steps, searching for his house key. "Gave the chief a hundred zaires."

I stopped. "Moody did?"

"Moody and his ministers. He bought it the week after we left. Bought the tusk, bought the chickens and rice for the *mwamba,* bought the monkey for slaughter and the palm wine.

Opening up the territory, I suppose. What was it you said, an Indian agent on the Wyoming frontier?" He laughed in despair. "So stupid, all of it. Chief Job said he thought we'd given Moody the money."

"Did you tell him?"

He shook his head, looking at the stars overhead. "No. I'd like to think he would have done it anyway."

"I think he would have."

"Maybe."

We talked about it for a while lying sleepless in our bunks under the mosquito netting. By then McAuliffe felt a little sorry for Moody and I suppose I did too. I thought of a shirttail boy from some gopher-hole town in Kansas hanging on a picket gate, watching the Indian circus come to town, churning up the dust of the streets as it paraded toward the fairgrounds. I wondered what had inspired him to become a foreign missionary. Maybe the same wanderlust that once tempted me.

We decided that if we'd been responsible for breaking the power of Chief Job's enemy, the chief and his village were better for it, but in our hearts we couldn't convince ourselves. Both had survived all these years. Would they be better off now the fetisheur was gone? What would now follow? Mobutu's political cadres, the territorial administrator, the local pastors? We couldn't answer that.

The next morning McAuliffe was up and dressed before I was. It was a little after seven. Moody was at his ham radio in the far rear of the dormitory room, trying to arrange a phone patch with someone in some small town in Iowa for Colonel Harris's wife. His back was to us. "Be with you boys in a minute," he shouted without turning.

"Take your time," I called. "Get the mail through!"

107

"Yes, ma'am!" Moody shouted into his ham radio microphone. "Reverend Virgil Moody, WDXZQ, Mbuji-Mayi, the Congo. You hearing me now, sister? . . ."

We had an hour or so before the morning schedule began and walked down to the *marché* and wandered around for a while.

The rest of the day went pretty much as planned. The AID director and economic counselor met with their counterparts in the provincial offices. There was a tour of the diamond mines and the diamond-sorting operation, followed in the afternoon by a trip to a Presbyterian clinic and a Catholic vocational school. The local director of tourism took the ambassador's wife, Blakey, and the other wives to visit the local curio shops. That evening over drinks at the ambassador's rest house at the Belgian compound, I talked to Blakey for the first time since our trip to the village. Her shopping trip had been a disappointment. She had seen nothing of any value. The masks and fetishes were newly carved. Jeffrey soon joined us.

"Any new tall tales to frighten us?" he asked. She bit her lip and turned away without a word and after a minute he followed, a little annoyed. I saw the two of them arguing in the far corner near the door. A few minutes later they both left.

Late the following morning, we were on our way back to the capital in the creaky old C-119 that had dropped in to pick us up on its way back from Lubumbashi. McAuliffe and I sat in the back of the cargo hold, surrounded by crates of fresh fruits and vegetables being brought back by the military mission's flying crew.

"It was perfect," Blakey said, pausing in the cargo door to turn to me as we disembarked, a flush rising to her cheeks. Jeffrey was standing impatiently behind her and so were the Johnsons. "I didn't get a chance to thank you or Ken, but it was lovely, all of it."

After the Mbuji-Mayi trip, Ambassador Graham's wife came to depend on Blakey more and more. She and Jeffrey were drawn more into the social life at the residence: cocktail parties, receptions, and dinners, large or small. Popular at the residence, they were more active on the diplomatic circuit as well, out every night, or so it seemed from my lonely upstairs flat. I began to see less of her. At a reception for a visiting Chase Manhattan banker, she told me she'd dropped her classes at Louvanium.

"I had to, I really didn't have a choice."

"But you don't mind." We were standing to ourselves.

"Not really. Genevieve's a very sweet woman, very lonely too. Most people don't realize that. She's planning to redecorate the guest rooms upstairs and needs help." She gave me a smile, a gentle reminder of her old self, and I felt it down to my toes. "I put your name on the list for tonight, by the way. Try to make the best of it." Then she was gone, just her lovely fragrance left behind, on her way to rescue the wife of the minister of finance standing helplessly by herself near the buffet table.

McAuliffe's days were winding down and soon he would be moving on to the Sudan. We took one last trip together to Bukavu in the east. I had too much to drink the first night in the hotel bar above the lake, sitting there alone trying to sort things out after McAuliffe had gone up to his room. I had trouble climbing the stairs and unlocking my door; I fell over my suitcase, crawled across the floor, and climbed into bed with my clothes on. I awoke the next morning disgusted with myself, still dressed, took a cold shower, and went downstairs to the dining room. McAuliffe was already there, having coffee and croissants. The light splintering from the water glasses was so blinding I put my sunglasses on. I had with me Blakey's illustrated text on Warega ivories published in Brussels. The Warega people are found up on the northeast frontier in the mountains below Bukavu. I'd never been there and each time McAuliffe and I had planned a trip, we'd had to postpone it. Warega art was among the most interesting as well as the most elusive and the most often faked.

McAuliffe said he'd never seen me drink that much before and wondered if I had a chaotic personality or maybe just fractured.

"You mean now or always?" My head ached.

"Both. But it needn't be. You know what it is, don't you?"

"No. What do you think it is?" I thought he would say something about Blakey but he didn't. He told me he was leaving the foreign service and he thought that in time I would too. "It's a kind of controlled schizophrenia, the diplomat's life," he said. "You wonder which side of the brain you really want to live in, the public one or the private one."

My head ached too much and we didn't talk about it again. It was a short trip, and after two days we were bored and hitched a ride to Bujumbura across the frontier in an Oxfam Land Rover and spent two days with a grateful American ambassador and his wife at their hillside residence. They seldom got visitors and except for their tennis court and swimming pool where their houseboy kept us supplied with beer, roasted groundnuts, and stale pretzels, had little to occupy themselves. The ambassador asked if we would talk to the embassy staff about the Congo and so we did. He gave us a cocktail party the night before we flew back to Kinshasa.

The week of McAuliffe's departure, Kim Johnson and his wife gave a small informal party for him at poolside on a Saturday afternoon. He brought Gretchen and they arrived in her old

Fiat, not in tandem on his Honda. There were just the five of us; it was informal. Kim Johnson proposed a toast but McAuliffe didn't respond, just nodded. "It's so sad," Marcia Johnson said to me afterward. Her husband was annoyed that McAuliffe hadn't answered his toast. McAuliffe was happy to leave; Kim Johnson hadn't given him a very good efficiency report.

I was on the esplanade of the air terminal at N'Sele the morning he departed, standing with Gretchen as he boarded the East Africa jet for Entebbe and Nairobi. There were just the two of us and she was in tears. He'd left me his Honda to sell. I heard him say he'd see her in a few weeks and she told me she was packing up too, reassigned to East Africa by the Scandinavian relief organization she worked for. He waved from the top of the step and we both waved back. Standing there, watching the jet sprint down the runway, all of it came flooding back, the villages we'd seen, the rivers we'd crossed, the savannahs and rain forests we'd traveled, all seemed to shimmer there like a kerosene fume mirage in the bright noonday sun. I thought Blakey might come but she didn't.

One Sunday at the ambassador's pool Blakey asked me about Beirut. She'd asked a few questions before, but never so pointed. "You regretted leaving?" she asked quietly. It wasn't yet noon and we'd arranged to meet, had driven out separately and were alone. I didn't know what was on her mind. She wasn't in her orange bikini but in a skirt and blouse, working on a guest list for Genevieve's luncheons, her green portfolio on her knee. She had on her tortoise-shell reading glasses and no makeup, looking very schoolmarmish. Maybe she thought they made her appear plainer and less attractive. I couldn't help wondering if that's how she saw herself each morning in the mirror, a married woman who no longer interested anyone.

"In some ways."

She didn't look up. "It's hard leaving friends, I suppose."

"Sometimes. A few maybe. I don't know. I liked it." I had told her once about hunting in the Bekaa and among the Shiites in the south.

Her head was still down and I couldn't see her eyes behind the sunglasses. "You're a wanderer, that's all. Here today, gone tomorrow. A drifter, a vagabond turned diplomat."

"Who told you that?"

"You did. One afternoon at the Belgian Club when we were talking. I sometimes wonder why you joined the foreign service. I wouldn't have thought it. Not you, not Ken McAuliffe either."

"No? Why not?"

"I just wouldn't."

"Maybe I like being on the move every two years."

"That's what you said that afternoon at the Belgian Club."

She returned to her guest list and said nothing more.

But after the witch doctor episode in Mbuji-Mayi had been repeated around the embassy, I was pretty much the odd man out. Nothing I did or said seemed to surprise anyone. My evenings were my own and I spent them listening to my old jazz records, remembering better days and sometimes drinking too much. Occasionally I heard Jeffrey downstairs, fingering a few lonely études at his piano.

During a trip to West Kasai near the Angolan border I visited the house of a trader I'd met in the marketplace in Tshikapa, a Maluba who had a two-truck transport company and dealt in African art on the side. His trucks traveled into Angola and he kept the wares his drivers picked up in a small room in the front of his house before taking them back to Kinshasa and Brazzaville to be sold to French buyers. I bought two Tchokwe masks, both very small and very old. One was half covered with monkey fur, had a rotten raffia collar, and smelled of fish oil. It was so ugly I had the trader double the burlap and paper wrapping before I left his shop.

I looked at the masks again back at the Baptist missionary cottage where I was staying. When I did I was reminded of something an English general in New York had written in 1767 during the French and Indian War. Instead of Colours and Cannon, the British trophies of war would be "stinking scalps." And at that moment, that's what the Tchokwe mask reminded me of, a stinking scalp. That bothered me for some reason.

I returned on a Thursday. On Friday night I stopped by Blakey's flat to drop off the burlap sack with the two Tchokwe masks.

"Ah, more pelf from the provinces, I see," Jeffrey said irritably as he opened the door. A tie was looped around his neck. His thin face shriveled in disgust as he saw my sack. "What is it this time, a shrunken head from the Amazon?" The cook and houseboy were there, preparing the table. They were giving a small dinner party. Blakey came running from the back bedroom wrapped in a terry-cloth bathrobe, her hair in a towel. "Don't you have enough of this rubbish?" he said. "I mean, let's be sensible about it. And for God's sake, put some clothes on!"

"How was your trip?" she asked, ignoring him. I said it was fine and she took the sack. "I have to dress. Fix yourself a drink, please. I'll be out in a minute."

"There's no time, Margaret!" Jeffrey called, turning his back on me. "They'll be here. I mean, for God's sake!" She went into the bedroom and slammed the door and he followed. I left.

That night I stood on my little balcony overlooking the ivory market and heard the voices drifting up from below where she and Jeffrey were giving their little dinner party, Blakey's among them. Falling in love is humiliating enough, but falling in love with a married woman is worse. I decided I wouldn't see her again.

That same weekend I finally understood her questions about Beirut. One of the two weekly pouches came in on Sunday afternoon and late in the afternoon Rudy Lamb, an NSA communicator on the first floor, picked up the apartment house mail and left it in the box in the concierge's office downstairs. As I sorted through the mail I never noticed the letters others were receiving. But someone else did. That evening a letter from Simone Coulet in Beirut lay atop the others in a blue airmail envelope, scented as always by the cachet in her stationery drawer. As I picked it up I wondered how many times Blakey had seen the same blue envelopes waiting for me downstairs while I was off in the bush.

I didn't show up at the Belgian Club or at the pool the next few weeks.

Travel is the best remedy. Get out, get away, and stay away, anything to get her out of your mind. Go where you've never been before, get lost in the bush, stay a week, ten days, then come home tired and fix a drink and wander through your empty flat listening to the ten-year-old records you've heard too many times and admit nothing is working, nothing will ever work. By then you're a mental case. You know that if your thoughts were ever taken in deposition and made public in a court of law, you'd be hauled off to the loony bin. I didn't see her for a couple of weeks, maybe longer.

I took the ambassador and a smaller group to Luluabourg

in West Kasai. Genevieve was ill with a fever and didn't accompany him. The trip was a disaster and typical of what was to come. Unlike N'Debo, the governor was a small cruel Congolese from the north, an ex-policeman out of the national political party, not the parliament, and something of a xenophobe. I learned he'd thrown a few former administrators in jail, including the two Lunda officials McAuliffe and I had dealt with, both held without formal charges. One of them smuggled out a note to me at the hotel, brought by a cousin, asking for my help. He didn't know why he was in custody.

I asked the governor's *chef du cabinet* if I could visit him in jail but he refused. He also told me I could play no part in the itinerary and I didn't. We were all pretty much his prisoners. The ambassador was annoyed but resigned when he saw the schedule the governor had planned. I suggested he ask about the two imprisoned Lunda officials, and he took their names and said he would but didn't get the chance. He didn't see the governor alone. It rained for two days. We weren't even able to manage a trip out of the capital.

The visit concluded with a large and lavish dinner at the governor's residence. After the banquet, a troupe of Bakuba dancers led by their chief performed on the side lawn under the trees, illuminated by the dim orange light of smoking flambeaux stuck in the soft turf. Most of them were old men and women, all clad in smoky raffia, beads, bracelets, and feathers, their dark wrinkled bodies oiled, a petrified remnant of the once-great Bakuba kingdom of the high plateau whose oral tradition could trace their royal lineage back to A.D. 400. I doubt anyone at the banquet knew that.

I remember an indolent Greek trader in a gray shantung suit who sat at my table far in the rear during dinner. He ignored the speeches and the toasts afterward. As the dinner broke up and the guests assembled on the side balconies to watch the dancers, I saw the Greek come awake, light a cigar, and take a zaire note and some coins from his pocket. He wrapped the coins in the zaire note and tossed it out on the lawn. I was curious as to whether the dancer nearest the bank note would stop to retrieve it, and he did, breaking an old taboo, snatching it up before another dancer got to it. Bored by the dancing, the Greek was trying to provoke a few more entertaining antics, like setting two fighting cocks together. Colonel Harris was out among the dancers with his DIA camera. I went back inside.

The day after I got back I called the minister of interior's office and asked a Congolese vice minister I'd worked with about my two Lunda friends being held incommunicado in Luluabourg. He said he'd look into it and call me back. I didn't hear from him. After three more unanswered calls, I decided to send him the letter smuggled to me from prison accompanied by a letter of my own typed on the ambassador's letterhead. But I didn't, knowing if word got back to the governor in Luluabourg, it would only make their imprisonment worse.

After the visit to West Kasai the ambassador lost his taste for bush travel for a few months. My trips continued but didn't change things: Roads and bridges were still out, teachers still went unpaid, cotton and coffee farms were abandoned for lack of credit or transport, villagers were still beaten senseless by the MPR political thugs for no reason at all and then tossed in the slammer and held for months with no appeal. Unable to do anything about it, I went my own way, enjoyed the freedom and the solitude, despite the feeling of helplessness, knowing it was taking me further and further from everything back in Kinshasa. The diplomatic life had become a lonely one for me. I'd seen it happen to McAuliffe. Proud, arrogant, and ambitious men are protected by their pride, vanity, or self-esteem, but not everyone. Vagabonds or semiexiles had nothing to insulate themselves against self-discovery but themselves and their own memory. Nothing matters more. It was essential never to forget who you are. In the Middle East and Africa far from the Ohio River Valley I had discovered a sense of the frontier, of borders not yet crossed, a future still to be found. Now it was my own future I seemed to be losing.

I visited the abandoned coffee plantation above Lac Leo II a few degrees south of the equator where apart from a night on the beach at 'Aqaba with Simone Coulet I'd spent the hottest, most miserable night of my life. I stayed in the same guest cottage and walked up through the morning sunshine to the house where I had had breakfast with the Polish couple. The front door was open, creaking on its rusty hinges; two dusty coffee cups sat on the dusty table. In the saucer of one lay two brass .45 shell casings. The other rooms were empty, the house abandoned. No one could tell me what had happened to the Polish-born couple.

One night I was invited to a bachelor dinner at the residence given in honor of a pair of visiting foreign service inspectors. There were eight of us from the embassy. Jeffrey Ogden was there, his Shavian wit as tiresome as ever, charming everyone, or so he thought. After dinner Ambassador Graham brought out the port and we sat around the long dining room table and our elders talked about the old foreign service and how the diplomatic tradition they remembered wasn't what it used to be. Everyone agreed, everyone had a word or two of regret about that.

I hadn't said anything and was listening as usual. A middle-aged foreign service inspector sitting at my end of the table was curious about my silence. He'd been an ambassador to some pint-size Caribbean island and had spent much of the evening telling me about it. He was a tiresome little man with nervous hands, a name-dropper who lived in the past and would never get another post. I always thought name-dropping a kind of social disease, like incontinence among the elderly. We'd been invited that night to give up our secrets and I hadn't said anything. He asked what I thought about the modern foreign service. I said it was always that way, that diplomacy had always been an old whore trying to remember when she'd been a virgin.

That didn't go down very well and I shouldn't have said it. Irritated, Kim Johnson mentioned it to me in his office afterward, plucking at his French cuffs behind his closed door:

"Now look here, we were trying to have a serious discussion and we tell everyone diplomacy's a bawd! A tart! What in heaven's name's got into us? I have a feeling we've been spending too much time in the bush."

Maybe he was right. That same week I got a few strange telephone calls in the early-evening hours. When I picked up the phone, no one would answer. But someone was still there, standing in the shadows, holding an open phone. I wasn't sure what to do about it.

I was at a cocktail party at Pickersgill's that evening, stand-ing in a corner of the crowded dining room. Two visitors from Washington were there and so were the usual cocktail-party crowd from the Western embassies, one of whom had cornered me. The room was in shadow and as I was listening to him I saw a woman at the buffet table across the room. Her head was inclined, her face in partial profile, silhouetted by the candlelight. I didn't know who she was except that she was a stranger whose loveliness set her apart. The mystery of her silhouette, the upswept blond hair, the tilt of her head as she listened to someone hidden by the glow of the candelabra told me that she was there without wanting to be there, like me, listening to someone who didn't interest her any more than the French cultural attaché who'd cornered me interested me. For some reason I imagined she was waiting for something miraculous to happen. I wondered about her nationality and if she was married. For some reason I didn't think so. I felt better seeing someone as lovely as Blakey, but then her head turned and I recognized her. It was Blakey Ogden but not the Blakey I so often met at the pool or the Belgian Club.

She had transformed herself. Her hair was drawn up, exposing her long neck and wide shoulders in a way I'd never seen before. A few minutes later she glanced toward the front salon where a few guests were leaving. As she turned back she looked at me, a long searching look that told me she shared something with me she shared with no one else on the face of the earth. I didn't know what it was but I knew it was there, alive in those distant gray-green eyes that saw more than she would ever admit. By the time I worked my way through the crowd, Jeffrey had appeared to lead her away. She looked back over her shoulder as they disappeared. It was just as well. I wouldn't have known what to say. How can you tell a woman she married the wrong man?

I should have continued to stay away from her but didn't. At the Belgian Club the following evening I found her sitting alone in the far corner of the verandah, dressed in a dark-blue suit, as if she had just come from an afternoon tea. I don't think she was surprised to see me. It was dusk, the first stars were out, and the cocktail crowd was beginning to leave.

"I wondered where you'd been," she said, looking up. "Tired of tribal art, ethnology, and intellectual relationships?"

"No, I've been busy. I've missed you, missed seeing you." I sat down. "You might as well know that. It hasn't been the same."

She looked away. "It hasn't been easy for me either."

The waiter came. I ordered a gin and turned toward the flood-lit tennis courts, wondering if Jeffrey was there.

"He's not here." She didn't tell me where he was and I didn't ask. The early diners were arriving and two Belgian couples took the table nearby. We sat in silence for a few minutes, as if neither of us knew how to begin.

"It's hopeless," she said finally, still looking away. "Absolutely hopeless, all of it. It's never been like this before and it frightens me."

I didn't know what she meant. "What frightens you?"

"Everything. Me. Who I am, what I'm doing. I've always known I wanted to be someone other than who I am. But it was always my secret, something I couldn't share with anyone. Don't look at me like that. It's true."

"Completely different? You? That doesn't make any sense."

"You don't know the world I live in." She stirred and picked up her drink. "I'm leaving Jeffrey."

I felt like a short mortar round had exploded above the terrace and taken off the top of my head.

"There's nothing else I can do. It's just not working. Nothing makes any sense. Not only my marriage but who I am, where I'm going, or what I'm doing. It's hopeless. I have to get away. I can't go on living this way."

"You can't leave." I didn't care about Jeffrey. All I could think of was that she would leave and I would never see her again.

"I can't stay here like this."

I still didn't know what to say. We sat there for a little longer and I told her she ought to sit down with Jeffrey and talk it through. The waiter brought my drink and left. She looked at her watch, picked up her purse, and took out her car keys. "I've got to get back. We have a dinner at eight. Would you mind walking me to the car?"

She got up and I left my drink on the table and followed her through the crowded terrace and down the steps. We walked down the flagstones and through the shrubbery to the parking lot. When we reached her car in the shadows, she turned. "I tried to call you, I did, I don't know how many times—" But her voice broke and she looked away. I took her and held her and she didn't move, her face hidden against my shoulder. "I shouldn't have called you. I'm sorry. But there was no one else. No one—"

A car's headlights found us and she drew a deep breath as she stepped away, her head down, fumbling with her keys. "I'll be all right now. I've got to go. I'll call you."

I watched her drive out and saw her hand lift and wave through the back window. I should have followed her but I didn't.

I didn't sleep well that night. The next day I couldn't keep my mind on anything, remembering what I had told her and wondering if I had made a mess of it. Frère Albert and Frère Felix were down from Bumba on a buying expedition for their mission station, and Frère Albert called me from their hotel. At eight thirty I gave up waiting and joined them for dinner. The three of us put away two bottles of claret. They were both high when I left them and I was feeling a little reckless. I thought about getting off the elevator at her floor and ringing the bell but didn't.

She still didn't call. I thought maybe she and Jeffrey had patched things up. The next evening I was on my way to a cocktail party when I passed Jeffrey on Avenue Joubert in the green Fiat convertible. The top was down, his feathery hair blowing in the wind. He was dressed in his tennis whites, on his way to the residence tennis courts. I followed him to make sure and parked my car along the river to watch him join three others on the ambassador's court. I ripped off my tie and turned around and drove back to the apartment.

"It's me," I said when she opened the door. "You didn't call."

"I know." She kept her face hidden in the shadows. "I'm sorry. I tried but I couldn't. Maybe you shouldn't come in."

"That's probably true but who cares?"

"Shhhh." The door opened and she led me down the dark hall and into the dark living room where the lights from the cars on the boulevard drifted across the ceiling. She didn't turn on a lamp and stood at the bar behind the sofa, her back to me, wearing a dark skirt and a white blouse. She didn't want to turn on the lights because she'd been crying and didn't know why. Her lank hair was in tangles and after a minute her hands stopped moving. "We shouldn't be doing this."

"That's probably true too but I'm not going to leave you alone. Not like this. Did you talk to him?"

"No. Not yet." After a minute she struck a match and lit the two candles on the bar. "My hand's shaking. That's better." I was standing behind her.

"You're all right now?"

"I think so. Just a little out of breath. I'm not used to this."

She turned to look up shyly, the candlelight in her eyes the way it had been that first night. I don't think she knew whether to put her arms around my shoulders or my waist or just stand there but it didn't matter. I took her, her head went back, and her arms came up, both of us yielding to everything we'd been so stubbornly denying all those months. After a minute we moved backward to the couch, out of breath and unconscious of the cars passing or the closing of the elevator doors at the end of the hall. Half undressed, her blouse and brassiere slipped aside, she roused herself and we groped our way through the darkness to the bed in the guest room and undressed. The soft cry that finally came from her seemed to me as much a cry of pain as of joy, as if finally yielding her physical existence to another had awakened her to her utter solitude. It was like the cry of the stormy petrel I once heard beyond landfall crossing the Cabot Strait on a lonely, windswept sea, and it went through me like a knife.

Released at last, she had enormous energy, even after mine was exhausted and my body weighed a ton. We lay in the darkness afterward, cramped together on the guest room bed. I asked her if she remembered the night I saw her at Pickersgill's cocktail party, and she buried her face against my shoulder and silently nodded her head again and again.

As I said good-bye, I asked when I would see her again. Tomorrow, she said, her hair a tangle of blond curls. She wasn't sure of Jeffrey's plans and said she'd put her skirt on backward and her hair was a mess. She promised to call me.

She phoned at seven the following evening, her voice a whisper. Twenty minutes later we were in my bed. I don't know where Jeffrey was. We were together three or four times that week, sometimes in my bed, sometimes in hers.

I knew long before she told me that she had always concealed her feelings. I didn't know her emotional shyness went far deeper than I had ever suspected. I couldn't understand why a woman as lovely as she would lock her emotions away, didn't understand why someone so sensitive could deny the power of her own emotions, believing they were less important or authentic than the feelings of others. But I knew she believed that. I listened, remembering the gentle grace that had first drawn me to her and the night she had looked at me from the buffet table, that long, bold, naked look that finally tore away the secret of her solitude. If this wasn't what she said, this was what I learned.

During the first weeks she no longer concealed anything. She was irrepressible, every feeling admitted, none denied. She had never had a lover, no one had ever undressed her and made love to her the way we had made love. She told me everything and wanted me to share everything in turn: what I'd done during the day, who and what I'd seen, what I was thinking. She would sometimes laugh at what we had said, and her pure sudden laughter lifted out of the darkness was like bright water breaking from an underground spring. I knew the woman lying next to me wasn't the woman her husband had married at all.

I gave her the key to my apartment and some afternoons she would wait there, running to meet me as the door opened as if afraid we might lose even a moment of the little time we had together. Other times she wasn't satisfied with our lovemaking and wanted it never to end, even after we were both exhausted and there was no more to be had. Her back would arch and she'd pull me to her fiercely as if trying to reach some point of pure physical annihilation, nothing left behind, she told me once, nothing left of me, nothing left of her, nothing remaining for Jeffrey or the world to find, nothing left but the damp imprint of her naked shoulders on the bed. We'd both be gone, not just for this night, but forever.

One night we were in my apartment and heard Jeffrey at the piano downstairs. She froze in the darkness and released me. After the music stopped she asked in a whisper if hearing him at the piano bothered me. I said no. She didn't say anything and we lay side by side, like two figures on a Greek sarcophagus, I told her, or maybe two nuns in a Pullman berth. I could feel the mattress tremble as she turned her face against the pillow. I thought she was crying but she was laughing. Later she told me marriage was all she had been taught to expect of her life and the same was true of her friends and classmates. Jeffrey had been her first and only romance. Before their marriage he'd talked so much about chastity she realized he was asking if she was a virgin. He'd thought it important. He believed in the old-fashioned virtues. Did I?

I said that as a Southern gentleman I believed the old-fashioned virtues were important. She rolled over and covered my mouth with her warm hand. "You don't believe that at all." I don't know what she told Jeffrey those nights to explain her long absence. Saying good-bye and returning to an empty bed was the hardest of all.

It was all right those first weeks, but mistrust dies as hard as solitude and when I couldn't give her the assurances she needed, she began to have doubts. One night she came back from the bathroom, walking naked across the bedroom with a boldness that would have been impossible earlier when she always covered herself with a knee-length cotton chemise. Awakened to her passion and spontaneity, she was a different woman now. Impulsively she leaped on my back. "I'm not promiscuous!" she cried. "Did you hear me! Wake up!" We'd been talking about nothing in particular before she slipped from my side. I rolled over, half asleep as she straddled me, shaking my shoulders. "Look at me! I'm not! Did you hear me? I'm not!"

What could I say? I'd never said anything about promiscuity and wondered if her sexuality had begun to frighten her. I wasn't sure what she wanted me to say and since I'd never believed that words were reliable or by themselves could ever resolve anything, I didn't say anything. But silence isn't enough to sustain trust, and after that she would sometimes watch me through her lowered lids as we made love, as if wanting to know if my passion was genuine and not merely the solitary joy of erotic male workmanship. And through the dark lashes lowered against her cheeks, I sometimes saw the eyes of another woman.

"How did this happen?" she asked one night after I'd come back from a three-day trip. "What have you done!" She lay at my side, her face hovering over me, her damp hair falling over my forehead. She said she'd been upset during the day, hadn't dared to go out, and had finally dissolved in tears. She rolled away, propped on her elbows, her slim hands covering her face. She had the most beautiful hands I'd ever seen, her fingers long and delicate, her palms slim and narrow. There was something miraculous about her hands, and I think it was her hands that first told me there was something miraculous about her.

"I can't believe we're doing this. I can't. It's unforgivable, not like anything that's ever happened to me. I look at poor Jeffrey, sitting there at the breakfast table in the morning as if nothing had ever happened in his life and never will, and I feel so sorry for him and ashamed of myself. But at the same time I can't wait for him to leave." She raised herself again. "Why have we done this? Why? What kind of a crazy world do we live in? Are we out of our minds? Tell me."

"It's the way we feel," I said. I thought this her concession to the Furies who'd been pursuing her that day, that she was trying to forgive herself, so I let her talk about it and after a while it was all right again. She didn't mention leaving Jeffrey and I didn't ask. But after a few weeks when I still hadn't said anything about the future and what I planned to do, her doubt returned. She reminded me of a few mindless remarks I'd made in the past. She remembered my comment at the ambassador's dinner table about diplomacy being an old strumpet. Jeffrey had told her and Genevieve Graham had mentioned it.

"I don't understand why you'd say something like that. I don't. I don't understand, don't understand you, your cynicism, what you want, or anything else. I thought I did once but I don't. Do you?"

"I was fed up with the protocol of lying, that's all."

"That isn't all. I know it isn't. You're the strangest man I've ever met." Another evening she said, "You frighten me sometimes, you really do. I sometimes think you're crazy, coming up to me on the stairs just outside Jeffrey's office or calling me at the residence like that. You really are"; "What's going to happen tomorrow? You don't care, you don't care about anyone or anything"; or, worst of all: "Please don't make me hate you. Please."

Hate me? How could she hate me? I thought it was her way of denying me. And if she was in bed with me now, why did she have to ask about tomorrow? I couldn't understand her doubts and wondered again if the passion she'd finally conceded after all those years of denial had frightened her. But I was wrong. She wasn't like the other women I'd known. In my clumsiness I didn't realize how fragile her trust and how lonely the truths she'd lived with all those years. My not saying anything may have been disappointing but that was the way I'd always been. Maybe adultery is like that too. To be together those nights she had to tell lies, not exuberant, funny Rabelaisian lies, like I did, but cunning, ugly little lies that in a far deadlier way began to infect the few hours we shared.

One night when we were unable to meet, I went to a National Day reception, knowing Blakey would be there. I found her with Jeffrey and another couple standing near the doors to the terrace. I got a drink and joined them and stood listening to Blakey and the other couple. After a few minutes I was conscious of Jeffrey studying me. I thought maybe I'd been too obvious in searching Blakey out. Or maybe he suspected our affair. After the other couple left, he continued to look at me.

"Do you mind if I ask you a question?" he said.

"Not at all."

"I was wondering what happened to your nose." I have a small scar in my right eyebrow and another across the bridge of my nose.

"An eight ball, I think it was. An Indian pool hall hangout in Raton, New Mexico."

He didn't ask me what I was doing in a pool hall in New Mexico, how the fight started, or how a half-drunk Indian attendant so clumsy with a cue stick could eight-ball someone from twenty feet away during a pool hall brawl. "I've never been to New Mexico," he said after a minute. Satisfied, he took Blakey's arm and wandered away.

Two nights later Blakey reminded me of it. We were in bed and she turned to me suddenly. "Why on earth did you tell him that?"

"Why not?"

"He thinks you're odd enough as it is. Is it true?"

"Sure it's true." I was hitchhiking to San Francisco but had gotten off the main track and the pool hall was near a bus stop where a six o'clock bus left for Denver.

"I can never tell with you."

"Tell what?"

"Tell whether you're fibbing or not. Sometimes I think you invent yourself as you wander around, the way medieval troubadours used to do. Here today, gone tomorrow. Is the truth really in you?"

"It's in me." I turned to her, pulling her to me and dragging the bedcovers over both of us. "It just gets buried sometimes."

I think she wanted to believe me but was no longer sure. Not long afterward she refused to go to bed with me. After a long and exhausting night together, we met the next morning at the ambassador's pool. It was early and the pool hadn't opened yet, so we were alone. She had decided we shouldn't see each other that week: no clandestine telephone calls, no sneaking up or down the back stairs, no calls for her at the residence, no meetings at the Belgian Club or anyplace else. She was lying on the lounge chair in her orange bikini, her head back, looking determined and very lovely, wearing sunglasses, and refusing to look at me at all. Maybe she'd found the truth or thought she had, but she wasn't certain. We had to discover what our true feelings were and discover them alone. Then in three weeks, I could call her.

I didn't believe her. "If that's what you want, never mind that it's a little silly, but just tell me why."

"I told you. We're still discovering each other. Anyway, it's not what I want but what you want."

I still didn't believe her. She'd temporized before, making excuses for not seeing me, but each time had relented when I called. But when I called her the next night she refused to see me.

I was annoyed those weeks, annoyed because I was miserable and didn't want to admit it and angry because I thought she was playing out a neurotic feminine role as dishonest as her life with Jeffrey. Then late one morning Colonel Harris stuck his head in the door and said he was flying to Bujumbura with the C-119 the next day and asked me to go along. I had no reason to go to Burundi and asked if he could drop me at Kindu. The next morning I flew to Kindu where I spent a couple of useless days before driving on to Uvira and Bukavu in the east by road. I swore I wouldn't think about her while I was gone, that I'd get her out of my mind, but it didn't do any good. I imagined I'd return and not call her at all.

In a sudden downpour under dark clouds on a lonely stretch of track above Lake Tanganyika a crippled old woman hailed my Land Rover, waving a bundle of rags tied to her walking stick. I told the driver to stop and we gave her a ride to Uvira. She didn't speak Lingala or French and I asked the driver to find out her tribal language. He spoke to her in Swahili. She was a Warega woman, a wrinkled old woman with malarial eyes whose flesh hung from her arms like rags from a stick. She had just buried her husband and son after a ferry accident and smelled of raw fish. I asked if she had anything to sell and she said no.

From the damp bundle of rags she carried she proudly brought out two small Warega ivory masks to show me, as smooth as amber and discolored by age. I asked her if she was interested in selling them. She smiled a wrinkled smile and shook her toothless head. I mentioned a price but she said no. We rode on and I thought she'd change her mind but she didn't. When she got out I doubled my offer. She hesitated as she stood outside, her bony hands still on the leather seat to steady herself before setting out again for the long walk ahead. She thought about it, smiled again, shook her head, and walked on. The rain had eased and I called out my final price, annoyed at her stubbornness and determined to have them one way or another. She stopped, turned, looked at me, and finally limped back to the Land Rover.

The C-119 brought me back from Bukavu the day before the end of our three-week separation. I called Blakey from the embassy, although I'd told myself I wouldn't. She was excited, knew I'd been away but didn't know where. She'd been worried and couldn't wait to see me. Only an hour off the plane, I hadn't slept well the night before and was a little hung over. I'd spent the previous evening alone in a dark little hotel bar, drinking too much and thinking about the mess I'd made of my life and Blakey's.

She was waiting for me inside her front door, wearing shorts and an apron and holding a bottle of wine. She shut the door and I held her for a long time, as if we were beginning all over. We had the entire night to ourselves, no returning to an empty bed. Jeffrey was in Goma. A charter flight carrying two American elephant hunters and their Belgian guide had gone down on the airstrip there during a thunderstorm. He'd flown up to the Kivu to inventory the effects and close the caskets.

We had dinner and she said she'd finally found herself, finally discovered her true feelings. She and Jeffrey were going on leave, three weeks in Crete, or so Jeffrey had planned, but she wouldn't go if I would rather she stayed. Or maybe I could take leave in a hotel on the other side of the island. Jeffrey wanted to sail to some of the other islands for a few days with a locally hired charter. We could meet while he was sailing.

We went to bed and made love and she told me she had finally found a meaning to her life she never thought she'd find. In the futility of her life with Jeffrey, she'd come to believe she was alone and always would be, but that was no longer true. In a way she didn't understand, everything around her, everything in the universe made sense in a way it never had before.

Her words bothered me. Love her or not, I didn't know any more about the universe than I ever did and never would. She slipped from my side and after a few minutes she came back from the bathroom, walking naked across the bedroom with a joyful innocence that declared her self-discovery, unashamed and unafraid. She was feeling playful and kicked aside our sheets, free of inhibitions, free of doubt, free of indecision, free of Jeffrey and his unexpected return.

She was pleased by the two figures I'd brought. They were identical to a larger Warega mask she'd seen in a Sotheby's catalog. "They're so rare, so marvelous," she said, lifting the two Warega ivory figures from the lamp table. "So terribly strange, so mysterious, like what's happened to us."

I was still tired. I'd thought of nothing but her for three weeks and now she was going to Crete with a man she didn't love.

"Do you know their story? They must have an interesting story, like our trip to Chief Job's village. How did you find them? Tell me everything." She sat up cross-legged in bed and danced the two masks around on the pillow. "They insist you tell me their story. Please."

I didn't want to tell her about my shameless badgering of the old woman who'd just buried her husband and son, so I said I didn't know their story, only mine.

"Then you'll have to tell me your story, won't you? What you found these last two weeks." She stretched out in bed, her chin on my chest, her green eyes lifted. They seemed especially sly that night, like a fisherman's cat, never satisfied, always eager for more. "So tell me your story."

She wanted to know everything, what I'd been thinking the past weeks, whether I missed her or not, if I'd been as miserable as she'd been, what I'd done on the trip, whom I'd met, what I'd talked about, what I'd seen. She wanted me to share everything, just like those earlier weeks, but what more could I tell her?

We'd emptied a bottle of wine and I was exhausted, tired of words, tired of believing in words, my bones still vibrating from the long trip back in the rattling C-119. As she lay against me I seemed to be outside my life, looking in from far away, seeing Blakey lying in bed, seeing the green corrugations of forest under the wings, seeing the dark rain clouds and the wrinkled old woman smelling of raw fish who had given up some rare tribal antiquities for a handful of zaires, seeing Blakey's foolish cuckolded husband in Goma closing a casket, and remembering a dead American of Lebanese ancestry whose effects I'd inventoried one weekend at Zahleh in the Lebanese mountains when I was duty officer. He'd owned a grocery store in a Black neighborhood in Richmond, Virginia, and the wad of soiled shirts and underwear I recovered from his suitcase were damp with the sweet sickening smell of spilled hair tonic. I remembered the Tchokwe mask I'd brought back from Tshikapa that reminded me of a stinking scalp.

The little truths that shrivel the soul are always uglier than the ones you brought back. I'd wanted to get her into bed and so I had and now I loved her but what was left? More nights like this? In a week she'd be gone, making the best of my hesitation and doubt, conspiring to share my bedroom in Crete while she shared her marriage bed across the island with a man she didn't love, shared with him the physical freedom she'd discovered with me. What had I done to her? What had we done to each other?

Jealousy is like that. I'd freed her from nine years of the Jeffrey-Margaret diplomatic duet, a barren marriage to a sexually illiterate husband who romped out his passion knocking tennis balls into the net or nimbly dancing his way through a cocktail-party set, and now she'd rediscovered herself and her freedom. How often had her pure sudden laughter lifting from the darkness of our bedrooms told me that? I'd once been free that way myself but no more. Maybe I resented her spontaneity because it denied my own. Love is like that too: Nothing gives greater joy but nothing can be more destructive.

It wasn't like going to the moon, I told her in that clumsy way I have of denying the pretense of the permanent and the eternal or that anything makes sense and ever will—you and a couple of half-assed forty-year-old Annapolis or West Point graduates in aluminum skin suits, America's adolescent diplomats to the world, skylarking around their gravity-free capsule like gibbons in a zoo while seventy million Americans are watching on the living room boob tube back home. Like every place else worth exploring down there at the rock bottom of things, when you went to the bush it was better to go alone. I'd brought her two Warega masks. What more could I say? What more did she want me to say?

It was a stupid, insensible remark, half false and half true, half angry, half mocking, like everything else I knew, and had nothing to do with her. I don't know why I said it, maybe because I was tired and it was my way of clearing my head, but I'll never forget the expression on her face: pain, loss, confusion, something whole shattered, her freedom, joy, and passion suddenly denied. I saw a desolation I couldn't explain, forgetting how fragile the trust she'd just shared with me. I'd gone too far and said too much. How terribly far we'd both come from that first night on Pickersgill's terrace and at what terrible cost.

She turned away, reached over to turn off the lamp, and lay for a long time in the darkness, not saying anything, retreating again to that unreachable solitude she'd lived with so long. I tried to talk to her, tried to explain, but it was too late. I'd denied a world she'd just discovered and she wouldn't answer. An hour later, unable to sleep, I got out of bed and stumbled around in the darkness and got dressed. When she didn't say anything I let myself out.

I didn't see her the next day and she didn't call. Two days later Jeffrey came back. That night I phoned her but no one answered. I tried to reach her during the next two days to explain and apologize, to talk to her and hear her voice, but I got no answer in her flat.

I didn't know she'd left until Marcia Johnson told me two afternoons later at the commissary. The day before Blakey had packed her bag, taken an embassy car to the airport, and boarded a Sabena flight for Brussels. "I knew they'd been having difficulties," she said, "maybe for months, who knows. I don't know why. She just decided she'd had enough, I suppose. He's so possessive, but very reckless on her part too. But I'm sure it's only a temporary separation. Poor Jeffrey's devastated."

But I knew it wasn't reckless at all. She'd looked at herself and her future and decided to take back her life and begin again. "Do what you want to do," I'd told her, and she had. "It's not what I want but what you want," she'd told me, but I was doing the same things in the same way, the same trips to the bush where nothing would change, the same arguments with Kim Johnson who edited my drafts and didn't want to put too brutal a face on the misery of the interior. She'd learned to withhold her trust and now she mistrusted me. I thought of going down to the admin section and asking about her travel plans and if she was still in Europe joining her but I didn't. She had more courage than I did.

The following week Jeffrey went on leave and didn't return. Two weeks later word came from Washington he was being reassigned. An officer in the administrative section who'd been substituting took his place. Each week I thought I might hear from her, but I didn't. Even so as the months passed she was never out of my thoughts. I tried to patch up my life and move on. I doubted whether she and Jeffrey had worked things out, but I didn't want to know. I sometimes consoled myself by thinking she'd taken the freedom she'd discovered with me and made the most of it. There was no comfort in that.

I never again stayed with Moody during my solitary visits to the Kasai but took a room instead at Mama Onema's hotel on the edge of the *marché* where the *mwamba* was always overcooked, the beer always warm, and the air-conditioning and water faucets never worked. It was easier that way, even if I never knew who might come knocking at my door in the middle of the night, woman, girl, or child—*"hotel du put,"* as N'Debo once described it to me a little less elegantly. You could always find someone in the bar and restaurant below with a story to tell, as true of Mbuji-

Mayi as it was of Kindu, Kisangani, or Bukavu, some brutal tale from the old Belgian days or some unreported massacre during the bloody rebellions. You could always find a trader with something interesting to sell: an ugly fetish, a half-rotted mask or bundle of bones and feathers, some talisman you'd never seen before and never would again, even in Blakey's books. You could never tell from their rags, their broken French, or their uninflected Swahili or Lingala who they were and where they'd been, sorcerers, soothsayers, chiefs, village thieves, or gravekeepers to the kings who were once the repository of the great oral tradition that could trace the royal ancestry back a millennium, now sleeping on cardboard or copra mats as they sold off the last of the relics from one of the once-great tribal kingdoms to the east or north before buying a seat on a truck headed west for the great sprawling slums of the capital I was fleeing.

When I visited Mbuji-Mayi, I always called on Governor N'Debo, who greeted me as warmly as ever. We drank together and swapped lies on his terrace under the bougainvillea and frangipani, old pals by then, well oiled by quart bottles of Simba beer from Katanga, but we never talked about the night of the sorcerer's storm or the financial help that hadn't yet reached his province. He told me one night he was in hock up to his ears and had borrowed against his real estate holdings in Kinshasa to keep body and soul together. He wanted nothing more than to go back to his commercial interests in Matadi and Kinshasa and was negotiating to represent a Japanese appliance manufacturer. I met his wife, a plump, laughing woman who'd studied nursing in Brussels and drank more beer than I did one afternoon on the rear terrace and afterward fell asleep.

The building sites were still abandoned mounds of rubble, the school and clinics still empty shells. My visits were brief and uneventful. I sometimes saw his frog-eyed *chef du protocol,* who'd found himself a new tailor, a new jeweler, and a few local girl-friends who must have given more spice to the local *mwamba* he once complained about. He was often in Mama Onema's bar, seated far off in a corner, usually with the same gold-toothed Senegalese in a white boubou, come to trade in diamonds.

Blakey called me cynical and maybe I was. It was the corruption that bothered me most, ours as much as theirs, mine as much as everyone else's; not only the corruption but the rottenness that followed, that crept into your clothes, skin, and mind as invisibly as the smoke from the savannah fires I brought back with me after my trips to the interior and finally followed me into Blakey's bed. But it wasn't just the corruption.

Time itself, so generous to the Greek and Roman ruins along the Mediterranean, punishes things African with a rancor all its own—the fragile wooden masks, the small delicate wooden figures with their omniscient brass-head eyes, the woven raffia, the intricately carved bowls and masks that crumble, turn to powder and dust, are eaten by termites or dry rot, are plundered and sold to hang odorless and identityless on museum walls in Brussels, Paris, or New York or country estates in Greenwich or East Hampton, denied everything that gave them meaning. Time devours Africa's memory like no other. No wonder mine seemed to survive only as an immensity of color, sky, savannah, forest, and river. The smell of smoke was the smell of Africa for me, its being and essence, as insubstantial as that but as powerful as my feelings for Blakey. How do you define that, get it down in words and on paper? You don't.

When the smell of smoke was gone from the figures I'd collected for Blakey but never given her, they no longer had any meaning. I often wondered whether she felt the same now, wherever she was. Traveling by myself so much I knew why McAuliffe had so little to say. I ended up as isolated as he was.

Ten months later I got a postcard from her mailed from New York. It was Picasso's *Les Demoiselles d'Avignon* and on the back was a note. "It wasn't your fault," she wrote. "You opened new doors for me and I'll always be grateful for that. Put it behind you, like I have. I know you will. Love and Good Luck." There was no return address.

It was a far more gracious farewell than I ever deserved but it was typical of her. We had had a passionate affair, too passionate for her gentle grace, but it was over now and she was the same sensitive, forgiving woman she had always been, returned to the civilized proprieties that had ruled her life. She had probably found someone else now, at ease in her new beginning. How else could she have written such a note? I was still the diplomatic vagabond in search of the miraculous who had found it once and let it slip away.

I went on to an embassy in East Africa after my tour ended. I reported on the interior and worked the political margins, not the center, just as I had in Central Africa. My responsibilities began where governance ended a dozen kilometers out in the scrub where the tarmac road petered out to a laterite or sand track, electric power dimmed to the flickering glow pulsing from gasoline generators or a kerosene lantern, and civil authority was confined to isolated police or army posts. I traveled most often among the Arabized Cushitic pastoralists in the north who were still suffering the effects of a murderous two-year drought and got to know the country by its victims in the interior, not its ruling claque in the capital. Like Chief Job's villagers, the semi-nomadic Moslem herdsmen had yet to receive the benefits of independence. Heirs to a tradition of blood feuds and violence, they weren't like the village agriculturalists I'd known in Central Africa. Some of the more remote clans were arming themselves.

Get close but not too close, those were my instructions. I remember the heat rising from the long desolate stretches of wasteland and the track suddenly gone when you weren't sure where you were or if you could ever find your way back. I remember stone villages that were no more than mounds of sun-bleached rock on the horizon and then coming over a rise and seeing the magenta sea in the distance. I remember the smell of the salt sea and flat-tailed sheep being herded through the narrow stone passageways to be loaded after sundown on dhows at an Indian Ocean port without electricity because there was no fuel for the generators. I remember the light fading and the sea surging quietly against the quay and the hawsers creaking and where that afternoon had been nothing but blinding sunshine and a sullen sea were now illuminated dhows lit up like carnival Ferris wheels lifting up and down in the swells as barefoot seamen from the Persian Gulf walked the rails as nimbly as goats, carrying lanterns. Under the boxes of Oman dates they had brought in were guns. Waiting somewhere beyond were other dhows from Aden, bringing more guns.

I remember arriving at dusk in a thorny wasteland village where the only light for mile after aching mile belonged to a solitary rock-walled compound where a lonely Australian with a gray beard and a Cockney accent ran a modest little UNDP program and had taken a concubine who didn't show her dusky face, but her scent was in the hall and the bedroom where I slept. That night we ate roasted goat, roasted chicken, and fresh tomatoes and cucumbers in the light of a kerosene lantern in the inner courtyard. Even then I didn't see her face, just the long slim hands that brought the plates, and heard the rustle of her skirts that left behind the lingering fragrance of jasmine. I remember lying on my hard pallet and thinking how remarkable it was to find jasmine, fresh cucumbers, and tomatoes in such a godforsaken outpost.

I remember leaving a Lutheran missionary cottage one morning and seeing a battered Land Rover in the shadows of a stone wall. A dark-skinned youth in a straw hat stood next to the driver of the Land Rover, a carbine across the windshield. Four ragged nomads sat lazily in the Land Rover, all carrying weapons and carrying them carelessly. They were the local constabulary, looking for cattle thieves, they claimed. They were brigands and extortionists, come to collect their monthly tithe from the middle-aged Lutheran couple for keeping the track free of thieves.

I remember standing to the side of my Land Rover under the stars and looking up at the immense African night when it seemed I stood on the far edge of the universe, looking back across the dust of drifting galaxies toward our own constellation. But I also remember the desert wind, always the wind, hot, ceaseless, and haunting, a wind that parches, eviscerates, shrivels, and kills without remorse and blows away the bitter dust of spiritual and physical extinction.

The week of my arrival I had a long talk with Ambassador Barnes in his third-floor office. He was a cheerful, red-cheeked man in his mid-fifties who radiated a robust, physical energy I always thought of as a kind of unconscious denial of the dismal futility of his responsibilities (lesser men might have gone mad). The regime was brutal and corrupt and there was little he or anyone else could do to change it. One evening as I stood with him in his rear garden waiting for a reception to begin, he questioned me about the lingering effects of the devastating drought in the north and said something about the cruelty of nature. I told him it wasn't only nature; no regime could be crueler than the one in power.

"There's that too, but sometimes it's better that change not come too quickly." He wasn't an apologist for the status quo. A devout Presbyterian, he was conservative by nature. Anarchy frightened him and so did the possibility crueler men might prevail. But I respected Barnes, who always listened, even when my cynicism puzzled and occasionally amused him. He was a conciliator, not a thinker, as he told me once. A decent, well-intending man, he never let an original or daring idea crowd out a cautious or consensual one.

"Dammit, Mathews, don't do anything stupid this time!" he called out to me one evening as I was leaving his office before a five-day trip, and I stopped in the door, trying to remember what I'd done last time. And then I heard Blakey's voice, as clear as a bell, and it didn't matter. She was seldom out of my mind. For some reason I assumed she had married again, settled down to a socially predictable life on the eastern seaboard.

I had an isolated walled compound on the northeast edge of the capital in a quarter favored by the northerners. There was a small tea shop and restaurant not far away with an open terrace shaded by laurel trees to one side facing a bus turnabout and a dusty plain where twice a week cattle, goats, and sometimes camels came to be bought and sold, the long caravans turning the dust of the streets to clouds of boiling brass. One dusty rock-strewn corner was used as a soccer field. The tea shop was owned by a Palestinian trader with Lebanese nationality who had a few rickety Mercedes trucks traveling to the north. His Palestinian wife ran the restaurant, which featured a Lebanese cuisine.

I would sometimes walk over through the warm evening dusk and have a mezza and a glass of beer on the terrace. On starry nights the radio in the bar would pick up the Arab music from Radio Cairo. In the evenings a few Egyptians and Palestinians from the UN would gather on the terrace with the northerners from the surrounding quarter. It was there I met Dr. Mohammed Hassan, a London-trained epidemiologist with the Ministry of Health whose compound was a hundred yards down the sand road from mine. Not far away the British charity Oxfam and the American Friends Service Committee shared a concrete block building behind concrete block walls near the UN compound. Dr. Hassan told me later that seeing me there alone at the table in the corner, he thought I was with either one or the other.

He was in his late forties, a pipe-smoker with a fringe of short white hair below a narrow bald head as brown as a chestnut. His father was an Egyptian cotton planter and his mother a northerner. He graduated from the American University in Cairo and later studied in London. His wife was an Egyptian pediatrician who worked long hours at the national hospital. They had met while working with the World Health Organization in the Sudan. We sat together at a table in the rear under the laurel trees at the tea shop as the evening lengthened and the stars came out.

143

He didn't know Central Africa or Turkey and was curious. He was a listener like me and in time we became friends.

I was often invited to his small back garden where he and his wife entertained on Friday or Sunday evenings. It was there I met other northerners. One night we were joined by Major Osman Farah, who had a small house a few sand streets away. A major on detached duty to the Ministry of Interior, he knew my name by my travel requests but we had never met until then. Tall and slender with deep-set brown eyes and a lean face scarred by smallpox, he was the son of nomads from a village deep in the camel scrag. Like Dr. Hassan, he was educated in England and Cairo.

From time to time two-man surveillance teams from the National Security Agency would drop by the tea shop and sit in the far corner. When their presence became an annoyance, we would move on to Dr. Hassan's rear porch or my own rear garden, which was larger and more secluded. I had a Hallicrafters shortwave radio, a dartboard, and a Ping-Pong table. By the end of my first year I'd met a number of their fellow clansmen from the north.

An article published one week in the *Economist* as part of an economic survey of the African continent was harshly critical of the old president, an ex-army sergeant from the south who'd ruled the country for over a decade with his clique of politicians, merchants, and bureaucrats from the south. Western economic and military assistance transfers had lined their pockets for years. Food imports had risen along with inflation and unemployment, the treasury was plundered, foreign loans went unpaid, and investment had stopped. The intellectuals were fleeing: journalists, teachers, economists, and doctors. The best qualified took up residence in that great expatriate rookery at the UN in New York or its agencies in Paris, Geneva, or Rome.

One anecdote in the article described a remark made by the old president a few years earlier when hordes of locusts had decimated the millet and grain crop. Asked by a UN official why his government hadn't been more active in bringing in anti-locust dusting teams, the old president had said it was a greater crime to kill a locust than a man. Men had immortal souls but not locusts. Once killed, a locust was dead forever. It was typical of the old president, a self-educated bully who, like many autodidacts, was dangerous in his ignorance and capable of believing anything. I met him only once at a reception on National Day at army headquarters where I was herded in line with a score of others and waited to shake his hand. Dressed in military uniform and without his presidential sash but wearing white gloves, he was a bull-necked figure of medium height. His thick impassive face and his unblinking bullfrog eyes reminded me of Governor N'Debo's *chef du protocol* back in the Kasai.

The *Economist* article didn't mention the worst of it, details hidden away in top secret intel reports that never saw the light of day. The president's security service—"knuckle-crackers," Crowder, the station chief, called them—imprisoned, tortured, crushed fingers, broke arms, kidnapped journalists off the streets, torched villages, and threw people out of airplanes. When one group of remote village elders complained about the army burning their crops, they were brought together at a rural police outpost to air their grievances. The doors were locked and a few grenades tossed in the windows. Because there were no laws, the killers had committed no crimes.

I suppose some of us were so contaminated by knowing too much about torture, mutilation, and death that we'd become infected ourselves. Colonel Wiggins, the defense attaché, had a bleeding ulcer; Crowder, thin, gloomy, and overworked, was a heavy drinker if not an alcoholic. He would sometimes call me late in the evening and ask me over to talk about events in the north. We would sit on his side verandah until he fell into exhausted silence. Then his haunted, hollow-eyed wife would appear and lead him off to bed. The details we knew may have been hidden away in top secret intel reports but burned in the mind like phosphorus each time you saw the chief of state and his minions at the UN assembled on the White House lawn to be greeted by the president, senior officials at State, and a claque from the White House clerical pool.

That issue of the *Economist* had been banned by the Ministry of Information but word had gotten out. Dr. Hassan asked me about it one night in his back garden. When I got my copy by pouch a few days later, I passed it along to him. After that I forwarded Dr. Hassan and Major Osman Farah my copies of the *Economist* and the *Paris Herald Tribune*.

Major Osman Farah began dropping by in the evening to return the newspapers and magazines and escape the confinement of his own compound, which he shared with two other families. Sometimes Dr. Hassan joined us. We would have a glass of beer and then a few more as the evening mellowed. Osman Farah sometimes reminisced about his days in England as an escape from his own intolerable isolation. One evening he described the uneasiness he had felt his first months in London when he was reluctant to sit next to a fair-skinned Englishwoman on the Underground. Then one day an Englishwoman sat down next to him and nothing had happened. But he had been punished that night, dreaming he awoke one morning to find himself in bed in Buckingham Palace with Queen Elizabeth. Ashamed and embarrassed, he didn't know what to say. Before he could explain a troop of palace guards burst in. He leaped from bed and crashed out the palace window. It was a very funny story and he laughed shyly as he told it. Dr. Hassan was also there that night and he said his feelings were identical when he first arrived in London, although his skin was lighter, but his psyche had never dared dream of sharing a queen's bed in Buckingham Palace.

It was on Sunday nights that we got together most often, sitting around listening to the news and drinking beer well into the night. We were sometimes joined by others, most often by Captain Hersi, a vice minister from Public Works who had a house nearby, and Nur Galal, a young Foreign Ministry desk officer. A few months later I tried to arrange a USIS leadership grant to the United States for the journalist brother of Captain Hersi but the request was denied.

"Hopeless, just hopeless," Osman Farah said the night he'd heard the request was denied.

"Smash it, just smash it," Captain Hersi said, but not Dr. Hassan, who had witnessed the brutal consequences of insurrection in the southern Sudan. He put his faith in the president's recently formed cabinet of national reconciliation to relieve the misery of the northern Moslem clans. Major Osman Farah and Hersi disagreed. With a laugh Osman Farah told Dr. Hassan that as a doctor he expected too much. Governments weren't like men and couldn't heal themselves. Their own was a corrupt fiction, one party, one man, one despotism that held together in mutual fear, poverty, and hopelessness agglomerations of peoples with no more stake in their nationhood than their own clansmen in the north. So long as the old president remained they had no future to share except their hope one day to declare themselves, as the insurgents in Angola and Eritrea were doing.

How was diplomacy possible with such buffoonery? young Nur Galal from the Foreign Ministry asked one Friday evening after he'd returned from a reception for a visiting Englishman from the foreign secretary's office. How could Englishmen treat so respectfully a regime that still hadn't yet discovered the Rights of Man? Turning to me, Major Osman Farah said it was a regime any self-respecting electorate in the West would have thrown on the rubbish heap decades ago, wasn't it? What could I say? Drinking beer with them and listening as they talked more boldly of the hopelessness of the present and their dreams of the future, I wondered when their anger would finally resolve itself in action. When it did I knew it would turn against me and everything I stood for.

One night in the late spring we were sitting around my back garden, celebrating Captain Hersi's promotion to major. Dr. Hassan and Nur Galal were with us, and we ran out of beer and piled into my Land Rover, half crocked, and drove out to the officers' club on the northwest edge of the capital. Major Hersi got us in the gate with his army pass, but the bar was closed, even though a few drinkers were still lounging around the tables outside. When Majors Osman Farah and Hersi insisted we be served, the argument got ugly and the bartender called a security detail. We left peacefully. As we drove out we were stopped by the armed guards at the gate. A young lieutenant took our identity cards and went inside the guard post. I suppose my presence aroused suspicion.

On my trips to the north I sometimes visited a village at the edge of the waterless scrub where the seminomadic people wandered that reminded me of Chief Job's hilltop village in the

Kasai. I'd first stopped there on my way north to follow the progress of an AID self-help and Food-for-Work project. Two wells had been dug and an irrigation system built for a corn, sorghum, and millet pilot project. One of the village elders was the uncle of the minister of commerce. In his seventies, he was as black and toothless as a crow and taller than the other villagers, which suggested he was of mixed blood, probably with that of the cattle herders to the north, like Major Osman Farah's clan, all taller and leaner than the agriculturists in the south. I don't know how many uncles the minister of commerce had but for reasons of his own this uncle had chosen to stay in the bush and not join the other members of his nephew's extended family who'd swarmed to the capital. Maybe his mixed blood had something to do with it.

A dignified old man with the bony face of an Egyptian pharaoh, he always received me dressed in a freshly laundered white dress shirt buttoned at the collar, a plaid cotton skirt, and rubber sandals. The whites of his eyes were stained as brown as a buckeye. He had nothing but scorn for the army. A military checkpoint in a thatched hut a kilometer south of the village was manned by undisciplined thugs and extortionists. His mud hut was larger and better furnished than the others. On the mud floor was a red-and-blue Belgian Wilton carpet and in the corner a small gas-operated refrigerator. Between the two upholstered European chairs was a metal table and on it an expensive Grundig shortwave radio the size of a suitcase. All had been supplied by his nephew, the minister of commerce, who had also given him a small gray Fiat truck. Because he didn't drive, he'd given it to the village cooperative.

Unlike his extended family back in the capital, he took no interest in politics and was content with life as a bush farmer, with his two young wives or concubines, his chickens, pigs and corn, sorghum and millet crops. I once asked him how many sons he had and he thought for a minute, counted his fingertips with a long polished thumb as smooth as soapstone, and gave up. Fifteen, he thought, but wasn't sure. All had left the village except one, a two- or three-year-old toddler I saw only once.

Early that summer I was asked to draft a cable on the internal situation and concluded the country would face serious problems if the president dismissed the so-called progressives in his recently appointed cabinet of national reconciliation, as rumors were reporting. I suspected by then that one reason my northern friends shared their dissatisfaction with me was to get their message through to the presidency. Barnes disagreed and so did Crowder, claiming certain subversive personalities in the cabinet were trying to "radicalize the nation," as he put it. Crowder reminded me apologetically that mine was bound to be a jaundiced view, traveling as much as I did in the north. I suppose others thought I was the one who had been radicalized. But Barnes was a reasonable man and let my language stand, adding his own paragraph in disagreement.

That July I took a few weeks' leave and visited McAuliffe on my way to Turkey. He'd left the foreign service, and he and Gretchen were working for an international relief organization in the Sudan, helping with the refugees who'd fled the Eritrean rebellion. I landed at Khartoum and caught a bus to Kassala. It was a long, bone-rattling drive south and then north over a road swarming with dust from the relief trucks we passed, and I'd brought no water bottle. Beyond the rocky road was a fiery yellow, rose, and purple wasteland where the suffocating heat lay like a fever. The ancient diesel bus broke down twice and the last time had to be repaired in the dim yellow headlights of a truck headed to the west toward Khartoum. The dozen passengers got out to escape the reeking interior that had begun to smell like tainted meat.

We were still outside in the warm wind filling our lungs when another bus headed west stopped and the driver joined the Nubian driver working on the engine. There was a dwarf aboard, returning to Khartoum, and he got out, carrying a vendor's suitcase. He opened the case, tied a band around his neck to support it, and hobbled among us, peddling his wares, calling out in four languages: *"Matahaba!"* *"Ciao!"* *"Comment ça va?"* *"How are you?"* It was too dark to see what his case held, cigarettes, candy, and Chiclets probably, but it was the parrot-like mimicry of his voice that struck me.

"C'est un fou!" A middle-aged Egyptian laughed. "A *madman!*" There was a French couple aboard our bus and the Frenchman spoke to him but the dwarf knew no more French than those three words. I don't know where he'd come from, this babbling colonial orphan.

I found McAuliffe and Gretchen in a thickly walled stockadelike compound on the edge of the town. It was fiercely hot, the wind swirled through the dusty streets, and the compound was thick with chaff churned up by the trucks and the smell of flour, sorghum, and diesel fumes. McAuliffe had lost weight and was slimmer than I remembered. There were touches of gray in his hair. "Rice dust," Gretchen said, smiling. "Me too." They lived in a three-room cottage within the compound. McAuliffe's habits hadn't changed much. He drank as much beer as he always had, repaired equipment, roasted chickens or lamb, and brought vegetables from the garden he was cultivating inside the rear wall. Gretchen was his bookkeeper. There was little furniture in the small living room. They had made bookscases out of old packing cases, but even so books were scattered everywhere, most of them paperbacks.

I spent three days following them about, watching and listening. Two hundred thousand tons of food and medical supplies passed through their compound every month. One evening we drove across the border toward Teseney in Eritrea under the stars but had to stop at a guerrilla roadblock and couldn't go any farther. Standing on the sandbagged bunker we could see the flashes of gunfire lacerating the night sky far in the distance. In the rebel-held territories beyond fields were planted by night and crops harvested by night because of the daily sorties of Ethiopian MIGs. The relief trucks came by night, always by night across the wasteland, along stony tracks and into ravaged villages, dim headlights in the dust among donkeys, chickens, dogs, naked fly-blown children, and an occasional camel, there to be greeted by young men in tattered green twill, some barefoot, some skin and bones, smelling of hunger and dehydration, men with little food and no medicine, all carrying rifles. Donkeys carried relief supplies the final miles to the front-line bunkers.

After we returned the three of us sat long into the night in the living room. The generators were turned off and we sat on lounging cushions on the floor and drank beer until McAuliffe fell asleep. Being with the two of them had brought back too many memories. Part of my life was still missing and I knew it.

The next day I went on to Port Sudan by another bus and arrived in early afternoon after an all-night journey. A few tabid palm trees lifted their crowns above the open square where the buses emptied their dark cargoes from the torrid villages of the littoral wasteland. The sky was a dirty yellow. A hot wind lifted spirals of dust from the sun-impacted earth and danced them out across the verges. In the distance the sun lay like scalded milk on the Red Sea. I was carrying a single nylon bag and had three hours to kill before my flight to Jidda.

Outside the open square fish merchants squatted before reeking baskets of tuna, skate, redfish, and sometimes small sharks taken from Red Sea. Beyond was a meat market of concrete stalls that looked like the rear washhouses of the old equatorial plantations. In a single row of dark, bloodstained stalls the carcasses of freshly slaughtered goats and sheep hung from iron hooks; their severed heads lolled at queer angles in rows at the rear, some with eyes open, tongues out, as if still stretching their severed necks for the feed trough. Bloody sheepskins dangled from posts. Both abattoir and meat market, the stalls were thick with flies; butchering knives as large as scimitars flashed against the bloodstained logs where the carcasses were quartered and trimmed. From the rear I could hear pitifully bleating goats.

The streets beyond were hard and narrow, lined by septic ditches thick with the fecal smell of the poorest Arab villages and filled with the filth of poverty, like those of the Shia I'd once traveled through hunting quail in the mountains of south Lebanon below Sidon or the native communes of Kinshasa. Arab women gathered at stone basins to draw water for the evening cooking pots from a single worn tap; their filthy children played in the narrow lanes where dead rats lay as flat as rusted tins. I moved aside in a passageway to let a barefoot herdsman pass with four sheep whose filthy matted coats smelled of piss and brine.

At the airdrome a mild wind from the Red Sea blew the punishing smells from my nostrils as I sat on the terrace where the ice dissolved in the tumblers and the conversation rose and fell like a sheen of flies over the melon rinds, custards, and beer glasses.

A few tourists sat staring emptily out over the horizon, mopping their necks and stirring only to look at their watches. Nearby were overdressed Sudanese civil servants, damp-uniformed military officers with thick black mustaches, and pale UN bureaucrats in black suits and black shoes who looked like defrocked clerics. Olive-skinned Saudi businessmen in black jackets and white robes sat fingering their worry beads. Two deranged-looking Moslem sheikhs with henna-colored beards were whispering in the shadows; closer to me a sweating Greek businessman in a white cotton shirt and white shorts was hunched over his Turkish coffee. A thick white stubble lay like salt grains on his jaws and a blue plastic case was tied by a long thin silver chain to his belt.

A beggar with a milk-white eye came to the top of the verandah steps, turned his head to give us its loathsome benefit, and piteously cupped his hand toward a French tourist in a Nairobi bush jacket. The Frenchman shrank away and a waiter chased the beggar from the steps with ice cubes thrown from a tumbler. The wail of the muezzin lifted from somewhere but no one stirred, all waiting for the overdue flight to Jidda and deliverance. Alone all day, I'd barely spoken to a human soul.

I'd been in pest holes before but there was something that got under my skin that day and it wasn't the landscape I'd crossed, the heat, the monotony of the sea beyond, or the faces of my fellow passengers. It was the nullity, so annihilating there was no reprieve, another dead end, and there I was, some sort of rice-and-curry concoction on the table I couldn't eat, a book on my knee I couldn't read, eyes drawn away to the feverish yellow sky, the crippled sea, the broken white hovels nearby scaled by the sun, and the narrow rodent trots in between. For those imprisoned here there was no escape. Up and down the sun-scorched littoral were more rat holes just like this. So I sat there trying to digest all this (I don't remember the name of the book on my knee), remembering instead other books in other times. I remembered a boy from Kentucky lying on the rug in his grand-father's study, reading from Hakluyt's *Voyages* and Saint-Exupéry's *Wind, Sand, and Stars* and imagining that one day he would find himself there where they had been, standing under the Saharan stars at the edge of the universe. The life of the spirit is intermittent, Saint-Exupéry once wrote as well.

Looking at the pale Frenchmen, the olive-skinned Saudis, and the Moslem sheikhs that day, it seemed to me nothing was more preposterous than the myth that all 3.5 billion people on the planet were contemporaries. Our common DNA said so and instant communication with the ends of the earth encouraged the delusion. So did the books I had read as a boy and so did the UN Charter. The faces I saw there at the airdrome resembled mine, just like the figures we see on the TV screen shouting, shooting, killing, starving, and dying were identical to my own, but it was a hoax, I thought as I sat there, one of nature's crueler jokes, like the emu, the great wingless bird of the Australian out-back, another of our dead-end contemporaries. Biological and zoological time may have brought us all together at the same planetary instant, but historical, social, and cultural time made each of us who we are and defined the crude truths we live by.

So I sat there in the swarming heat of the Red Sea coast thinking about all this, looking at the dozen or so escapees from the anthropological zoo surrounding me, caged by their own particularistic creed or nationality. The miracle of Homo sapiens' DNA may have survived in them but lay broken, dis-honored, disgraced, and gone haywire in this crowd of cultural, historical, and political freaks. They were no more like me than the idiot dwarf I'd seen on the track four days earlier.

But what could you say of those who only kept their sanity by moving on, like I did, always the vagabond, always on the move, in transit, another bus ride, another flight, another arrival or departure somewhere? What about those who couldn't escape, those I'd seen in the streets beyond that day, the des-perately poor so wasted, emaciated, and brutalized by their con-dition they belonged to another species entirely, like the rats that gnawed their bread or the parasites that infested their bod-ies? What about the barefoot insurgents in Eritrea and the southern Sudan, different only because they now had guns? What about friends like Gretchen and Ken?

What truths did they really serve? What could you say of those whose lives weren't committed so much to a cause, what-ever it called itself, but to the escape from suffering at any cost? And what of those whose cause was so hopeless there was no escape except extinction? Pathological cases? What truths did they serve?

Gretchen and Ken weren't like that but their life worried me. On the rattling bus trip up from Kassala, I'd thought they'd created a world for themselves out there and that pleased me, even if it wasn't my kind of world, but now I wasn't sure. If their feelings for each other sustained them, why was I worried? Anger came and went with me, cleansed my mind and then was gone and that was the end of it and I'd move on. There I was in the heat of the afternoon, down at the bottom of things again, another dead end, waiting for another bus or a flight some-where, sitting among strangers I'd never see again, listening, watching, indulging my curiosity and not minding it so much, thinking how lucky I was still able to find something left to discover, still alive and kicking, even if existence had shrunk to little more than two black pinholes in my aching skull and a desperate desire to get the hell on the road again.

I flew on to Jidda and caught a flight to Beirut and Iskenderun, Turkey. I took a diesel bus that chugged along the Mediterranean coast to Alanya on a narrow switchback road above the sea. The scenery was as I remembered, pine- and cypress-covered cliffs, rivulets of whitewater plunging over the rocks, and the miles of empty white beaches and the blue sea far below. Most of the Turkish peasants aboard were mule riders by tradition. Dazzled cross-eyed by the horseshoe turns, the dizzying views, and the leaking diesel fumes, most of them got sick and lay heaving on their seats, braying like sheep in a slaughterhouse pen, groaning, gagging, and pleading for an end to it all.

I spent six days loafing on the beach, snorkeling and exploring a Crusader castle at Alanya, but it wasn't any good alone, part of my life was still missing. I went on to Ankara and Istanbul by road. When I got to the Hilton in Istanbul I was dirty, hot, tired, and fed up. I walked to the bar through a verandah filled with murmuring English and German tourists politely drinking tea and whiskey, and a nervous Turkish waiter in a red cummerbund approached me and said I'd have to put on a tie. I told him to hell with it and left but on the steps outside thought about what I'd done, went back, apologized, and gave him a U.S. five-dollar bill. He must have thought I was as mad as a hatter and I suppose I was. I drove on to a ratty old hotel near the Blue Mosque where the Arab and Serb truck drivers overnighted on their long trek from the Balkans to the Persian Gulf. The two-week holiday didn't do me much good.

I was feeling pretty much the odd man out when I went back to my post and my walled compound on the edge of the city. The rains had come, the skies were gray and ragged. The weak afternoon sun did little to dry the flagstones in my rear garden or the pools in the sand road. The week after I got back, Major Osman Farah dropped by one evening to return some books. We sat for a while in the back terrace, listening to the BBC and drinking beer. He didn't stay long but from his silence I knew something was wrong. As he left he said he'd be busy the next several months. Two days later Dr. Hassan strolled down the damp sand road in the warm dusk, shared a pilsner with me in the back garden, puffed on his pipe reflectively, and said he'd sent his wife back to Cairo. He said trouble was brewing but he didn't explain. He left a heavy package with me for safekeeping. Inside was a Colt .38 wrapped in a chamois cloth.

Four days later the old president dismissed his cabinet of national reconciliation, removed the so-called progressives or northerners from their ministries, and dismissed the army chief of staff. The coup came in the early-morning hours three days later.

I heard the gunfire from my compound and tried to drive to the embassy but was turned back by an army roadblock near the UN compound. That afternoon the dismissed army chief of staff, supposedly the ringleader, was killed in a firefight at the radio station and two of his aides wounded. A second group sent to shoot its way into army general headquarters was pinned down inside the front gate and the two vehicles set afire. Had either survived the coup might have succeeded but it didn't. That night the government turned off the power in the northern quarter of the capital and sent in the army. I sat in the darkness of my back garden listening to my battery radio and the messages from the embassy evacuation net. I could hear the army's armored personnel carriers rattling by through the roads outside, hear occasional gunfire from nearby and the jangle of cartridge belts from the foot soldiers on the sand road.

Gunfire was sporadic the next morning. Soldiers in battle helmets and M-16s were on guard outside Dr. Hassan's compound and two other compounds nearby. Gunshots still echoed in the distance where a few rebels were under fire as they retreated to the north. I didn't know whether Majors Osman Farah and Hersi and Dr. Hassan were among them. I had to talk my way through two army roadblocks as I drove to the embassy. At the last barrier just north of the embassy a young sergeant in sunglasses tried to commandeer my Land Rover. The national currency was in crisis at the time and inflation was running at something like 26 percent. I told him my Land Rover was an embassy vehicle, gave him a U.S. twenty-dollar bill, and drove on.

The riot screens were down at the chancellery and the marine guards were in combat gear. The embassy was mobilized that day, all those lazily monotonous lives suddenly given meaning. People were running about, the defense attaché's office and the Agency station were scrambling their people in and out, off to debrief their contacts in the Ministry of Defense and the Internal Security offices. I watched from the second-floor window of the political section as two Agency officers wearing sidearms and flak jackets climbed into a Toyota Land Cruiser and rolled out through the gate of the compound. My contacts were out in the bush or on the run, and I was put to work helping draft hourly situation reports for the department.

Twice that day Ambassador Barnes was summoned to the presidency. I slept on a cot at the embassy that night as the coup began to fall apart. The following afternoon when I drove back to my compound the power was on again and three- and four-man army squads roamed the sand streets. The next morning I drove down the sand road past Hassan's house, turned past Osman Farah's compound, which was similarly guarded, and onto the bus turnabout and the Palestinian tea shop. The front door had been smashed in and the shop looted. A few old women were still picking through the terrace rubble. That afternoon I got a call from the ambassador's secretary on the third floor. Barnes wanted to see me at his residence at seven o'clock that evening. She didn't say what he wanted to talk about.

He was waiting for me alone in the front salon.

"You were right and I was wrong, I suppose," he began that evening. "A matter of being in the right place at the right time. Or the wrong place at the wrong time, whatever side of the fence you're on." His legs were crossed and he was rocking his loafer-clad foot on his knee as we sat over scotch and waters. I wasn't sure what he was talking about until he explained.

After reading from my cable predicting violence if the cabinet was dissolved, he again asked me about my conclusions and I told him what I'd told him earlier: I'd been talking to my contacts, most of them civil servants.

He nodded, put on his reading glasses, and consulted the penciled notes he'd scribbled on a legal pad. He told me about the night my Land Rover had been seen at the officers' club, gave me the time, the date, and the names of the northerners I'd been with, and asked if the report was true. I said it was. He gave me five or six additional dates a few of the suspected conspirators or their cars had been seen at my residence and asked what I knew of the coup. By then I realized the CIA-trained National Security Agency had had a watch on me those many months. I was annoyed none of my Agency friends down the hall at the embassy had ever mentioned it.

Not much, I'd told him. I'd known a few officers were unhappy with the regime but so was everyone else. They decided to do something about it and so they had. No, I didn't know the details. They were my friends and drinking companions but they weren't stupid.

I'm not sure he believed me but I didn't much care. A few of my seniors had stopped believing me long before, so I'd been feeding from that nosebag too long for it to matter much now. After all those years abroad, most of them spent in capitals where our embassies were busily but royally irrelevant, I was fed up and most of them knew it. But I knew he had something else on his mind.

The notes he was consulting had been taken two days earlier during a talk with the old president, his chief of security, and his minister of foreign affairs. Listening those many nights at the tea shop, in Dr. Hassan's back verandah, and my back garden had made me an accomplice. Either I left the country within forty-eight hours or I'd be arrested. The minister of foreign affairs had declared me persona non grata and demanded my recall.

Barnes had protested, insisting that if I'd met with or been seen with a few dissidents (he didn't call them rebels), I was only carrying out my duties and those of the embassy in keeping him informed. He proposed a solution to their problem and his own. I was leaving the country for reassignment in a month or so, he told them, and wouldn't return. It would be far better for the embassy, Washington, and the president if events were allowed to take their course. My departure would be speeded up.

That morning the minister of foreign affairs had telephoned him and accepted his compromise. Barnes was gratified by his success in avoiding an incident that would do no one credit, not me, not him, not the embassy, not the State Department, and not the old president. His pleasure was a symptom of everything that was wrong with him, me, and the embassy.

Since I wasn't due for a transfer for another four months, his solution was a little disingenuous. I asked him what choice I had. He laughed and shook his head.

"You mean what choice do *I* have. None at all." As we finished our drinks, he told me our conversation was between the two of us and he preferred to keep it that way. I suppose he thought he was doing me a favor, keeping it out of my record, and maybe he was. So far as I know, he never reported his conversation to the president and the foreign minister.

Two days later I boarded an Alitalia 707 and left.

Every year when the first frost comes and the maple leaves turn orange and yellow as autumn begins to die on the hillsides, something returns me to my early years, to autumn and winter growing up in Kentucky. The more the passing years separate me from the idylls of boyhood, the more acute the feeling I'm not a real person at all. I felt that way even more after all those years abroad returning to an America I no longer knew.

It was the second week of autumn. The Pan Am 747 from Rome bringing me home lumbered over the silver lakes of the Canadian Maritimes and the Maine coast where the long combers curled ashore under a cloudless sky. On the sea near

Cape Cod and Nantucket flotillas of sailboats drifted like duck feathers on a pond. Turbines droning down, we rumbled on over the villages of Long Island toward the sun-bronzed towers of Manhattan.

I was one of a handful of Americans scattered among the two hundred twenty Russians in tourist class. With their weathered faces and wrinkled shirts, suits, and dresses, they looked like derelicts from a Salvation Army soup line, filling the cabin with the smell of soiled laundry. The downy-cheeked woman sitting next to me told me in broken English she had worked as a packer in a state-owned preserves factory; her husband sitting next to her was a shoemaker. They were from Minsk and he had a cousin living at Brighton Beach who owned a kosher butcher shop.

After the in-flight movie the Russians crowded the aisles like gypsies, chattering with anticipation as they queued up at the rest rooms to make their final toilet. As we approached Manhattan, many of the Russians were standing, looking down into the canyons deep in shadow far below. I gave up my window seat to the Russian woman. As the 747's wheels touched down, many of the Russians cheered and whistled, and a few seats behind me someone warbled like a nightingale on a wooden whistle. They'd arrived safely, each destined for a new beginning, like me. As we made our way up the crowded aisle, I wished them the best of luck.

At Kennedy an X-ray machine outside the inspection tables had picked up Dr. Hassan's snub-nosed Colt .38 Cobra in one of my bags and someone had tagged the suitcase. At customs an immigration officer told me to pick up my bags and follow him. In an office down the corridor a second immigration officer went through the suitcase and brought out the Colt .38 wrapped in a chamois cloth. A thick-fingered man with reddish hair and beginning to bald, he was a Boston Irishman, or so his name tag and accent told me. I said I'd brought it from Africa.

After the other immigration officer left the Boston Irishman sat down and searched my diplomatic passport. Thick with added pages, it was twice the usual size. "You sure get around, don't you?" He asked me how long I'd been a diplomat and where I'd served and then opened a drawer and gave me a few forms to fill out. After I finished he glanced at the papers, initialed them, and put them in a box on the corner of his desk. "You gonna be stationed now in Washington?" He pushed the Colt and my passport back across the table. "Better keep it, fella. Washington's knee-deep in coon shit and crack these days. Better get it registered."

I rented a car and drove down the Shores Parkway and over the Verrazano Narrows. After all those years overseas I'd forgotten about the traffic and trapped myself in an inside lane, crowded by too many drivers in too many overpowered cars. After ten minutes or so I recovered the homicidal rhythms of the American interstate, broke free at 75 or 80 mph, and breezed down into New Jersey to spend the weekend with Sue and Frank Craven. I'd known Frank at the embassy in Ankara before he resigned and returned to a graduate fellowship at the Woodrow Wilson School where he now taught.

Princeton was an oasis of autumn tranquility, a secluded Cotswolds village of flintstone and cobbled walks under brilliant foliage. I sat with Sue and Frank high in Palmer Stadium that Saturday afternoon watching Princeton play Lafayette or Lehigh, I forget which, trying to be part of it, but sat looking out instead at the brightly colored maples and oaks beyond the stadium rim and not feeling a part of it at all. I don't remember who won. Not being an old Princetonian had nothing to do with it. I hadn't lived in the States for over ten years.

"Basically I'm a PR purist," I heard a man say at the cocktail party that evening. "No shtick." He was a short gopher-faced man wearing a dark suit, tasseled shoes, and dark glasses, even though we were standing in the afternoon shadows in the living room.

"No kidding. I'm shifting vocational gears, so to speak," said the woman he was hustling. She was wearing a green linen dress, green shoes, and green eye shadow. She told him her colors matched his tie. He stuck his thumb inside his jacket, rooted out the tie, and looked at it.

"I'll be damned," he said, "you're right." I didn't know how he could tell with his dark glasses. I didn't hear how it ended. We went to a dinner given by friends of the Cravens. It was an old-fashioned sterling silver, crystal, and candlelit sit-down dinner. I was shoehorned in at the end of the table on a library chair and didn't say more than a dozen words. As the host and hostess said good-bye at the door, they didn't remember my name.

On Sunday morning I woke up in the four o'clock darkness drenched with sweat, recovering from a nightmare I couldn't remember and forgetting where I was. Unable to sleep, I dressed and found a book on the table in the downstairs study and sat reading a mystery novel by an Englishwoman I'd never heard of, set in a 1920s English vicarage in a village I'd never heard of either. A few hours later I walked up to the drugstore through the deserted streets bright with early-morning sunshine and rustling with blowing leaves and bought the *New York Times*.

The mopping-up in the capital I'd left three days earlier was described in a back-page item: "Coup Smashed: Four Army Officers Executed." A few more plotters had been caught, sentenced, and shot. No names were given and I wondered which of my friends was among them. Dr. Hassan? Major Osman Farah? Major Hersi? Nur Galal? How many of them were dead, how many in prison, and how many had fled to the bush, gone back to family, kinship, and clan, the basic but most primitive unit of social existence, the refuge to which we all return when the political fabric is smashed or barbarized? I'd boarded an Alitalia 707 and left, a stranger returning to his own country, come back to an America I'd visited for a few weeks at a time during those years but no longer knew.

I turned in the car at Princeton, took a taxi to Princeton Station, and sat on the train to Washington looking out through the dusty, sun-glazed windows at the passing countryside on a sleepy Sunday afternoon. It was the first time I'd been on an American train in more than twenty years. Memory is that instant when past and present collide; two speeding trains hurtling toward each other on the same track, demolishing the moment and everything else, as it did that afternoon.

In Kenya the railroad clattered from Nairobi in the highlands to Mombasa on the Indian Ocean. In Ethiopia the railroad abruptly drops from Addis Ababa eight thousand feet in the mountains to Djibouti on the coast. Along both tracks a footpath winds along the ballast bed all that distance, crossing gorge, savannah, riverbed, scrub, and salt pan, pursuing you through the long afternoon like the lengthening shadows, a serpentine trail that loops, winds, strays, and for a moment falters and disappears in the scrub but then returns to pursue you all the way to the coast. Watching it you feel a certain uneasiness, sense the stalking presence the grazing gazelle and antelope must sense, head and nose lifted, tail twitching, an unseen host nearby, a century of ghostly footfalls, decades of invisible Africans, tirelessly padding along in silent accompaniment, as mute and faithful as dogs along the path that haunts your present.

So I'd failed, left it undone or half finished, left them behind too, gone to ground in the scrub. Maybe a few had followed to bid me bon voyage—ragtag rebels, unpaid civil servants, a vice minister or two, elderly tribal chiefs in their beaded caps and capes, territorial commissioners from deep in the bush, smelling of hunger and despair, a vanquished fetisheur or two on the laterite track, the last of the old barbarians, bags of bones selling off the last of the relics of their once-great savannah kingdoms to the foreign scalp-hunters on the African frontier. What postcards would ever reach them?

Looking out the dusty coach window I saw no footpath and none of my old friends on the cinder path along the ballast bed, just rusting railroad iron, broken bottles, beer cans, and clumps of ragweed and goldenrod. Ash and ailanthus trees sprouted in the shadows of crumbling concrete embankments scrawled with aerosol can graffiti. "I Love Maria Theresa!" read one that made less sense than the rest. A parochial school, a nun, or a girl? I remembered the ailanthus was called the tree of heaven.

I looked into the back streets of Philadelphia, Wilmington, and Baltimore, into narrow and board- or wire-fenced backyards. Some had small gardens, now as brown as winter bracken, others were filled with debris. Black men moped on street corners in front of boarded-up storefronts. A few abandoned cars sat at the curb, paint dulled to chalk, collapsed tires drifted with gutter debris and windshields thick with clutter.

Seeing all this I lost a sense of myself as well. I'd been out on the edge but not like they had, but still felt the desolation of what I'd known, all of it uncommunicable. Now I was beginning all over. The last ten years of my life had dwindled to a five-line dispatch at the bottom of page fifteen of the *New York Times*. I felt like someone out of a displaced persons' camp.

I'd reserved a transient flat in a yellow brick apartment across 23rd Street from the State Department. The taxi that picked me up outside Union Station was a ten-year-old red-and-black Chevrolet with the name Red Sea Taxi Company painted on the door. It was a one-car cab company and the owner-driver was an Ethiopian, most probably an Eritrean. I didn't ask. It was a drowsy Sunday afternoon, the taxi queue was long, and I suppose he'd been bored senseless, eager for conversation. He asked if I'd ever been to Africa. I didn't feel like talking and made it easier for both of us and said no, but maybe one day I would. I felt bad afterward and overtipped him. I carried my bags to the second floor and in a nearby delicatessen whose windows were protected by steel security grills bought rye bread, pastrami, and beer for the American meal I'd promised myself.

In my second-floor suite I saw color television for the first time in years. A golf match was being held at Pebble Beach. The pastel-colored clothes, the smiling faces, the carpetlike turf, and the Pacific Ocean had the artificial tint of cafeteria Jell-O. Seeing all those faces I remembered a few lines from W. H. Auden borrowed from a Cole Porter lyric I hadn't thought of in years: "America addressed/The earth: 'Do you love me as I love you?' "

I fell asleep on the couch waiting for the six o'clock news and woke up at three in the morning with the television still on and sirens screaming in my head. The sirens were outside. Old habits die hard, and I went to the window and looked out. I could see a stoplight a block away. The nearby streets were decently lit.

So I'd come back to the State Department after a dozen years with no assignment, an uncertain future, and an awkward reputation to live down. Except for a fifth-floor debriefing at State that lasted a couple of hours and didn't amount to much except to tell me the desk officer and country director were still confused about the failed coup and what I knew, my State Department bureau didn't have anything for me. I was cut adrift. Two weeks later for lack of a better opportunity I was given a fifth-floor desk in Intelligence and Research. Although the title was more impressive, it was little different from the desk I had been parked behind years earlier. By then I'd decided to stick it out.

"We all make mistakes," my father used to say after I had abandoned one university for another, and I'd made my share of them. "You learn to pick up the pieces and begin over again," he added, although he never did. He was a newspaperman but never the success he'd hoped to be. Long before the end he knew he was a failure. That was his misery and he accepted it but the drinking made it easier. I remember putting him to bed in a Frankfort, Kentucky, hotel room where he lived alone those last years when he was reporting on the state legislature. We'd been drinking in the dining room, moderately, I thought, until he got to his feet. He adjusted in that sly way alcoholics do, but on our way through the lobby two legislators called to him in their dry Kentucky brogues. He didn't want to stop and pretended not to hear them, but their voices carried through the lobby and he had no choice but to stop and talk. They saw and heard what I'd seen and heard: the slurred speech, the damp eyes, the smile of shame that denied both. They were grinning as they talked to him and I despised them for that. Upstairs in his room I helped him off with his coat, took off his shoes, and lifted his feet onto the bed. As I did he remembered a scrap of Yeats. I wouldn't have recognized it if I hadn't known the lines:

> *I must lie down where all the ladders start,*
> *In the foul rag-and-bone shop of the heart.*

Terribly rich in memory, he was terribly poor in practical things. My mother couldn't forgive him that, even after she'd left him and remarried and I'd gone to live with my grandfather. I thought sometimes that if he'd remembered less, he might have aspired to more. Poets have the ability to entertain themselves in solitude, and maybe that's one of the pleasures of alcohol as well. Rye and bourbon unlocked his imagination the way verse once did but his work suffered. He was eased out and the last five or six years lived alone with his books.

Tired of being a vagabond, I didn't want to fail. Not wanting to fail, I wouldn't take risks, wouldn't offend, wouldn't stick my neck out. I'd grow comfortable with the conventional life, join a metropolitan dining club, bank my salary, find a broker, stay away from married women, meet a few interesting divorcées, read the *Washington Post* and the *New York Times* every morning, and confine my sedition to my lunchtime talks with my colleagues in the first-floor cafeteria where I'd entertain but not instruct and in the end no longer be taken seriously by anyone, another failed bureaucrat in the Washington boneyard.

But I'd find my place, learn to be dependable, would try to make it work, and so it would work. These were the disgusting little lies I was telling myself, which show how corruptible I'd become.

I rented a house out in suburban Virginia, a brick rambler on a wandering lane sheltered by oaks, maples, and dogwoods on the far side of a small creek meandering along the road. My neighbors were nice, friendly, and hospitable. They lived in similar houses half hidden among the trees, worked in their yards, played golf and tennis, planted gardens, had children, and owned dogs. They drove their kids to school or the bus stop, talked to each other over their lawn rakes, and entertained each other on their backyard patios. That autumn their quiet laughter, the clink of glasses, and the smell of charcoal, sirloin, and barbecued chicken sometimes drifted over the lilac and rose bushes.

Drinking alone on my back terrace, the sounds and smells of suburban life consoled me in a way. I wanted to live like an American again, recover my privacy, restore my self-respect, rediscover the books in my library, work in the yard, shop at the local supermarket, and see snow in the winter and not have to fly to the Swiss or Bavarian Alps to find it. It would be there, thickly floating down through the winter twilight, accumulating on my woodpile and covering my lawn, a recovery of all those lost seasons. But I was kidding myself. I was still an expatriate.

My air freight came and I got my household goods out of storage and tried to fix the place up. I didn't have much furniture. Most of it was pretty ramshackle, bought secondhand in Washington years earlier. It rained a lot the last week in October. One evening the power failed during a thunderstorm. I was drinking vodka on the rocks when the lights went off. I lit a few candles and stood at the window of the family room, looking out into the storm-whipped back garden, remembering the afternoon thunderstorms out on the African savannahs. The rain was coming down in buckets. On a low table at the bay window I'd put some of the sentimental bric-a-brac I'd brought back: an Arab coffeepot, a Roman terra-cotta, and a small, wooden Janus-faced African figure.

A brutal crash of lightning lit up his copper eyes the same way it had shocked me near Bumba on a long-ago afternoon on the mission station verandah. He turned and looked at me, wondering what the hell I'd brought him back to. A second bolt rattled the window as it crashed through the trees a block away. He quivered, danced around, and looked at me again. I decided he didn't belong there, wrapped him in a napkin, and put him away in a drawer. By the time the lights came back on I'd had a few more drinks. What I'd done wasn't rational but I knew why I'd done it and it wasn't just the drinking. The *Bena N'Kuba* had come home with me and so had she.

Escape was still the best remedy. Get out, get away, take a tramp steamer to Fiji or a ferry out of Vancouver to the Yukon, hire a dogsled and a pack of huskies. Go to Moscow or Tashkent, book passage on the Trans-Siberian railway. If you're deskbound, like I was, go shooting out in the Rappahannock on weekends, go duck hunting on Chesapeake Bay, the colder and more miserable the day, the better. Go in the rain, sleet, and snow, get yourself wet, soaked, numbed stiff, frozen senseless. Then come home like a drowned dog, duly punished, and stand at the kitchen window, fix a drink to thaw out and wander through your empty house, don't answer the telephone, and admit that without her nothing is working, nothing will ever work.

I didn't have a basement parking pass, and every morning walked to the bus stop at the end of the lane to board the bus for the State Department and my windowless fifth-floor cubicle in Intelligence and Research. It was a grim way to begin the day— the waiting, the creaking bus, the smells of diesel, the wheylike faces around me. Some had been riding the same bus for years, like a few of the analysts in INR, dedicated civil servants who'd never served abroad and never lacked for good intentions.

It was a long dry autumn. Analysts from the Defense Intelligence Agency at the Pentagon and the Agency often called me those first months, searching for more details about the September coup and worried about the rebellion spreading farther to the south. The rebels had reorganized after their flight to the north and attacked police posts on the edge of the nomadic grazing lands. Army units sent in relief were undermanned, undisciplined, and unreliable. Occasionally units sent in pursuit mutinied and joined the rebels. A DIA major was especially annoying. He must have called me a dozen times.

"Major Mohammed Hersi, Mathews?" he asked one morning, reading from a list of military officers who had been reported missing. "U.S.-trained. That ring a bell?"

"Hersi? I met him a few times. I don't know what happened to him."

"I wish to hell we knew who these people are but we don't, not yet anyway. Anything you can come up with will help."

Caught unprepared, his ignorance had offended his self-respect, DIA's as well, but that wasn't surprising. Washington can manage everything but the unpredictable.

Established in pursuit of a philosophy of natural order that believes every event in the universe harmoniously predictable, Washington still pretends this is true. Order, routine, and predictability manage its cosmos as much as they did John Locke's, Isaac Newton's, or Alexander Pope's. Spontaneity is dangerous, the enemy is the irregular, the lawless, or the unexpected, which suspends natural law and introduces chaos. But America's daily compass swings wildly free, irrepressibly spontaneous, a reminder of how immense, complex, and unruly is our daily national existence and how partial, limited, and preposterous are Washington's claims of mastering it. A city whose thousands of executive decisions are refined to the ultimate adverb, adjective, and semicolon, it pretends their end result is a physical absolute, like Planck's constant or the speed of light, but isn't since all this is done in prose and on paper, hundreds upon hundreds in each executive agency with each combination of words possessing some eucharistic meaning to some group of experts somewhere in the labyrinth, however banal or opaque the language appears to the rest of us. In finding their way through this maze of bureaucratic scholasticism, it's no wonder the White House or the State Department seems bewildered or paralyzed, no wonder either that the committee of experts responsible for the policy's final "crafting" or "fine-tuning," both popular Washington catchwords that convey the experts' Augustan pride in their own microartifice, could be so suspicious of an unpredictable vagabond like me who believed these paper constructs had little relation to the reality of everyday lives and that those who lived so obsessively among words, as Washington does, couldn't help telling lies.

One day outside the seventh-floor Ops Center I bumped into an old CIA officer I'd known in Beirut. "What's this I hear?" he said, grabbing my arm. "Blotted your copy book, did you?" He was Harry Donahue, a rumpled little man with thinning gray hair who'd lost part of his larynx as a seventeen-year-old marine rifle-man in Korea and had a voice like a wood rasp gnawing an ax han-dle. He was deputy director of the Agency's Middle East division and had just come from a strategy session with an Afghan task force. We went down to the first-floor cafeteria and had coffee. The failed coup and the rebellion had raised questions about the CIA station's operations, or so he said, and he wanted to know why the station had been caught unprepared, who the insurgents were, and what they wanted. I suspected Crowder, the station chief at my old post, had told Langley about the government's demand for my recall, but he didn't mention it and neither did I.

The National Security Agency at Fort Meade had begun reading radio signals from one of the rebel headquarters in the northern bush. The cryptanalysts hadn't been able to identify the code names of the rebel commanders or the force size of the separate rebel units. Telephone intercepts from Libya, Belgium, and Hungary told them the leaders were dickering with Euro-pean arms brokers. A few days after my talk with Harry Don-ahue, I got a call from Tim Bowles, a CIA officer I'd talked to a few times. He thought I hadn't been very cooperative in our pre-vious conversations but now there was a hint of reconciliation in his manners. I assumed Harry Donahue had talked to him.

"Mathews, this is Tim Bowles. How's it going?"

"Not too bad. How about you?"

"Still chasing your old crowd through the high grass. Lis-ten, I've been looking at some stuff we just got in. Did you ever know a Major Osman Farah?"

"I knew him. Why?"

"We think he's one of the rebel commanders. You ever heard of something called the National Democratic Front?"

"No. What is it?"

"The guerrilla front. At least that's what they're calling themselves. The NDF. We think maybe Osman Farah's one of the leaders. He's in Libya, looking for arms. You knew him?"

"I knew him. In Libya?"

"Yeah. We have an intercept. Maybe you should look it up. Looks bad. Harry Donahue told me to tell you. We don't have much on him. Kept a low profile, disappeared in the bush after the bungled September coup. Anything you know about him would help. I mean his politics, his military training, his bio."

"He's a northerner, a Moslem, worked as a vice minister at Interior. I talked to him a few times, that's about all. His villa wasn't far from mine."

"If you can give me a piece of paper it would help. I'd really appreciate it."

"I'll give it a try."

I wrote up a brief memo and sent it to him, feeling a little guilty, the way I always did in writing up official bio material drawn from personal reminiscences. A week later I got a note from Bowles including a photograph Xeroxed from a Libyan diplomatic passport. The photo was circled in red pencil with a question mark in the margin. The photograph wasn't of Osman Farah.

By December the rebels were in control of the north and sent marauders south toward the central agricultural regions, attacking army outposts, torching sorghum and millet fields, stealing cattle, and burning villages. After two kidnappings, the missionaries from the Lutheran World Federation evacuated their remaining stations and retreated to the capital where martial law had been reimposed. More northerners were rounded up and imprisoned, there were random shootings at night, and bodies of northern tradesmen began turning up on the streets in the morning hours. Following the execution of two northern army officers for treason—they were shot and their bloody bodies hung in the public square where they remained for forty-eight hours—a rebel group seized a village a hundred kilometers north of the capital, well beyond the borders of the occupied territory. It was the village I had often visited that reminded me of Chief Job's village in the Kasai.

A week later regular army units reoccupied the village. The government claimed its first victory but DIA analysts believed it was a tactical withdrawal, not a defeat. The national radio and the Ministry of Defense claimed the rebels had massacred women and children, slaughtered livestock, burned huts, and poisoned wells as they retreated. The old president had appealed to the United Nations and the Organization of African Unity in Addis to send in observers and asked the International Red Cross and the Red Crescent to supply relief teams.

An *Agence France Presse* reporter and photographer hitched rides with a company of regular army soldiers sent to reinforce the unit reoccupying the village. That Friday the first photographs appeared. Scores of black bodies lay twisted in the dusty road outside the village and in the village itself among the still-smoldering hut ashes where they'd been shot. Many were piled atop one another, fly-blown, bellies swollen, limbs missing or flung akimbo. The AFP dispatch and the accompanying photographs appeared in the U.S. press the same Friday.

There was another detail not mentioned in the AFP dispatch but included in a CIA cable. According to a source in the capital, the village elders, including the commerce minister's uncle, had been mutilated by the NDF guerrillas before they were killed. The last time I passed through the village, his gas-operated refrigerator wasn't working. I couldn't fix it and neither could my driver. I told him he should put the refrigerator in the Fiat truck and take it to the capital to be repaired, and he said no. The soldiers at the army checkpoints would steal it, just as they stole everything else. I suggested he tell his minister nephew but he only laughed. That was the last time I saw him. His ears, nose, and right hand were cut off, and he'd bled to death in the sand track outside his hut with the others. Before the NDF retreated, the bodies had been dragged back inside, soaked with gasoline, and the hut torched.

A week later a pair of American journalists together with a French photographer visited a rebel faction in the bush. After making contact with an exile group in London, they had flown to Nairobi and were led in across the border, traveling by night through the scrub. When they returned they filed their stories from London. USIS obtained a full text of the interview and put it on the wire the same day the story and picture appeared in the U.S. press.

The grainy photograph accompanying one newspaper dispatch showed an NDF commander sitting outside a rebel command post. He was unshaven, wearing a sweat-darkened khaki shirt and shoulder holster; a cigarette was in the fingers of his right hand clasping his left wrist, one foot was across his knee. His lean face was now gaunt and hollow, the smallpox cusps high on his cheeks clearly visible. His eyes were narrowed against the piercing sunlight outside the rebel command post—cruelly, some might have said if they'd never heard him speak in that voice that carried the anger of a man who never doubted what he believed. On the shadowy verandah of the small tea shop where we once sat in the evenings, those sitting nearby would fall silent when he spoke, listening to their own hearts and minds. A few blurred figures stood behind him, only their tattered trouser legs or bony ankles and the AK-47 gun muzzles showing. He was Major Osman Farah, who'd once drunk beer in my back garden and talked long into the night about his youth, his hopes for his countrymen, and his dreams for the future. He refused to answer the journalist's questions about the atrocities, but from his other comments I knew he had turned against everything he believed I stood for. He was wrong but what could I tell him?

A madman was loose on the Capital Beltway that month, terrorizing lonely women motorists during the midnight hours from an old pickup truck painted a dull primer gray. The newspapers said he wore an orange wig, a set of novelty store Dracula fangs, a pair of scruffy running shoes, and red long johns. Keeping up with his midnight escapades in the paper, I wondered where he hid his sickness during the day. The police were searching garages and body shops along the Beltway. I thought they were looking in the wrong place. He was probably sitting behind a government desk, like me, hiding himself behind a facade of cheerful irrationality.

I wondered if he'd been driven into the midnight streets by a failed romance, a woman who'd thrown him over, a lovely face seen from his truck, an abstract smile he'd been trying to catch up with ever since, maybe the reflex of some nostalgic ballad heard on an FM radio that lulled commuters through the Beltway snarl every morning. People think of romance or love as affirmation but forget the darker side; nothing is more destructive, nothing wrecks more lives.

In early December the first snow fell late in the afternoon but was gone by the next day. I saw Kim Johnson on the seventh floor at the Department one morning, waiting to log in at the watch center.

"Mathews, old fellow! Here, are we? I thought you were in Zanzibar, still trotting the bush!"

"Maybe next time. How've you been?"

"Chomping at the bit." We talked for a few minutes. He had been named ambassador to a Caribbean nation. He and his wife were having a Christmas party and he dutifully wrote down my address. The invitation never came. On Christmas Eve a group of grade-school carolers holding candles stood outside my front door and sang carols. There was a neighborhood party on New Year's Eve and from my bedroom I could hear the drunks staggering off until dawn.

I didn't have much of a social life except for an occasional date with a young woman met at a dinner arranged by friends. They never worked out. The younger women liked chic restaurants, new movies, and loud bars; the divorcées preferred intimate dinners, soft music, and fireside chats. I spent many of my weekends looking for rural property in western Virginia and Maryland. Intrigued by an abandoned farm out in the Shenandoah against the Blue Ridge Mountains, I thought of making an offer but didn't. It was too remote, even for me. I had been too many places, seen too many things, caught between two different worlds.

The rebellion in the north continued into the new year. A minor bush war among a half dozen in Africa, it had never attracted much notice apart from an occasional Reuters item in the back pages. Afghanistan and Iran were dominating the television screens, the bloody flowering of that electronic revolution that had begun in Vietnam. Its brutal imagery brought into American living rooms the suffering of distant people in remote places they once knew only as print media abstractions. Americans were now sensibly present as witnesses to distant catastrophe whose awful truths seemed brutally self-disclosing, requiring nothing more for a common revulsion and a common humanity to declare themselves. For a nation so passionately dedicated to self-evident truths, television's revelations were all the more overpowering, much to the dismay of Washington's foreign policy intellectuals whose conceptual vision was never graphic and rarely self-disclosing. Television is a world of visual events, not words, and when the images are authentic, the words count for even less. But no television cameras ever reached the far wastelands where I once wandered whose atrocities went unrecorded.

One week in February Harry Donahue's wife called and invited me to dinner. I don't know Bethesda very well and that Saturday night I had trouble finding Harry's address. It was a nice Tudor house with leaded windows and a high sloping rock garden in front and a glassed-in terrace in the rear overlooking a pool. I was one of the last to arrive. A dozen or so guests stood in the shadows of the glassed-in rear terrace.

Standing among them that dark evening with the candles flickering on the tables and the smell of charcoal drifting from the open door near the rose bushes where Harry had his brazier, I was suddenly disoriented and didn't know why. It was a chilly evening. There were six at my table. The silver-haired man opposite me asked me where I'd served abroad. When I told him, the dark-haired woman to my left turned to look at me without saying anything. "I don't know Africa," the silver-haired man said. "The Middle East, yes."

"Coups and countercoups," said the woman to his right, and sighed. She was the wife of a Washington lawyer who was seated at a table somewhere off to my rear. "One can hardly keep track these days. One never knows."

Coups and anarchy everywhere, someone said as the candles fluttered under the storm chimneys and the sky darkened. It all came flooding back, recovered by the smoke from the brazier behind me and the gathering darkness I still couldn't explain: the darkness of the rain forests and the savannahs like no other I'd ever known, the smell of smoke and the smell of Africa mixed together. How do you explain that to others?

The blond Dane to my right was from the World Bank and had recently returned from a mission to Khartoum. "Frightful," he said.

"Just awful," added a dark-haired woman from across the table. She was a congressional staffer who'd twice visited Africa and had caught hepatitis.

"You said you were in the Congo," she said to me after a few minutes. She'd known someone who'd lived in the Congo but that was a few years ago. "Margaret Ogden," she said. Did I know her?

I felt like I'd just been kicked in the head by a horse. "How's she getting along?"

"She keeps to herself pretty much. She had an interior design business, a shop in Georgetown, I believe, but I think she closed it. I'm not sure."

I didn't want to know if she was married and I didn't ask. I don't remember the rest of the conversation. As I left I asked Harry and his wife if they knew Blakey Ogden. They didn't.

The next day I looked in the Virginia, Maryland, and District phone books but couldn't find a Jeffrey or Blakey Ogden. I called three M. Ogdens in the District directory without any luck. Then I looked under the yellow page for interior designers and decorators and found the name.

It was chilly and overcast that Monday in Washington and I

hadn't brought a raincoat. I took a taxi from the C Street entrance at State and had the driver drop me off in Georgetown halfway up Wisconsin Avenue. On a side street just a few steps away I found an oval sign above a doorway entered by a pair of steep iron steps. The sign was black and the scrolled English letters were in gold: OGDEN & CONGREVE—INTERIOR DESIGN.

At the top of the narrow steps inside an identical smaller sign hung over the door to the right. The door was locked and through the glass I saw an empty room, not a stick of furniture in sight. A woman in the office down the hall said Ogden and Congreve had vacated the office a few months ago. She didn't know where they'd gone but gave me the name of the building's rental agent. I called that afternoon but the office manager had no forwarding address. I asked if Ogden and Congreve had another address, persuaded her I wasn't a collection agent but an old friend, and she told me the billing address was the same, Ms. Margaret Ogden in Georgetown. I telephoned a few interior decorators in Washington asking if they knew about Ogden and Congreve and finally got an answer from the third firm I called. A woman told me Blakey's partner, Grace Congreve, had died and she thought she had moved to New York or Boston but she wasn't sure.

At the State Department library on the third floor I looked through the Boston and New York telephone directories but couldn't find her name. I called information but the operator had no Margaret Ogden in Manhattan. I tried a few of the boroughs but with no luck. The only Margaret Ogden given was in the Bronx but the woman who answered had the wrong voice.

The old president died in late May, although few people in Washington or elsewhere were aware of it. He wasn't overthrown, wasn't assassinated, wasn't disemboweled in bed like the president of Liberia, garroted on his prison pallet, like Haile Selassie, or shot in one of his own filthy dungeons. Illness, old age, diabetes, heart disease had finally settled a long-overdue account.

Five days before his fatal seizure a French medical team was summoned from Paris. The senior French doctor delivered its verdict to the president's personal physician, who hadn't the courage to pass it on. The Frenchmen were fetched to his bedside in his second-floor Louis Quatorze bedroom. The senior French doctor said he wouldn't survive unless he relinquished his responsibilities. The presidential entourage stood sweating in terror waiting for the old man's reaction. The windows were open so the dying man could hear the crowds herded outside the presidential gates by the national police, all clamoring for his recovery.

Wasted by illness, his left side paralyzed, and too weak to lift his head, he was propped up on pillows, his black eyes roaming the roomful of terrified faces. Then he delivered his judgment: *"Why should I listen to you quacks? If you're like I am, you're just a pack of sheep turds!"* So the old tyrant had finally admitted his swindle. Late at night two days later, he suffered a diabetic seizure followed by a massive coronary that catapulted him out of bed. His servants found him convulsively rattling his heels on the floor. He died without recovering consciousness.

We would never have known of his final outburst if the senior French doctor hadn't phoned his wife in Paris that night from his hotel. A garbled version was repeated by a bedside attendant who claimed the old president had told the Frenchman their European medicine was too weak for his immortal African soul. NSA eavesdroppers had plucked the French doctor's conversation from the air and put it on the wires. The transmission is still buried at State, Langley, and out at Fort Meade in a top secret code-word UMBRA vault no historian will ever crack.

Two weeks later the dead president was succeeded by the prime minister. In late July, after an unpublicized visit from a deputy assistant secretary and a senior staffer from the National Security Council, he reluctantly agreed to ask for Washington's help in arranging a cease-fire with the NDF rebels. A protocol or nonpaper was signed, the assistant secretary for African Affairs came back triumphant, and the White House staffers were satisfied, never mind that the so-called National Democratic Front had splintered into four hostile factions, each of which controlled sectors of the northern front and each as much at war with each other as the new government. The instructions went out, our diplomats were sent scurrying, but the exiled rebel factions in London, Tripoli, and Nairobi proved difficult to manage. The London rebel faction insisted on one set of preconditions, those in Nairobi another; the group in Tripoli wouldn't talk to our diplomats at all. The fourth and most important rebel front, led by Major Osman Farah whose guerrillas occupied the largest sector of territory in the far north, had no liaison office abroad. And so the discussions continued—the memos from the secretary to the White House, the endless meetings in the old executive office building, the long cables, the renewed hopes and repeated failures, all kept alive by the White House staffers' hope of achieving a diplomatic coup for a president who was only dimly aware of the initiative.

But in late August, the NSC imagined it had identified the opportunity for a diplomatic breakthrough. The Nairobi-based

NDF group had agreed to begin talks leading to a cease-fire without preconditions, or so it was claimed.

An embassy car met my flight from London in Nairobi and drove me to the embassy, a tall, ugly, congested building that reminded me of a down-at-the-heel hotel in some tropical backwater. Our delegation was led by Dickson Lawrence, a deputy assistant secretary for African Affairs, and Norman Collier from the National Security Council. Lawrence's African tours were in Tunis and Rabat and he knew little about the darker side of the continent. I briefed him occasionally on sensitive intercepts from NSA and back-channel reports from the Agency. A curiously remote man, his hobby was painting toy soldiers. He kept several companies of the Coldstream Guards on his credenza in his sixth-floor office at State. Collier was a forty-five-year-old political appointee. A former academic with an anxious squint behind steel-rimmed glasses and thinning blond hair, he had come to the NSC out of the Rand Institute as a Soviet expert. He had no experience among the moral indigents of the Third World. It was Collier's enthusiasm as much as the political naivete infecting the NSC and White House, both anxious for a pre-election foreign policy success, that had kept the initiative alive the past months.

The plan called for us to meet an NDF delegation representing something called the Unified Northern Command that evening at a villa on the outskirts of Nairobi. There was to be no press coverage, no official acknowledgment that we were even there. The meeting had been covertly arranged by Carl Doggitt, a rumpled, overweight CIA officer at the Nairobi station who maintained contact with the single NDF exile group in Nairobi and had done the preliminary planning. I had never heard of the Unified Northern Command except in Doggitt's cables and it mystified me. But late the previous night the NDF liaison office telephoned to say the NDF delegation had been delayed. Doggitt was furious the NDF had used an open line, worried the mission might have been compromised. That morning the liaison office again telephoned and Doggitt went off to meet with them. He returned to say the NDF group refused to come to Nairobi and proposed to meet instead at a remote border village. Upset, Lawrence phoned Washington over a secure line for instructions and Doggitt hustled off to see if he could arrange a charter. State wanted to know if the village was in hostile or neutral territory. Lawrence wasn't sure. A by-the-book diplomat who imagined the emerald-green suburbs of Tunis were the African outback, he recommended the mission be scrubbed. Collier disagreed and so did Doggitt. I had been asked to go along, not as part of the negotiating team but because of the possibility I might know some of the principals. They were still arguing when I left and walked back to the Hilton and had dinner. At midnight the call came from State after clearance at the National Security Council. Collier, Doggitt, and I were to proceed but not Lawrence, the deputy assistant secretary.

At seven the next morning five of us flew out of Nairobi in a sand-colored C-130 without markings. The NDF liaison officer Doggitt claimed would accompany us didn't show up. Doggitt had two tall Shooters with him from the Agency, two rawboned ex–Special Forces NCOs in their early thirties wearing khakis, sand-colored fabric combat boots, flak jackets, and sunglasses. The C-130 was piloted by an Australian from Perth and a sandy-haired American pilot from South Carolina, both middle-aged bush pilots who'd flown in Angola and Mozambique for an Agency proprietary. The cargomaster was a tall, bearded South African. Empty except for stacks of cargo mats, the shadowy bay with its few patches of sunshine was as cheerless as a railroad reefer car and just as noisy. We waited thirty minutes for Doggitt's NDF liaison and finally lifted off without him.

A young technician with thick dark hair wearing blue jeans and a Chicago Bears sweatshirt was with us. He was from the National Security Agency. Collier pondered his briefing book, glasses on, chin on his hand, plump knees pressed together. As I stood to look out the porthole, the NSA technician fiddled about with an electronic device resembling a laptop computer. I asked him about it. It was a monitor programmed for pinpointing radio transmissions. He pressed a few keys and the monitor lit up like a racetrack tote board. I couldn't read it and I couldn't see much from my window either. We flew through drifting cotton clouds, chasing a droning gray shadow against the reddish-gray scrub far below.

Two hours later we overflew a dirt strip near the border, came around again, and landed, rumbling to a stop near a tin shack fuel dump where a few drums of aviation fuel were stored. The cargomaster dropped the ramp and we uncramped ourselves and stood outside, watched by a handful of nomads a half-kilometer away and two guards with carbines sitting in the shadow of the fuel shack. There was no one else about, no vehicles, no militia units. Neither the nomads nor the two guards moved. There was nothing but the hot wind, acrid and constant, thick with the smell of dead, parched earth.

"See any hostiles out there?" the NSA technician called from the shadows of the bay before he joined us.

"Negative," the taller Shooter said.

The two Land Rovers had been parked some distance away in an acacia glade near a draw. We watched them come, two very old, very battered Land Rovers, once painted gray, cream, or pale green. They were without roofs, stirring up rooster tails of billowing yellow dust. A dark-skinned youth in a straw hat stood next to the driver of the lead Land Rover, his arms folded across the windscreen, an AK-47 over his shoulder. Eight nomads were crowded in the Land Rover, some sitting, some standing, some in tattered street clothes, some in blue coveralls, in shorts and underwear shirts. None wore helmets, brevets, or insignia, most wore cartridge belts, all carried weapons: AK-47s, M-4s, old carbines, old rifles. Except for the guns, they were identical to any mob of idlers and layabouts you could find in any open-air tea shop or dusty street in the torrid Moslem villages of the north. They carried their weapons indifferently, muzzles bristling in crazy angles, up, down, and sideways, sometimes pointed above you or near you, sometimes at you. I'd seen the same marauders before, their indifference as vast, cruel, and mindless as the wastelands that bred them.

Doggitt didn't know the rebel in the straw hat. He asked if the NDF delegation had arrived. The rebel leader silently beckoned us aboard the two Land Rovers. Doggitt looked at me, his two Shooters, then at Collier, and suggested we discuss it inside. We went back up the ramp and into the bay where one of the pilots and the cargomaster were waiting. After talking it over, we decided to continue. Doggitt tightened his belt over his paunch, buckled a .38 on his hip, and suggested we wear flak jackets. I said no, it was too hot. Collier agreed.

Outside again Doggitt nodded to the squad leader and said we were ready. Six rebels climbed morosely from the rear of the

Land Rover and pushed their way into the second vehicle. Collier, Doggitt, the two Shooters, and I climbed in the back of the first with the remaining guerrillas. They studied us as we drove away, their brown-stained black eyes silently taking in every detail, our clothes, shoes, faces, and skin, the Shooters' automatic weapons, as childishly and mistrustfully curious as those in the most primitive African villages. We were from another world.

The rendezvous point was three kilometers away on the other side of the border, an abandoned village of no more than eight burned-out huts in a shallow depression partially sheltered by blowing laurel and acacia trees on the edge of the grasslands. None of the rebels left the Land Rovers. Despite the wind the smell in the back of our vehicle was suffocating. We got out to stretch our legs and wander about the sun-speckled shadows. The rebels continued to sit or stand, watching the sky, the track to the east and west, and us.

"What do you think?" Collier asked me, mopping his neck.

"I don't know. Wait, I suppose." I didn't know the area but I knew the desert wind, always the same, a wind that kills without remorse and afterward blows the dust away.

The NDF group arrived twenty minutes later in two open Land Rovers and an old blue Fiat truck whose cab top had been cut away. Mounted in the rear was a .30-caliber machine-gun ring. There were twenty of them, all with guns, dressed like the guerrillas who brought us there. I didn't see any radios or ammo boxes, just a few battered jerry cans lashed to the front bumpers. Two emaciated prisoners sat in the back of the Fiat truck, arms and hands bound with sisal rope. Filaments of bright fresh blood streaked their dark faces and glistened in their woolly hair. One man's eye was swollen shut.

The commander was a short dark-skinned northerner dressed in dirty khakis and wearing sunglasses and dusty boots. Preceded by two bodyguards he climbed heavily from the front seat of the Land Rover and gave Doggitt a clumsy embrace. He was Major Yusuf Ghalib, chief of the Northeast Sector, so Doggitt said. I knew his name from Doggitt's reporting cables but nothing more. His black hair was thickly oiled with what smelled like animal grease. His hand tugged nervously at the sling of the machine pistol on his shoulder as he looked from Doggitt to Collier to me and the two Shooters. He seemed disappointed there were only five of us.

Collier asked about the remaining members of the unified NDF high command. Were we to wait for them?

No. This was his sector and he would speak for the NDF high command. He waved someone from the second Land Rover, and we were joined by a man in a white shirt and dusty serge trousers who fumbled with a worn leather dispatch case hanging from his belt like a kilt, drew out four creased, wrinkled pages, and gave them to Major Ghalib, who passed them to us. They were in English, badly typewritten on yellowing government paper whose letterhead had been crudely slashed through with a ballpoint pen. Collier and I looked through the pages. A number of inserts had been scrawled in with ink.

It wasn't the list of negotiable demands promised Doggitt but an angry, confused, and sometimes unintelligible denunciation of the government. It was hardly a document to open the long-awaited dialogue between the prime minister and the guerrilla factions, as Doggitt had claimed.

While Collier and I studied the paper, Doggitt stood to the side talking with Major Ghalib, as if they were both back in some bar or Nairobi safe house where they regularly met. The Land

Rover engines were still running, the rebels were still standing or sitting in the vehicles, some watching us, some looking uneasily to the east or toward the sky. Except for Ghalib, the clerk, and the two bodyguards, no one else had left their vehicles.

Collier asked if this was what they intended to discuss. Major Ghalib launched into a long tirade that so closely resembled the typewritten screed he'd given us I knew he had written it. Collier tried to say something but Ghalib's voice grew even louder. He wouldn't be interrupted. Collier took a notebook from the pouch pocket of his safari jacket and began taking notes, occasionally looking at me or at Doggitt, who was now studying the typewritten paper, wondering what the hell was going on.

Collier should have known what anyone with any common sense had known from the very beginning. Major Ghalib and his ragtag rebels represented nothing more than control of a small fragment of the Northeast Sector and the villa they rented in Nairobi, funded in part by Agency money. They weren't like Major Osman Farah, Major Hersi, Dr. Hassan, Nur Galal, or the others, men who read the *Economist* and could sit in a rear garden and discuss politics, parliamentary ideals, and their hopes for the future. Ghalib's rump brigade were brigands and foragers with guns and vehicles who ruled territory, villages, roads, and what little commerce there was, but nothing more. There was no National Democratic Front, no Unified Command, as Major Ghalib had promised, just a collection of warring clansmen and killers, eager for Washington's recognition and support. Both were fictions, abstractions created as much by the NSC and their intelligence analysts back in Washington, eager for a presidential success, as by Agency operatives in the field like Doggitt, all anxious to identify some collective rebel entity with whom they could deal, if only on paper. Major Farah might have told them their folly: Who can negotiate sensibly with madness or barbarism?

Ghalib would now claim he had met with the Americans and would demand a price for it, recognition by the other guerrilla fronts. I wondered how much Doggitt was paying him. Far across the wastelands to the north lay Major Osman Farah's sector, somewhere else Major Hersi's. Maybe after a few more years of butchery the warring factions would come together out of exhaustion, death, and defeat, but not now. The killing would continue.

I was back where I had begun, the same anarchy, the same hopelessness, standing uselessly at the side of Ghalib's Land Rover, listening to the wind, to the dry rustle of leaves overhead, to the throbbing of the nearby engines, to the clank and jingle of guerrilla weaponry. At Ghalib's side the two guards and the clerk kept glancing up at the drifting cotton clouds, anxious to move on.

Major Ghalib beckoned to his driver for a plastic water bottle and stepped to his Land Rover to drink. Earlier he had mentioned the NDF demand for the release of all political prisoners. As he lifted the water bottle, Collier asked about their own prisoners. Ghalib turned, spat out the water, shot his jaw forward, and said they had no prisoners. His face dripping water, Collier nodded to the two men sitting in the back of the Toyota truck. "What about those men?"

Ghalib's flushed, angry eyes were fixed on Collier. "Thieves! Cattle thieves!"

"So what happens to them?" I asked.

He turned savagely to me. "We *shoot* them! They are not pairsons, sir! They are dogs!"

A few rebels came alert at his angry voice. The two Shooters looked at each other from behind their mirrored sunglasses and stepped back, as if to double their field of fire. The leaves rustled overhead, the wind sang, leather cartridge pouches creaked, metal rattled on metal as other rebels watched the sky. With a sigh of defeat, Collier put his pen and notebook away and looked at me. I tapped my wristwatch, said it was time to go, turned, and looked up at the sky, my back to Major Ghalib. Collier, Doggitt, and the two Shooters might have looked up too. I heard the rattle of cartridge belts and weaponry as Major Ghalib and his two guards scrambled back into the Land Rover.

Whatever else Ghalib and his killers represented, as I told Collier later, we'd come from a world they didn't understand. They weren't like Major Osman Farah or Dr. Hassan. We were Americans, capable of the unimaginable. We hung satellites up among the stars where their herdsmen saw them by night and gossiped about their meaning over their dung fires. We invoked aircraft, helicopter gunships, and murder from the skies by incomprehensible wizardry, sometimes by electronic gadgetry, sometimes by other mysterious means, sometimes just by lifting our eyes, as I had one day a year earlier in the distant scrub in the north when I'd stood on a rarely used strip, scanning the sky to the south an hour before sundown, watched by the skeptical truck driver who had driven me there and a few goat and cattle herders who had silently gathered, curious as to my lonely presence and what I was up to. The UN charter arrived fifteen minutes later out of a cloudless sky. Those who had been silently watching couldn't imagine how I'd done it. They couldn't comprehend our sorcery any more than we could understand the magic of the *Bena N'Kuba*. But anecdote won't explain to those back in Washington why foreign people think or behave as they do. I don't know whether Collier believed me or not.

Two minutes later Major Ghalib and his rebels were gone.

"Crazy fuckers, right, sir?" One Shooter looked at me with a suddenly boyish grin. Maybe he was as relieved as I was. We turned, watching them go.

A single Land Rover drove us back to the airfield and dropped us half a kilometer from the strip and sped away. We walked the rest of the way through the blowing powder and hardpan. Collier was puzzled, Doggitt was angry, winded, and out of breath, trailed by his two tall Shooters, his face flushed as red as a strawberry from the exertion. The C-130's engines began to feather as we approached. I stopped and turned to look back from the ramp but the Land Rover that returned us was far out of sight. Our boots were white with dust as we tramped aboard and our wet faces seemed to tell the South African cargomaster everything he needed to know. The sun was low on the western horizon as we lifted off. I unstrapped myself and got up to look through the porthole but the plane had banked too steeply toward the east.

Collier wanted to talk but I could barely hear above the roar of the engines and had to watch his lips. Doggitt was bitterly silent. After a while we gave it up. It was dusk when we reached Nairobi. The field perimeter was brightly lit and three or four 747s were waiting in the glare of the terminal for their midnight departures for London, Frankfurt, and Paris.

That evening during dinner at the Hilton Collier and I talked about the futility of our meeting. There would be no pre-election presidential policy success in East Africa. He blamed Doggitt, of course, but I told him Washington's isolated executive culture was as much responsible. He didn't completely understand. How could he? He was its product. We fiddled with a cable reporting our failure. At the last minute he decided not to send it but to give his report orally to the National Security Advisor.

I left for London and Washington the next morning.

Major Ghalib would be dead within eight months, murdered late one night by his own bodyguards during a violent quarrel at his bush headquarters. Shortly afterward his brigands were scattered southward by Osman Farah's units moving down from the north as they consolidated their territorial authority. It was Osman Farah who told me the details. We met a year later in New York where I'd gone for the opening of the UN General Assembly. He was there to plead the cause of the northern clans in their struggle for independence. But I'm getting ahead of myself.

It was autumn again, the days bright, cool, and lovely. The leaves were turning in my rear garden. I was still monitoring the faraway war, still followed events in faraway places that wouldn't change my life one iota. In late September I was approached about a position in the Middle East Bureau beginning in January but didn't know whether I would accept or not. That October weekend I had planned to drive west toward the Shenandoah to look at rural property but a thunderstorm took down a heavy maple limb in my backyard. I borrowed my neighbor's chain saw and spent the day clearing it out.

On a wet Sunday afternoon, tired of the Sunday papers and looking for something to do, I drove down to an exhibit at the National Gallery. I hadn't been there in years. I had to park six blocks away, a fine mist was falling, and the corridors were filled with Sunday visitors. The exhibit advertised at the Hirshhorn was crowded and a long queue had formed. I turned back and crossed through the drizzle to the main gallery, thinking I wouldn't stay long.

Her back to me, she was walking through the crowded main corridor ahead of me, a slim blond woman in a dark-blue coat and dark-blue stockings, leading a group of girls dressed in blue jumpers, blue jackets, and berets. She attracted my attention for some reason, maybe because of her height or the grace with which she moved through the congestion in the corridor and the mob of Sunday tourists, but I lost sight of them as they turned in one direction and I turned in another. I was drawn to the intimacy of Vuillard, Bonnard, and Utrillo that afternoon, I'm not sure why. It was a little like window-peeping through the back streets of Paris into late nineteenth- and early twentieth-century domesticity. Thirty minutes later I was back in the main corridor and saw her again through the crowd. Far across the way she had turned near the door to one of the exhibition rooms to make sure her group was together, her face in partial silhouette. I stopped, thinking how much she resembled Blakey Ogden. A guided tour straggled between us and she disappeared. After a moment I moved on.

In the shadowy main rotunda I stopped to put my coat on, looking out through the doors at the grayness beyond, remembering the tall blond woman and thinking how improbable it all was. Blakey was in New York or New England, probably married by now. But I wanted to see the woman again, not to satisfy myself she wasn't Blakey Ogden, but because she might remind me of Blakey. Following a woman because she reminded me of another was so much an admission of weakness I almost left. But I didn't. I walked back through the corridor and moved randomly through the crowd. Ten minutes later I found her with her group in an empty exhibition room. I stopped in the doorway, wondering how I could approach without making myself too obvious. As she turned away from the painting on the far wall, I saw her clearly at the same instant she saw me. The expression on her face was impossible to describe and I suppose mine was too. Neither of us moved. She still hadn't stirred as I joined her. She managed to smile as she looked up, as gracious as ever.

"You surprised me."

"I surprised myself." I felt light-headed. "I wasn't sure it was you."

"It is, I'm afraid. Much older, not much wiser." Her gray-green eyes were flushed and the color had risen to her cheeks. "It's been a long time."

"It has been, hasn't it? Much too long."

She glanced toward her wards who were watching us, her hand lifted to the scarf fallen loose at her throat. "Go ahead, please. I'll join you in a minute."

They trooped out obediently, as gangly and long-legged as colts, but not without looking back. The two tallest girls in the lead were smiling.

"I found your old shop in Georgetown." My voice was still a little husky. "The trail went cold after that."

She looked up in surprise. "My shop?"

"Off Wisconsin Avenue. Someone told me you'd moved to New York or Boston. She wasn't sure."

"Oh, no. I've been here. Out in Virginia. How long have you been back?"

"Since last year."

"At the Department?"

"At the Department."

"I don't imagine that's your style, is it?"

"Not quite. What about you? How have you been?"

We crossed the empty gallery to the next room and she told

me she had worked in New York for a time and then had been invited to join Grace Congreve, an older woman with an established interior design business in Georgetown. She had closed the Georgetown business after Grace died of cancer. Now she was freelancing as an interior designer and teaching two courses in art and art history at a girls' private school out in Loudoun County in the Virginia countryside. The six girls she had brought in that day were her best students.

They were waiting in the adjacent gallery, whispering together on the leather couch in the center of the empty room, probably exchanging fantasies at their middle-aged teacher's liaison with a stranger in a public gallery. They stood up when we entered, silent, smiling, and ready to move on. Their restlessness made her uncomfortable. "I'm afraid the afternoon has grown too long, even for them. I promised them tea. We have to be back by six." She looked at her watch and I knew this wasn't the time or the place to talk.

"I'd like to see you again. Maybe this week sometime."

She nodded but didn't answer, looking toward her students. I wondered if like so many schoolteachers approaching their autumn years she had yielded her own future to the hopes, dreams, and unconscious cruelties of a younger generation. I didn't want to give her a chance to say no. "Maybe Saturday. What about next Saturday?"

She hesitated, still looking away. "Saturday?" Her lips barely moved.

"Next Saturday. I could drive out. Maybe we could have dinner or do something."

She hesitated. "I have a dinner invitation that night. But maybe you could come in the afternoon if you like."

"The afternoon's fine. Just tell me how to get there."

She gathered her skirt under her and sat down on the leather couch to write her address on one of her old Ogden & Congreve cards. Then she drew a map on the back and added her telephone number. I stood watching her, seeing in the lowered head and figure that same combination of beauty, power, and grace that had first struck me years earlier. As she finished she looked up at me silently, a long searching look, as if about to say something. But she didn't speak and in her eyes I saw a terrible, distant sadness I'd never seen before.

"Until Saturday then."

"Until Saturday."

The look in her eyes had emptied my mind like a shot. Outside a light mist was still falling. I'd forgotten where I had parked my car. I wandered around blindly for twenty minutes looking for it. I stopped, started, began again, down one street then into another, stopping, starting, retracing my steps, remembering nothing except her face and that haunted, faraway look.

It was a long, miserable, interminable week. My restlessness was made even worse by the certainty that she was involved with someone. Dinner that night, she had said. How could she not be after all these years?

Saturday was a raw dark day. A few light snow squalls danced around the kitchen windows that morning. To keep busy those final hours, I helped the West Virginia truck driver unload the cordwood he'd brought for my fireplaces. The wind had died down by then. I left my house a little after one and drove out Route 66 toward the Shenandoah. Traffic was light going west. Fifty miles out I turned onto Route 17 and turned north again at Delaplane.

I followed a narrow gravel road and crossed a couple of single-lane bridges and climbed a hillside. The entrance was marked by a small sign: MILL RUN FARM. I drove back down the gravel lane past another road that led to a small stone and stuccoed cottage off to the right. Lined with shaggy pines, the road climbed to an old stone house with a circular drive enclosed by holly trees and boxwood. A gray BMW with DC plates and a green Ford Bronco with Virginia plates were parked near the wide front steps. I couldn't see anyone through the tall windows. I knocked at the door under the fan light. I didn't know the smiling woman who stood there. Dark-haired and in her forties, she was wearing a denim shirt and riding jodhpurs but no boots, and holding a drink.

I told her I was looking for Margaret Ogden and supposed I had the wrong house.

"Oh, no. You passed it on your way in. I'm Shelly. Who are you?"

I said I was an old friend. In the rear of the long hall I saw another woman crossing from one room to the other; she saw me and lifted her champagne flute and waved. "Cocktail hour," Shelly said, and came out on the wide porch and pointed to the cottage I'd passed. "I don't know who you are but have fun," she called as I left.

I drove the half mile back down the hill and parked in the gravel drive next to the newly renovated cottage. There was a small pile of old brick, plaster scobs, and scaffolding at the side of the shed where a gray Volkswagen Rabbit was parked. I could smell the smoke from the fireplace as I got out, cedar smoke from a kindling fire that had just been lit. The deeply recessed windows were small and low, and I thought the cottage had once been a log cabin. The front door was lit by two flanking brass lamps. The door was of old pine planks, recently sanded and stained. I knocked and almost immediately Blakey opened the door.

"I went to the wrong house, sorry."

"Did you? The big house, you mean. People often do. Come in. Please."

Inside was a low-ceilinged hall. A coat and a hat lay on the old cobbler's bench in the hall. To the right was the kitchen and to the left the living room. A fire was burning in the fireplace and in front was a couch flanked by two antique pine tables. The pine floor behind it was bare except for a burnt-orange Turkish rug. On the mantel was the only piece of African art in the room, the Bapende mask I had bought on my first trip to the bush, mounted on a black enameled rod on a wooden pedestal. Her eyes didn't take it in as she looked around, and my glance didn't linger.

"It's quite small but it suits me. It's all I need." She was wearing a dark-blue cardigan, a long gray skirt that reached well below her calves, blue stockings, and loafers. Her ankles were as slender as her wrists, and I remembered how lovely her legs were but they were half hidden now. Her pale-blue blouse had a high collar and pleats that smoothed away the full breasts. An antique silver brooch was pinned below the collar. There was something matronly about the way she was dressed.

"It's nice, very nice."

"It is, isn't it? I moved here after I closed the Georgetown shop. It had been remodeled by an architect friend for the German owner who lives in Argentina." A woman by the name of Shelly Farnum-Smith found it for her. She taught riding and dressage at the school and rented the big house with her sister Susan and her horse-trainer companion.

She showed me the small library and the kitchen and suggested we walk out through the fields. She found a jacket, changed into gum boots, and pulled a gray woolen cap over her head. We followed the road out across the hill where the pastures were dying. It was a gray smoky Saturday afternoon with a nip in the air. A brisk north wind blew the leaves from the fencerows and rattled the russet and red leaves on the oaks.

"I often walk out here. Almost every afternoon." She stopped at a small graveyard behind an old iron fence. There were a dozen or so gravestones, so old, weathered, and worn blank by the wind and rain the epitaphs were illegible except where green and gray lichens defined them. "It's an eighteenth-century graveyard. I took a rubbing with a crayon and drawing paper one afternoon." An old man arrived occasionally to attend it, coming in an old truck with a lawn mower in the back and accompanied by a black dog. He cut the wild grass and raked and cleared away the fallen limbs and always left behind on one of the graves a small clump of wildflowers gathered from the hillside. At first she thought it was the same grave but then realized it was always a different grave. She'd never tried to learn the names on the gravestones. It was his secret, she thought, not one to be shared with strangers.

We moved on and stopped at the crest of the hill.

"There's a lot I want to tell you, Blakey. I mean about what happened."

She didn't look at me. "That was a long time ago."

"It doesn't seem so long."

"It never does, does it; time passes so quickly. But you've been managing, haven't you. I never had any doubt about that."

She led me on across an open field toward a hilltop where a pair of craggy old oak trees were outlined against the dark sky. Rain clouds were moving in from the west. The remnants of an old stone fence lay on the hillside, and she stopped to kneel among the stones scattered and fallen in the grass.

"I remember something I once read about an English cathedral. I told my class about it. Lincoln Cathedral, I think it was.

The most beautiful stained glass window there was built by an unknown apprentice. He used the scraps thrown away by his master." She turned away and we walked on. "I suppose someone will come to take the stones away. Use them for something. That's what some lives are like, isn't it? Using what's left over. The scraps, the remnants. I don't know where I read it. Do you live alone?" Her question surprised me.

"All the time. Very alone."

"It takes courage."

"You think so?"

She nodded. "Very much, yes. Do you have your own house?"

"I rent a house."

"When I moved to the country I wanted to buy a house rather than rent but I was afraid of making a mistake."

"Why would you think that?"

"I suppose I didn't want to fail again." She stopped again. "In those first months working with Grace Congreve, I would sit for a long time at my desk, incapable of dialing a number, unable to phone a client. Have you ever done that?"

"A few times."

"Then here, getting ready to shop at the village grocery last summer, I would change my clothes several times and give up, wrap myself in a raincoat, pull a scarf over my head, and put on sunglasses. I wore sunglasses even on cloudy days and never shopped at the same hour." She stopped and looked back toward the cottage. "I thought the grocery clerks recognized me and believed me neurotic. It was terrible. Indecision, paralysis, I don't know what to call it. As if I no longer had any reality as a person."

"I know the feeling."

She turned. "I'm sure you don't, not you."

"Sure I do. Every year when the leaves turn and the first frost comes. Something in me takes me back to my early years and I get the feeling I'm not a real person at all."

"You're not serious."

"Sure I'm serious. My problem is simple. I read too many books as a boy."

She smiled. "That's ridiculous and you know it."

"No, it's not. I'm serious. I'm always serious."

"You're not. I'm sure you don't do odd, crazy things."

"Sure I do. All the time. I'm a perpetual screw-up and you're the sanest, most complete person I know."

And then she laughed, head back, her face to the dark sky, her hands deep in her pockets, a laugh so delighted, natural, and spontaneous I knew she hadn't changed, not in those ways that mattered. I wondered how often she had a chance to laugh like that. A few raindrops fell, the afternoon light was dimming, and she turned back toward the cottage.

"Would you like some tea?" She was going out to dinner that night, the birthday of one of her colleagues at the school, a young Frenchwoman who was homesick for her family in Lyon. But we had time for tea.

We left our coats on the cobbler's bench in the low-ceilinged hall inside the front door. I stood with her in the kitchen while she put on the kettle. It was a low shedlike room, recently modernized with a new iron gas stove, stainless steel sink, recessed ceiling lights, and cherry cabinets. Attached to the refrigerator by magnets were cards from her students. More cards and amateurish watercolors were pinned to the corkboard above the telephone. Her back was to me and I moved to the side, watching her hands, her shoulders, the matron's blouse with the antique silver brooch pinned below the collar. I seemed to see it all then.

Nothing makes sense; nothing is what it seems.

I followed rebellion in faraway places that wouldn't change my life one iota in one way or another, a skeptic searching out the logic of doubt in the endlessly overwritten abstractions of diplomatic cables and intelligence reports that changed nothing at all. She walked the autumn hills, watched the leaves fly, heard the trees creak, and returned to her cottage to boil water on the stove, brew a cup of tea, and sit at this table for her evening dinner and afterward review her lesson plan or her design sketches by the fire. Upstairs was a bed where she would sleep alone, dream alone, and rise alone. I listened to Boswell, back from the Sudan, to Cromwell on his way to Mozambique, to professors gathered from their university classrooms across the country come to peddle the annual produce from their little scholarly gardens in the INR-sponsored colloquiums and talk about the winds of political change sweeping a distant continent while she taught her daily classes and when evening came would sit and quietly fade into a fog of genteel impalpability, of benign and gentle nonbeing.

I wanted to tell her what she meant to me, wanted to say that with most people I knew, even those who believed themselves more sensitive and civilized, moral discovery was as fitful as epilepsy, and maybe that's why they wander through the National Gallery on gray afternoons or attend Beethovan, Mozart, and Bach concerts, trying to recover again for a few hours a sense of the miraculous, to know that courage they'd lost touch with in their daily lives. But with a few rare people courage of spirit is more or less constant, never dims, and in their presence you discover what you might never have known at all. That's what she meant to me, but how would I tell her that?

I wanted to say all this as I sat listening to her describe her days there, reconciled to her solitude in the Virginia countryside. As I said good-bye, I told her I had never stopped thinking about her. Surprised, she looked up in that same gently forgiving way. "But that was a long time ago," she said.

On a mild day two weeks later she suggested we pack a picnic hamper and a Thermos and drive west into the mountains. In the early afternoon we had a picnic lunch in a roadside park along the broad Cacapon River plunging over gravel, rock, and shale. Coal trucks and campers passed from time to time. The leaves were gone and the hillsides were bare and patched with snow. A solitary fisherman in waders was spin-fishing in the rapids. We sat on the sun-warmed picnic bench and watched him as the wind moved high in the trees. He hooked a smallmouth bass that flashed silver as it broke water to dance on its tail and shake the silver spoon from its jaws.

Afterward we walked along the river. At the far bend on the hillside above the opposite bank, she saw the ruins of an abandoned building half hidden through the trees and was curious. A barn or a house? We went down the river shingle to look. Once a single-story log cabin, it had been boarded over with siding. The snow-reefed roof had collapsed, like the stone chimney. The forest had reclaimed it and it sat in abandonment, stippled with sunshine in a tangle of wild creeper and patches of snow.

Like the ruined cabin, the country around us had once been the true wilderness, not the sentimental farce imagined by New England poets and pedagogues, trotting the board sidewalks of Boston and Cambridge in their high-button shoes, heads filled with the transcendent rubbish of German scholarship. Here was the genuine American article, crude, cruel, unwashed, unlettered, and barbarous; a cabin in a clearing, a spring nearby, maybe a salt lick, fox and badger pelts nailed to the rough walls, windows of oiled parchment or deerskin; inside the stink of bear grease, bear furs, and hominy gruel.

"Your people, were they?" she said, smiling, still studying the cabin.

We walked along the river looking for Indian flints and arrowheads and afterward packed up the hamper, drove on, and found a historical marker at the edge of a pasture where guernsey cows grazed, and got out and walked over to look at it.

In 1756 an Indian raiding party under Shawnee Indian Chief Kill-Buck attacked the fort, massacred most of the inhabitants, and took the others prisoners, including George and Isabella Stockton, a Mrs. Edna Horner, and thirteen-year-old Sarah Gibbons. Mrs. Horner, the mother of eight children, never returned to her family. Only three limestone cornerstones remained of the pioneer fort.

I told her I was going to leave the diplomatic life and write a book about the French and Indian War, mad Frenchmen, mad Englishmen, and mad Americans doing unspeakable things to barbaric Indians out on the eighteenth-century frontier. I would pour the bloody present into the safely distant past, the way historians do. No blood, no mayhem, no butchery, no contrition, the bones all safely buried in scholarly buckram.

"You're still a romantic, still looking for some last frontier to cross. You'll feel better when you're back overseas."

"I think that part of my life is finished." She looked at me skeptically but only smiled.

She fixed dinner for the two of us that night. It was late

when we finished and she didn't want me driving back. She brought some blankets and sheets from upstairs and made a bed for me on the couch.

There were steeplechase races near Upperville in Loudoun County that Saturday and it rained, a light cold steady rain that invested everything—raincoats, woolen clothes, face, neck, collar, rubber shoes, common sense as well, and finally soaked to the bone.

I stood with Blakey in the crowd watching the timber races among people I didn't know—the BMW, Jaguar, Mercedes, and Toyota Land Cruiser crowd with their Bean boots, tweedy caps, and brandy voices. Our faces were wet, water dripped down my collar despite the umbrella I was holding over Blakey, and I didn't know one muddy horse or mud-splashed rider from the other, didn't know which horse I should be watching, the color of the silks, how many jumps, or the distances, and didn't much care. Horses thudded by, the rain drummed on the umbrella, the sodden crowd came alive. Between races a few spectators wandered over to say hello to Blakey. I think my anonymity troubled them, even after Blakey introduced us. Their eyes wandered over me like livestock brokers at a cattle auction, especially those of a thin bespectacled man in his forties who removed his hat as he shook her hand and mine. In his sad blue eyes I thought I saw the wistfulness of a failed suitor. He stood in the distance afterward, turning his thin shoulders to watch us from time to time.

"An architect from Leesburg," Blakey said, taking my arm

and leading me away. "He did the cabin. His wife died last year and he used to call me from time to time."

She had come to watch Shelly Farnum-Smith and Susan race, and both finished well back in the pack. We watched them dismount in the distance among the other riders but it was all confusion there and raining harder. There was a shot off in the distance and someone said a fallen horse had broken a leg and had to be put down. The trunks of the nearby oaks, maples, and ash were polished to silver by the rain; in the distance the tree-tops were a haze of dark brush against the gray sky.

"Are your feet as cold as mine?"

I said they probably were. She wanted to leave before the final race and not get caught up in the traffic snarl. As we were walking back through the rain and mud, she said she was glad we'd come, despite the rain.

It was still raining when we reached the cottage. We took off our wet coats and our shoes and she made drinks while I built a fire in the fireplace. The rain was coming down harder and the wind had come up, bothering the chimney. The cottage creaked from time to time like an old schooner in a gale. A car climbed the hill toward the house on the hill.

She was kneeling on the hearth, feeding cedar scantlings to the fire.

"I screwed it up once, Blakey. I don't want to screw it up again."

She stood up, her loose hair falling over her face. "Don't say anything. I understand."

Her hair was scented by cedar chips from the scarf she'd worn and her face still warm from the fire. If she'd stiffened the way a blue-stockinged matron from a girls' school might have or turned away in anguish, I would have conceded she was no longer the Blakey I knew, but she didn't. We turned off the lights and the room was in darkness except for the orange flames flickering from the fireplace. As the embers faded and the room grew cool, she brought an afghan from upstairs and we shared it sitting on the rug with our backs against the couch. We talked about everything that had happened since that first night years ago, the time lost, the missing dates, the missed opportunities, lost by us, by others, by people everywhere.

She had had an abortion in Paris four months after she left Africa. She had flown to Paris the same week Jeffrey had filed for divorce. She had gone to Paris because she was a stranger there and had been given the name of a French doctor who could do such things. She didn't know how to describe it, didn't know the words because it had no words and that was what made it so terrifying. If she had to put it into words, she would say she'd discovered how fragile her existence, how slight the emotional bonds that held everything in place, and how destructive what waited below: mindlessness, madness, or absurdity, whatever name it went by. She had seen it, felt it that rainy night in Paris, lying on a soiled table in an underheated abortion clinic wearing a thin cotton gown as she waited for the surgeon, her head turned to one side, frightened and shivering, staring at the flaking green paint scrawled with watermarks a foot away, hearing the shrieks of a woman in a nearby room and listening to the rain. She'd flown all that way and there she was at the end of her journey and there it was, waiting for her. Her sanity depended on finding the truth of that flaking hieroglyph in the scaling green paint. She saw nothing else, heard nothing else, her body rigid, eyes burning, focused on the scrawl of paint and plaster, praying its message would somehow give her hope. But it had no meaning. It was just an ugly watermark left by a leaking sill, a formless shape that made no more sense than her own life. As she walked the streets two days later trying to recover herself, in the faces she passed she recognized how fragile the civilizing balance, as fragile as her own sheltered existence, and how terrifying the alternative when that equilibrium was destroyed.

I moved in with Blakey a week later. I kept my house in northern Virginia where she joined me a few days a week, but we spent most of our time in the country. I didn't leave the foreign service but decided to stay on after I was moved up to a deputies' desk in my old bureau. Since it would be a few more years before I would be posted overseas, in January we began looking for a country place of our own.

The following spring I attended a conference on the Horn of Africa organized by the World Bank in Nairobi. Blakey couldn't go because of her work schedule and I didn't want to go without her. Times had changed in other ways as well. No longer was it possible to roam the bush, the countryside, or even the nighttime Nairobi streets as I once had. Random terrorism, kidnappings, car bombs, and urban crime now had made us all vulnerable.

She drove me to Dulles Sunday afternoon. She bought a book for me to take along, a paperback copy of the first volume of Lewis and Clark's journals she'd found in a secondhand bookstore. After I checked in at the United Airlines counter, we sat at a table in the international departures lounge. It was the first time we had been apart for more than a day since we started living together.

"It'll be all right," I said as she silently watched the crowd waiting outside the departure gate. I wondered if she was as miserable as I was.

We overflew the Sudan on my way home. As we soared high above the wastelands, an Englishman at the window seat behind me said how peaceful it was. I remembered stone villages and flat-tailed sheep being herded through narrow stone passageways to be loaded on dhows at an Indian Ocean port where there were no lights because the generators had no fuel and the barefoot seamen from the Persian Gulf walked the dhow rails carrying lanterns, oblivious to the murderous cargo below. I remembered Chief Job's village and wondered whether anyone had ever come to dig his well. I remembered arriving at dusk in a thorny wasteland village on the far horizon where the only light for mile after mile belonged to a solitary rock-walled compound where a lonely Australian ran a UNDP program on a shoestring and I no longer wondered if that was where I belonged. But that was very far away and the district capital was now in rubble.

We passed high above Fezzan, where ten thousand slaves from the Congo were sold as late as 1864. I looked down to try to identify a landmark but at that altitude it was an unbroken rug of coarse brown burlap. I heard an English passenger across the aisle say to someone else that Hubert Satterwaite was leaving Nairobi after their safari and going back to Cape Town. Poor Hubert, divorced from his third wife but still so active in African animal conservation. Did anyone miss the Judds? Did anyone remember how vulgarly they'd both been dressed during the steamer ride to Abu Simbel last year?

Eyes on my book, I sat listening to these horrors as the sunlight streamed in the windows and the air was thick with the smell of warm muffins, steaming coffee, and air freshener. In Eritrea off to the east the relief trucks still came by night across the rocky wasteland. MIGs still bombed and strafed the roads by day and tanks still roamed the red hills but the rebel-held territories were still intact, fields were planted by night, the villages still ravaged, the poor smelled of hunger and dehydration, and young and old men still carried rifles. The crater left by the land mine that killed Ken McAuliffe had been filled in by then and someone else had taken his place in the walled compound near the Sudan border. His Land Rover had broken down one night. After he got it repaired he had gotten on the wrong track in the darkness. At his funeral in a working-class section of Hartford two months earlier, I learned his father wasn't an Episcopal minister but a machinist retired from a Connecticut brass factory. He hadn't taken a degree at Harvard where he remained only a year, but was a graduate of the Merchant Marine Academy. His picture in his academy uniform stood on the piano in the family parlor. Why he had reinvented himself in Africa I would never know, but maybe that was what the continent did to many of us.

I got into Dulles at four fifteen, a day earlier than I expected. I didn't call Blakey, thinking she was still at her school and hoping to surprise her. I took a taxi out Route 66 to her house near

Delaplane. She was inside and heard the taxi door close, left the front door open, and came running to meet me. I dropped my bag and stood holding her for a long time.

"I tried to imagine," she said. "Every night I tried. Where you were, what you were doing. But I couldn't. Was it all right?"

"Awful. I missed you."

There were still a few hours of sunlight left. We changed clothes and took a walk up through the rear meadow and across the hillside past the graveyard.

She was looking far to the west where the sky was still luminous. "I think I've finally found the house we've been looking for. Very old but very lovely."

It was an old frame and stone farmhouse on a hilltop two miles to the west. It had been empty for two years and needed work. Secluded at the end of a long gravel lane looking west from a copse of oaks and shaggy cedars toward the blue-green haze of the Shenandoah, it was larger than Blakey's cabin, with four large rooms downstairs and three upstairs bedrooms. We found a contractor and worked on weekends ourselves. Unpacking the books and putting them on the shelves, she would find an airline boarding pass stuck between the pages, Alitalia, Air France, Sabena, or East African Airways, or a receipt from an airline terminal bar or a foreign exchange slip and ask me about where I was going or what I was doing and I would try to remember. And afterward if I seemed more silent than usual she would sometimes ask me where I was. I was always there, no place else. There was no place else I wanted to be. It took her a long time to be convinced of that.

On some nights the rain wakes me, sometimes the wind, sometimes dreams, old ghosts on the prowl, their rags heavy with the smoke of woodfires and charcoal, come to seek me out. Some find me, some don't and wander on, lifting their smoking lanterns away from my face to wander back down the stairs and search elsewhere before they quietly fade into eternity. How many are still living, how many are dead, I don't know. With some, I'll never know. I watch the winter snow and spring rains falling past our windows after all those lost years. Sometimes the rain bothers Blakey. Or the sound of the surf breaking on the distant beach. It doesn't matter where we are. When I hear her cry out, I wake her, remembering that whatever people are doing, whatever their hopes or dreams, whether in politics, government, painting, composing, or anything else, whether Bach, Stravinsky, Klee, Miró, or anyone else, at one time all were just a quarter tone from dissonance, a knife's edge from shrieking mindlessness, an excremental scrawl on an asylum wall, an idiot's sobbing delirium, the smoke from a butchered village fading on the horizon, or a pale-green watermark in a Paris abortion stall. And maybe someplace, somewhere, someone will be there, waiting to summon you back from extinction.

But that is a never-ending story and this one has gone on long enough.

Date Due

FEB 4	1998
FEB 2 8 1998	
MAY 2 7 1998	
NOV 1 0 AUG 1 0 1998	1998
MAR 2 5 1999	